LAND OF ICE,
A VELVET KNIFE

Spatterlight
Amstelveen 2023

LAND OF ICE,
A VELVET KNIFE
THE SECOND NOVEL OF PULSIFER THE ROGUE

WM. MICHAEL MOTT

A novel inspired by Jack Vance's Dying Earth

Published by Spatterlight, Amstelveen 2023

Cover art by M.J. ter Brughe

ISBN 978-1-61947-493-2

www.spatterlight.nl

Foreword

Fantasy fiction is a strange beast — an amalgamation of mythical, science fiction, adventure, historical, esoteric, and often satirical inspirations, thrown into the fevered stewpot of an author's skull.

There was a time when old maps were labeled "Here be dragons"... but the fantasy author asks not just "Where?" but also "When", and even "Why?" and "How?", and then "How do I go about building a world filled with dragons or other bizarre, original creatures, races, and civilizations?"

All I can tell you, dear reader, is this: More than 3 and less than 7 million years after the collapse of the civilizatons of the Gaean Reach (along with various other star-faring civilizations), when the universe finally began to wind down and rules of reality slowly started to change, there came about a variety of epochs and civilizational cycles which preceded, by a much longer period of time than the aforementioned, the final dimming of the Old Sun and the advent of the Dying Earth. During such a vast span of time many old personalities re-emerged as new ones, lost knowledge was discovered anew, and schools of thought were molded by both necessity and caprice, along paths both identical and divergent from those which had come before. Humanity is adaptable yet intractable, wise yet foolish, tragic yet amusing. Within the greatest desperations often lie the richest jests.

The greatest ice age the world has had, or might yet know, could theoretically be the setting for just such an eventuality. And the most wanton and flagrant survivor of such an age might, in fact, survive in one form or another until the time of the final Dimming of the Sun.

—Wm. Michael Mott
November, 2023

Contents

- NORTHERNMOST · ICE -

·UMLAK·

DROSTHULI
· ICE-TROLLS ·

RISGAL MTS.

THE ∧ LAIRMANUL ∧

ROGTHULI
· ROCK · TROLLS ·

· SMALYU · SHAKAL ·
· THE · OCHER · STEPPES ·

THE ∧ SENEMENE ∧

·Spege

∧ HILLS OF MATASCORI ∧

Melgre ·   ∧ GWYPEDI MTS. ∧
(ICE-BURIED)

· Mysurl   ∧ YEMREN HILLS ∧

RASKURYE SEA
GREAT ICEBERG SEA

KALSURRIDIN ·

· Thimmen

· OUTER · ICE ·

THURADIN MTS.

Mt. Yawamris ·

· YINTER · SHAKAL ·
· HUNTERS' PLAIN ·

FORIASH

Sorondi Islands

· DISTIDAK ·

PITS OF
PHYSTYL

Kraberkrast ·   ∧ ZABATHI MTS. ∧

NISHAR ·

· Jeb

MAJI
SEA

200 miles

OEUAADOOH

·GORETH·

SILGIG·SEA

·ICE·LOST·LANDS·

·DADRATH·SHAKAL·
·THE·SILVER·STEPPES·

LAKE
RUTAKEN

KRUGENTHULI
·STEPPE·TROLLS·

THE·WASTALRES

·PURAG·MTS·

Kebbege

·JESBIDAN·

·COLUMNS·OF·KEGRESH·

·LAKE·SYRAGEN·

Skiggen

Parhimmion·

ROSKIL·SEA

Skurpe

·PESKELY·HILLS·

Lygoem·

·FORESTS·OF·
ISKIRUEN·

·Pacaras-Tem

Oriaber·
Imonber·

·YABLAST·SHAKAL·
·KILLERS'·PLAIN·

PELDRAIT·RIVER

·PHONTYQUE·

·Pegres

·Neshgrel

·PARUTHAIS·
·THE·GREAT·SOUTHERN·
GLACIER·

·Mishraen

Phaltomai Islands

(ICE·BURIED·MTS.)

·Aggaram

·IBRET·

Mouth of Peldrait

N

W   E

S

·OUTER·ICE·

Wm. Michael Mott '94

Part One

THREADS GATHERING

Chapter I

A Chance Acquaintance

Rain fell from a lusterless sky, each drop a freezing reminder of the impermanence of the brief season called the Warming. Before the wanderer the road was mostly clear of ice, though in places wagon-furrows were fringed with slush. The northwestern sky seemed suspended upon a mighty grey wall, which rose up from the ancient earth to curve southward. A huge volcanic mass, slightly smoldering, jutted near the central bend of this curve, where the Thuradin Mountains met the Aulothem chain. Despite the presence of the volcano the air held a heavy chill, for these were the plains of Distidak, on the continent of Teumdoth, and the Age of Ice was yet upon it.

The man was tall and rangy, handsome beneath several day's growth of stubbled beard. He was crafty of visage, a supercilious curled moustache upon his upper lip, his long face framed by a thick tumbling mane of chestnutbrown hair which bounced with his stride, despite its wetness. He wore trews of blue-dyed wool, vest and breeches in one piece, and about his waist was a beaten pouch-belt with locking compartments. A rusty, unscabbarded shortsword hung from a makeshift harness at his side, its worm-eaten wooden pommel an indication of both his penniless state, and its foundling origin. He stepped in a puddle and cursed, kicking to dislodge mud from his boot.

Pulsifer the rogue looked with disgust at the road ahead, which dwindled into a distant, late-afternoon murk. He was soaked through to his skin, which itched madly beneath the chafing of his coarse-spun shirt and woolen garments. His stomach growled in unfed rage, and his face was irritated from hours of continuous exposure to downpour and drizzle, wind and chill. He longed for a comfortable set of quilted traveler's clothes, with mask and pads to shield him from the elements. Mostly, however, he wished for a warm, dry place to pass the coming night. The nights of Teumdoth were not safe for solitary human travelers, for darklings and other creatures of unnatural derivation always rose from burrows and warrens with the sinking of the sun, to hunt for man-flesh beneath the stars.

Mount Yawamris, the volcano many miles away, shot a brief greenish flame into the clouds. Pulsifer had already resolved to give that mountain wide avoidance — not out of fear of the fires of the volcano, but rather out of worries of encountering one of the many enemies he now had among the Brotherhood of Mages, particularly the awesome Morskured Montath.

Yawamris was surrounded by a bustling town, which catered primarily to the needs and research of wizards and arcane scholars; even deep within the mountain, sorcerers worked, forging weapons and devices from the molten blood of the outwardly-frozen earth. Pulsifer thought of the civilized comforts there, and sighed.

Suddenly, for the first time in days, the road forked. He hadn't seen the branching-off until now, due to the low-lying haze of rain and ash particles in the air, and his own melancholy state of mind. One path led to the north, as it had for weeks; the other twisted off between hillocks covered in scrub, toward the volcano. He stood at the fork in indecision, fingering his moustaches, his thumb on his stubbled chin.

He felt a desperate urge to take the leftward path, toward the volcano and the nearest human settlement. His wary nature screamed no to this direction, however — his hunger, his discomfort in unison cried yes. As he stood considering his eyes strayed to the ground; a broad set of four-toed footprints, each a yard long and nearly as wide, were sunk into the frozen earth to a depth of four inches.

He dropped into a wary crouch, grasping the pommel of his sword. The prints were either those of a day-roaming *malderg*, a monstrous ogre of the wildlands, or a southern olang, an ogre-like creature of near-human intelligence and savage disposition. Such day-wandering creatures were not as tainted with magic as the darklings of the night, but they were just as deadly. The prints followed the right branch of the road as far as he could see.

Accordingly, he scurried to the left, still bent-double, his decision made for him by circumstance. He would take his chances with the possibility of danger in the days to follow, at Yawamris, rather than risk the near-certainty of meeting an ogre along the other road today. He walked stealthily up the left road, looking toward the northward path to his right until it was concealed from view by low-rolling hillocks and jutting, igneous boulders. Although the sun would be sinking soon, and the malderg or olang would be squeezing into its burrow for the night, other dangers were all too plentiful; and when night fell, life in Old Teumdoth became truly perilous.

The dun-green landscape faded into swatches of blue shadow and grey expanses of bannis-covered ground. Yellowish patches of cinque-foil glowed eerily here and there, and stunted tamaracks twisted in frozen dances to either side. The rain stopped and a clinging mist began to curl and seep from the plain; shivering, Pulsifer hurried through the twilight with his rusty sword in his hand, looking for a place to pass the night, wary for newly-risen darklings in search of warm flesh.

As he went, he mentally cursed the enemies responsible for his outlawed state, and also the injured shaghorse he'd left miles behind. Darkness descended with a shudder on the wind. Bannis-weed and thorny shrubs rustled and clattered in the freezing blasts which swept down from the north; figures of fog leapt up before the wind, to be quickly tattered and dissolved; stunted trees loomed like hunched crones, or crouching parsennocs. He studied each dark shape with care, fearful that one of them would prove to actually be a man-eating parsennoc, or other nightwalker.

Fortunately, he saw no other being. Half an hour of darkness passed beneath the stars. A pale glow in the eastern sky spoke of the imminent rising of the moon — light to both reveal to him any nearby darklings, or show him to their preternatural eyes. He searched in vain for a sheltered nook between hills, or another place to build a fire and perhaps actually sleep, but he saw nothing that seemed suitably defensible. Rather than build a blazing beacon in the open, he chose to keep moving along the now ice-slicked road.

The wind cackled among ragged hollies and shrubs of bremphrey. Soon he became aware of an intense sense of presence; looking about circumspectly, he saw nothing threatening. He continued on, but could not rid himself of the impression that he was being watched; he tightened his grip on his sword-hilt and increased his pace, as chills not caused by the cold crawled along his spine.

Several minutes passed — he wheeled at a rustling behind him, to glimpse something long, low, and glistening slide from the east to the west side of the road. The pale thing vanished into the shadows and Pulsifer broke into a trot, ready in an instant to strike out to either side.

Now it slid along beside and behind him, apparently heedless of his glances at its amorphous form. From shadow to brush-clump and again to shadow it moved, almost silent, its surface spongy and flesh-like in the cold radiance of the moon. Pulsifer began to run with all his strength.

Still the shapeless entity slid and slithered at an equal pace, several yards behind and to his left. He ran a while, walked swiftly, then ran again — for twenty minutes he was accompanied by the seemingly-boneless lifeform. It was apparently content with its position, and a tittering, laugh-like sound rang out occasionally; finally he halted, his body aching with exhaustion. It would be folly if he fled until he dropped! He turned toward his pursuer, taking a confrontational stance and shaking his sword menacingly.

"Enough of this game!" he yelled. The thing lay ten yards away, shimmering in the darkness with a pale green luminescence. It heaved slightly, its form bulging and collapsing, a slow, bubbling motion beneath its slick surface. Pulsifer stared, yet hid his uncertainty behind a bluff demeanor, as the entity began to change form.

First it swelled into something that resembled a calf, eyeless and without legs, which thrashed toward him with fish-like motions. He steeled himself, but did not run — the nature of the thing was now known to him. It was a *kouool*, a shapeshifting ghoul which generally haunted desolate places.

Created by human-hating ochdeviants during the Wars of Wizards millennia before, a few of its kind still survived in the wilderness, preying upon animals and waiting for a final, human victim. If legend were truth, it would prefer to terrify him into fleeing, following until he fell with weariness — then it would pour upon him and steal his likeness permanently, walking away in his own human form. A residue of muck and bone would be all that remained of the scoundrel who had been Pulsifer, the Velvet Knife...

The kouool flowed and glistened like mucous, to become a headless, disemboweled corpse, groping with swollen fingers; it fell in upon itself, taking on the appearance of a trembling ball with a thousand lidless eyes upon its surface. It rolled toward him with a high-pitched whine, changing as it moved into a creature with lower extremities like the hind parts of a huge ewe, and the upper torso, arms, and heads of two pale-tressed women. The snapping heads of ermines darted from their mouths, and shrill laughter filled the air.

Knees shaking, Pulsifer stood his ground. He held one hand before his own mouth, supposedly the preferred point of entry for a being such as this.

"State your business, shapeshifter — I'm in a hurry, and tire of this display of sad exhibitionism!"

The kouool stopped twelve feet away and dissolved into a column of lambent protoplasm five feet high, which swayed and pulsated as if it would collapse at any moment. It emanated an angry hum, bulging repeatedly toward the man. Its lust for a human form, however, did not override its evident caution of a desperate man with a sword, as iron was one of the few materials which caused it pain. They stood at a stand-off, neither moving, and the kouool spoke mouthlessly.

Its voice was urbane and vaguely masculine, issuing in humming tones from its featureless surface. "To run is useless, of course — to resist the inevitable is, by definition, a waste of time. Your mass and likeness are needed, so that I might fulfill my function as an exterminator of humanity, a task more easily performed in human guise. I will absorb the permanence of your membranes and cytoplasm, and your brain will ride as an instructive passenger within a replica of your present form! You will not, therefore, cease to exist! The predacious experiences we shall share, heights of murder, genocide, and violence, will fill your consciousness with indescribable vigor! And the immortality of my unaging ectoplasm will be yours as well!"

Pulsifer shook his head. "I am afraid that I must decline your invitation, Master Slime Mold, for I am not fond of invertebrates such as yourself. You would do best to slither back beneath the rocks where dwell your smaller cousins — my flesh is quite comfortable upon my skeleton, thank you. Do not molest me, and I will not carve you into slabs of lard. Our interpersonal Equilibrium is kept at a healthy stasis, and we each continue upon our respective ways. I myself have appointments of great importance to keep —"

The kouool did not debate, but began to sink and flatten out into a carpet of sinister, creeping plasma. It flowed onto the road, and as it crept forward, Pulsifer found himself walking rapidly backward up the dark highway, unable to see other dangers which might lie behind him. The thought of walking backward into the arms of an amused parsennoc, or the talons of a pride of faceless jinmonanders, was not particularly appealing — but he had little choice.

A dozen snaking pseudopods of green-tinged plasmagel shot forward, to run rapidly at him and along the edges of the road, in an attempt to tackle his legs from either side. The creature's mass flowed quickly into these, and hands of human appearance began to sprout from the extremities, to scrabble at the frozen ground. Teeth clenched, Pulsifer lashed out at two which shot at him on elastic extensions, amputating them — then, despite his better judgment, he turned and ran. He found his weariness wiped away by terror and adrenaline.

The blue-white moon rose higher, light dancing from its glaciated surface, to illuminate the ribbon of grey road. As he ran Pulsifer hurdled loose bits of brush which had blown onto the road, occasionally glancing back at the swift-flowing plasmodium twenty yards behind him. He knew that he was reacting in exactly the manner preferred by the creature, but at the moment he saw no alternative. His breath rasped burningly in his chest, and twice he nearly stumbled and fell. Leaping over another tangle of icicle-laden limbs, he saw, too late, the slick glimmer of an ice-sheet across the road —

His feet hit the smooth surface, a flooded area over the lowering road, probably frozen the night before. Like a swooping hawk he sped sliding across the ice, hunched over, half-balanced, and fearful of thin spots which might break away and ensnare his legs. He slid for thirty yards, jumped as the road sloped up and out of the ice-gulley, and landed on his feet with the agility of the roof-walking burglar that he was. Pausing to catch his breath, he looked back at his pursuer.

The shapeshifter slid beneath the brush in the road, hitting the ice with the speed of a running man. Instantly the kouool was spinning madly, at last coming to rest in the center of the slick expanse — it sent out pseudopods in quest of anchorage, but its appendages were incapable of moving more than a few feet over the slippery area. It swelled and heaved like a baking pudding, but was incapable of locomotion.

Realizing the thing was stranded, Pulsifer laughed loudly and headed up the gradual slope. He halted at the top of the hill, to look back at the monstrosity below. The kouool bucked and thrashed in an effort to assume a legged form which would allow it to traverse the ice, but repeatedly the shapes it took collapsed into quaking jelly; the unsupportive ice was its undoing. The creature, although a sorcerous mutation, was not a darkling which moved solely by night; with a delighted chuckle Pulsifer realized that it would probably be stranded for days, until the ice melted sufficiently to create an uneven surface.

The kouool ceased its efforts — a hairless, noseless and earless head, lumpy and broad, grew out of its topmost layers of its pudding-like form. It stared at the man on the road above with an expression of hatred and disgust; Pulsifer waved merrily, turned, and continued on his way.

An hour later, he hid beneath a crawling stuntwillow, as thirty or more tambens, covered with blue splotches, swept up the road and past his place of concealment. Their heads were vaguely rodent-like, their stunted bodies hairless, bloated, and bow-legged. They chattered in consternation, and he listened to their fading sounds for several minutes, before rising to resume his journey.

He strode through the night, his sword thrust again beneath his belt; his freezing hands were in his pockets, fists clenched. Soon he made out the outlines of a low structure in the murk ahead — a traveler's shelter, marked with protective runes to keep out non-human passersby. A curling serpent, roses sprouting from its body, was emblazoned on the door; this was the mark of the Brotherhood of Mages, and meant that mighty spells guarded the traveler who took refuge there. Behind the shelter was an equally-low stable, likewise sorcerously-marked. With a cry of delight he ran toward the small door of the building, eager to be within, where his clothes could dry. He knocked, then opened the door and stepped inside.

The darkness was almost total. Fumbling for his tinderbox, he struck flint to steel and held up a burning scrap. The small, windowless hut was unoccupied — near the ceiling were ventilation-slits, and in the ceiling was a smoke-hole. The center of the floor was graced with a stone-lined fire-pit.

There was firewood in one corner, and soon he had his clothes off and drying before a crackling blaze, while he rubbed his aching limbs in the golden warmth. Outside the bolted door, the night howled viciously as hail began to fall; Pulsifer ate some smoked meat he found in a cabinet, glad to have avoided a storm which could have meant his death.

Soon his clothes were dry, and he dressed again. He reclined on the hard floor with his eyes closed, his face bent into a hostile frown. With an all-too-familiar bitterness, he recalled the last thirteen months of his existence, and the most recent circumstances surrounding his beggarly state. Once again he was an outlaw, hunted by both the Brotherhood of Mages and the Collectors of Knowledge, the two most powerful and select groupings of the Eight Upper Classes of Teumdoth. Once again, he wandered penniless, without a home. All monies of restitution that he had paid in good will to wizards and collectors had vanished with the djinn which had created them, and the Lord Collector himself, Moilerve, had placed a huge bounty upon Pulsifer's head.

It was said that he had heard from some mage or other that his beauteous daughter, Erhis Sulshaine, was now a slobbering, fifteen-hundred pound somomorph. This was the work of a recalcitrant djinni, but Pulsifer was blamed for Erhis' condition, since the djinni had been in his employ when the effectuation was enforced. But worse than the wrath of Moilerve Sulshaine was the enmity of Morskured Montath, a young and brilliantly-potent sorcerer whom Pulsifer had bested — rumor had it that Montath now searched Teumdoth for the Velvet Knife, with the intention of utterly destroying him.

In addition to this most-worrisome threat, he had also to contend with vengeful members of the now-defunct and dispersed Coalition of Equiponderous Lifestylers, an organization he had effectively destroyed with magical resources temporarily at his disposal; the founder of the movement, Megwurl Lunt, had been both humiliated and transported to a distant hinterland. Three times already, Pulsifer had narrowly escaped members of the crumbled Coalition, and twice they had informed constabulary of his whereabouts.

Despite a throbbing weariness, Pulsifer smiled to himself. Montath was no doubt frustrated by his inability to lay a curse upon the Velvet Knife, a condition the mage would have learned of from his brethren. Due to the largesse of the Singularity, Pammoth, Pulsifer was now known by all humankind as the Uncursable — all fulminations cast against him fell back upon their makers with three times their original force. This immunity, in conjunction with his natural craftiness, had permitted his survival over the last year and one month.

After his departure from Phontyque, he had wisely gone into hiding on the plains of Distidak, in a village near the steaming Pits of Phystyl. For a month he stayed with a crofter and his daughters, until the search for him had seemed to quiet down — his enemies had assumed that he, too, had fallen victim to the destruction which had devastated his own magically-gathered forces. But he was seen by a passing courier, and scarcely escaped wrathful swordsmen of the Warrior caste. After this began a period of wandering, across the nations of Distidak and Nishar; most recently he had departed the city of Jeb, in Nishar, with constables and the familiar vesps of a dutiful wizard on his trail.

He finally eluded the men, and the vesps he managed to trap in a bottle, which was now buried two feet beneath the frozen plain. He was not set at ease, however, by his fortuitous escape — by now the Brotherhood of Mages would be alerted to his latest actions. Again he scowled — his difficulties had increased a thousandfold! Not only was he an exile from his homeland of Phontyque, but he was now a pariah from every civilized land of Teumdoth! He had no goal, other than to continue to live.

He sighed. He was still alive, in spite of the animosity of those who hated him. Although lacking social position or magical might, he had by the very fact of his survival proven his superiority over all adversaries! His cleverness was a humiliation to the Collectors and Mages, his brief dominance over them, by the granted power of Pammoth, an aggravation they could neither forget nor forgive! Even the lowest of the lower classes still spoke of it, in tones half-outraged, half-appreciative; and such an affront against the social order could simply not be tolerated by the aristocrats of the Eight Upper Classes.

He folded his arms behind his head. The hunger within him somewhat satisfied, his face and body soothed by the dancing flames, he drifted into a welcomed sleep.

Waking some hours later, he refueled the dying fire. The storm had passed, and a heavy silence lay upon the night. Lying back to resume his slumber, he cocked his head at the jangling of metal and creak of wood which suddenly violated the stillness. He rose warily to his feet as a vehicle of some sort halted in the road before the hut — there came the sound of a door opening and closing, and the nicker of a horse. He went to the door and opened it a bit to peer out. An icy blast of air gusted in, herald of the oncoming nine-month winter.

The black silhouette of a long, peak-roofed wagon was stark against the moonlit sky. In the front was a rounded bulge, reflecting moonlight, an encapsulated cupola to protect the driver from the elements; from this, reins proceeded to the harnesses of six hefty, shaggy horses, which stood snorting clouds of steaming breath into the frigid air.

Pulsifer squinted; a slender figure moved about in the darkness, placing feedbags on the pawing horses, then unhitching them and leading them around to the stable. Pulsifer closed the door and returned to the fireside, hoping that the traveler would neither recognize nor speak with him. After a few minutes the door was opened, and the driver of the wagon entered the shelter. Pulsifer lowered his head in an attempt to hide his face in shadow.

The newcomer closed the door, shot the bolt, and raked Pulsifer with a dubious look.

He found himself returning her gaze. She held a fanciful but cheaply-made mask in one hand, baring her face indifferently. Her hair was blonde, her features chapped by outdoor rigor; her mouth was full-lipped, her eyes large and a peculiar light shade of green. She wore a brown overcoat, unfastened, over close-fitting shirt and breeches, and in her left hand she carried a large shagreen valise of sturdy fabric. A long dagger was at her belt, and on the thumb of her right hand she wore a ring set with a large garnet or ruby. About her throat was a silver collar, upon which was a medallion inlaid with the likeness of a leaping gazarel in lapis-lazuli. By this badge Pulsifer knew that she was of the League of Couriers, a lowling guild almost exclusively in the service of the Eight Upper Classes — the mask she carried was just an affectation she had adopted for her encounters with members of the upper echelons. She moved uneasily to the fire.

Despite his cautious reserve, Pulsifer sat up and smiled at her. He had not seen an attractive woman for many weeks, and she was pretty, after a rough fashion. She did not return his smile, but only glowered. She spoke in a threatening tone.

"Keep to your side of the fire — I will do the same. You have an untrustworthy appearance, and a rascally face." She reached beneath her coat and pulled out a forked wand which terminated in two squared-off ends. From her wrist hung a clattering bracelet, strung with the shells of munji-snails.

"This is the reinforcer issued to me by the Brotherhood of Mages; I am adept at its many uses, against darkling, man, or other beast."

Pulsifer nodded agreeably. "I'm sure you are. Have no fear regarding me; despite my present appearance, the result of much recent misfortune on my part, I am actually a gentleman of the Aesthetes. My pedigree should set your mind at ease."

"I do not know that you are of the Upper Classes — you could be of the pedigree of Liar. And if you are of the Aesthetes, then all the more reason for me to be cautious — none seek liberties with low-born ladies with more abandon, than do Aesthetes and Warriors. As I said, remain on your side of the fire, and you will live to see the dawn."

"As you wish." He waved a hand indifferently. "But we can speak a bit before we sleep, can't we? I have seen no other person for over a week — my name is Calim."

She relaxed somewhat, and almost smiled. "A common enough name. I have a cousin named Calim. I am Azahad Zuzirco, of Kraberkrast. Excuse my suspicious nature. As you can see, I am a

Courier, and as such I am alone for long stretches of days and weeks. The work is dangerous, for I often carry precious cargo. Highwaymen, snow-devils, hungry olangs — these and other terrors of the wild places I face day and night..."

"Hard work indeed, for one of such obvious refinement — your beauty must only make your life more difficult! I myself encountered both a kouool and a small swarm of tambens, this evening. However, I had neither a reinforcer, nor other magical devices, so I was compelled to elude death by my wits. Perhaps I was a bit lucky, as well."

She looked at him with a measuring gaze. "Had I not seen these things myself, I would indeed believe you a liar. The tambens you saw fled before the fire of my reinforcer — the kouool I found stranded three miles back. I assume you skirted the shapeshifter?"

Pulsifer laughed. "Ha! The repulsive creature was trapped by a maneuver of mine — I led it onto the ice, where it would be in effect neutralized. The thing was no match, mentally, for a man of advanced perceptions —"

Azahad nodded, an expression of appreciation on her face. "That particular kouool has haunted this stretch of road for two hundred years; many attempts have been made to capture it. I took advantage of its inability to flee, and performed a permutation upon its components with the reinforcer — its excess mass was evaporated, and its basic constituents are now contained in a jar in my wagon. Not only have you done travelers a great service, Calim — you have also enabled my early retirement and the negation of my guild-debt to the League! Sorcerers and collectors alike have standing offers for the capture of a living koooul which they can examine at their leisure, for the creatures are quite rare..."

Pulsifer shrugged with a self-deprecating smile. "I am glad to have been of assistance! Perhaps you could do me a favor in return — I would be thankful for transportation to Yawamris, or another civilized locale... If I may impose upon your gratitude, of course!"

Azahad Zuzirco studied him thoughtfully. "Hm. It is against the rules, of course, but insomuch as this may very well turn out to be my last run along this course — thanks to an action of yours — I believe I will give you a lift. Equilibrium will be served as well." She laid the reinforcer on her leg, and pulled her overcoat off with a series of dislodging wriggles.

Her close-fitting shirts revealed her attributes nicely. Pulsifer thanked her for her generosity and lay back — but his eyes were slit open, and he watched her with admiration as she prepared a meal for herself from articles in the valise. As she pulled packets of food from her bulky bag, a wooden box fell out with a bang, spilling its contents upon the floor. Pulsifer caught a glimpse of a glimmering golden bowl, wide and shallow, the inside of which seemed to be lined with a substance resembling mother-of-pearl. Azahad quickly scooped up the object and thrust it into the box, which she in turn placed back in the valise — she looked at Pulsifer suspiciously, but he continued to pretend that his eyes were shut. Eventually he fell asleep, dreaming of white skin and golden hair, and the fragrance of the woman who slept on the other side of the fire.

Chapter II

In Yawamris

The next morning, Azahad shared her breakfast of bread and cheese with Pulsifer. Shortly after dawn they were on their way, perched within the cab of the courier-wagon. The convex glass window before them was of an unbreakable substance created by a mage of Kalsurridin, so they had no fear of creatures they might pass on the road. Azahad explained that she only halted to use the reinforcer when the road was blocked, or the horses were attacked. With an eventless night under the same roof behind them, Azahad seemed without worry concerning the character of her new companion, and proved to be quite talkative. They spoke of many things, to pass the time — of the buried ochdeviant cities said to lie abandoned beneath the glaciers of the once-verdant moon; of the rumor that mages had engendered, which stated that the world was not after all on the way to a final freezing death as had long been thought by everyone, but would warm up progressively over many thousands of years; and they spoke briefly of the rogue called Pulsifer, the Uncursable, the Velvet Knife, last seen in Distidak and Nishar. Azahad exclaimed in astonishment and wonder at the nature of the criminal's outrageous crimes against the Upper Classes, and society as a whole; Pulsifer refrained from commenting overmuch on his infamy, nor did he mention his inadvertent role in changing the course of the Earth's destiny. He spoke of the outlaw Pulsifer with loathing and derision, eventually turning the conversation toward the topic of Azahad's hazardous occupation.

She pursed her lips in distaste, her eyes still scanning the road alertly. "I admit that this is an occupation I will not miss. I inherited the guild-debt from my father, for I was his only child. With the debt came this position. He was killed by a ribald grimkel, along the road to Pegres — only his head was recovered." She sighed. "Now, though, I will return to my former ambition…" She lapsed into silence, then changed the subject somewhat.

"Having a particular interest in the efficiency of Couriers, the Brotherhood provides plentiful protection for those of us in the League — not only do we carry reinforcers and hassle-nooses, but proximity-rings as well."

She held up the thumb upon which was the red-stoned ring; Pulsifer noticed that it had the appearance of a garnet after all.

He nodded. "I have heard of these rings, but I must confess my ignorance as to their exact function. Prior to my unfortunate disinheritance, my days were spent in pursuit of heights of artistic principle, and thaumaturgy I totally neglected…"

Azahad explained in an authoritative tone. "The ring alerts the wearer to the nearness of certain entities — for five seconds, it flashes red or orange if a human being is near, or green for parsennoc, tambens, and other darklings averse to the sun; yellow is for demonic or elemental entities, and blue for miscellaneous or indeterminate species. By virtue of the ring I anticipated both last night's tamben ambuscade, and the proximity of the kouool. You, also, were represented by a flash of red when I arrived at the shelter."

"A fascinating bauble," Pulsifer remarked, eyeing the ring sidelong. "Your freight must often be of great value, to command such precautions."

She nodded. "Even now I carry objects belonging to powerful mages and grand personages of rank — or destined for delivery to suchlike. The bowl you saw fall from my bag last night —" she grinned at him, "— is a gift to the witch-delver Tatimoi Murlda of Yawamris, from her aunt Dacaleevish the Sorceress. I am not certain of its properties, but it is to be used somehow in smelting particularly valuable alloys. It is priceless — and many such items are locked in the steel cabinet behind us. Or they are under my personal protection when the compartment is full, in the bag I always keep close at hand."

Pulsifer nodded and they became quiet, as the rolling landscape flowed past on either side. They saw a pack of wolfish eppeleros, and later a monstrous, broad-winged fottermee cruising the air above the steppe in search of prey. The Yinter Shakal was a hazardous plain, and he was glad that he did not have to worry about being chased across the open spaces by the flighted carnivore; even the duglouge they passed at one point, broad antlers tearing roots from the earth, were dangerously belligerent creatures. The ominous brown cone and crags of Yawamris grew larger every minute, and he mentally calculated that they would arrive by the end of the day.

The sun was already behind the mountains to the west when they arrived at the volcano and its surrounding city. The city, also called Yawamris, glittered with myriad lamps of many colors. Stone towers, conically-roofed, jutted from the slopes of the volcano, and long edifices curled about the mountain like giant, tortuous serpents of stone. Beautifully-gabled buildings of one and two stories were laid out along spiraling and curving streets. All around were an army's worth of black-garbed laborers, armed with broad brooms and buckets, sweeping volcanic ash from streets and structures.

Pulsifer took in the view with interest, for he had never before been to Yawamris. Yet he also looked about warily as the wagon bumped down the cobbled streets, for many mages and collectors, as well as others, knew him by sight or description. Now that he was in a civilized place again, his first priority would be to lift a purse and buy food, clothing, and lodgings! As if anticipating his thoughts, Azahad glanced at him with an unsure eye.

"Where will you stay, Calim? By your look I would say that you have no money — and Yawamris is not renowned for the charitable spirit of its citizens! Vagrants and vagabonds are generally seized and pressed into service in the mines and smithies of the mountain, and do not see the sky again."

Pulsifer shrugged. "I will take my chances, I suppose, and look for some method of earning an honest wage."

"This city is in the grip of a hundred guilds. If you are truly of the Upper Classes — and I cast no doubt upon what you say! — then you will find it impossible to secure even a position cleaning stables. Come with me to the Mournful Lute, a hostelry where I usually stay, and share my room until you hit upon a plan. To protect you from the press-gangs, we can pass you off as my cousin."

He considered for only a moment. "I accept your hospitality, Azahad — and your friendship! You will find your kindnesses reciprocated!" Azahad laughed, almost ran down a pedestrian with her team, and stroked Pulsifer's face boldly with her free hand. "To the Mournful Lute, then, where our friendship can blossom! You will share in my celebration after the kouool is sold, and I am freed of this wagon forever!"

Soon they pulled up before the inn. The Mournful Lute was a rambling, thick-limbed spider of a building, located on one of the volcano's lower slopes. Azahad Zuzirco checked her wagon and cargo at a nearby depot of the League of Couriers, and they walked to the hostelry, Pulsifer carrying her bag. As she stepped ahead of him, he flipped the catch and glanced into the valise — the box containing the bowl was still in the bag, among clothing and personal items. He squeezed shut the catch and did not voice the questions in his mind; as they entered the inn, he deftly lifted a money-bag from an exiting patron, and slipped it beneath his vest.

Their room was small. Pulsifer was pleased to eat, bathe, and give his clothing to the maid for washing and mending. After he had shaved and dressed again, he left his battered sword in the room and joined Azahad in the taproom downstairs. She already dickered with a dark-skinned, grey-haired man at a table in one corner. Most of the customers were maskless commoners, laborers of various types; Pulsifer judged from the man's attire of satins and gold-studded felt that, despite his maskless face, he was an aristocrat. His suspicions were confirmed when he saw the round blue badge which the fellow used as a brooch for his cloak. He was an hereditary scholar of the utmost social degree, one of the Collectors of Knowledge — and hence a potential enemy.

On the table between Azahad and the collector were a jug of wine, several glasses, and a jar of smoky glass sealed with a locking lid. Pulsifer approached the table with a grin of camaraderie, and seated himself beside Azahad — the collector glanced at him disdainfully. Pulsifer helped himself to the wine.

Azahad made the introductions. "Calim, this is the esteemed

bestiarist, Srod Yaorn. His menageries are the most varied in Yawamris! Calim is my cousin, Sir Yaorn."

"How excellent for him," the collector remarked, in a condescending tone. "You ask too much for the lifeform, Azahad — you are not licensed to sell such specimens in Distidak, in any event. This raises complications which, in combination with the amount you are asking, make the kouool no bargain."

Pulsifer examined the grey-tinted jar. Within, a slimy, folded mass of protoplasm moved ceaselessly, filling the container. A colorless eye swelled and formed for many seconds, to press against the glass and jerk erratically as it took in its surroundings. It gazed at Pulsifer for a moment, and he was certain that it recognized him. He grinned; it dissolved.

Srod Yaorn ran a finger along one side of the jar as he studied the creature within, presumably ruminating upon its value. Azahad Zuzirco shrugged.

"Twelve murtils of good Kalsurridin gold is a fair price; much danger was dared on my part to capture the thing. This must be considered, in conjunction with the intrinsic value of the creature."

"Your price is exorbitant," Srod Yaorn insisted. "I will go as high as six murtils, no higher. This amount will enable you to live comfortably for a handful of years, without undertaking labors such as folk of the lower castes must, to survive."

"It's not enough," Azahad muttered, frustration in her voice. Pulsifer could see that she was thinking of some private ambition or other which apparently required greater financing. He took her by the arm and leaned forward to address the collector himself.

"I have some experience in such matters — more than does my pretty cousin. You rob us, but what can we do? Of course, Jelremmit the Collector is just over the mountains, in Kalsurridin; he always exhibits generosity when making a purchase. But go one more murtil, and the creature is yours — if you also provide an additional service to sweet Azahad."

Azahad opened her mouth to protest, but he squeezed her arm sharply. Srod Yaorn narrowed his eyes as he considered, watching the sloshing thing in the jar. His desire was evident to Pulsifer, who read his tight-lipped countenance like a signpost. Finally, the collector nodded.

"This is satisfactory—but state the service you require. I am not a mage, and outrageous deeds are as unthinkable as excessive monetary demands."

Pulsifer slipped an arm about Azahad's shoulders. "My cousin wearies of driving a wagon through the waste places—with your influence, you might intervene and see that the League of Couriers cancels her guild-debt. This would enable her to advance in her own quest of personal development. A man of your refinement can certainly sympathize with such a harmonious ambition..."

Srod Yaorn looked at him shrewdly. "This might be done; I am not without influence with the League. Financing will be required, however—at least one murtil. Bribes must be paid, as well as favors collected. Sell me the plasmodium for five, and we have a bargain. How much is your guild-debt, my good woman?"

Azahad smiled sheepishly, brushing a wayward strand of hair from her eyes. Pulsifer found the motion alluring. "Five murtils."

"A hefty sum," the collector observed, his brows rising. He laid a bejeweled finger along one cheek. "Not impossible to have negated, however. The League of Couriers owes me much for services rendered in the past, and the promise of using them in the future." He smiled. "Done! Within a day's time, you will be free to wander wherever you wish—at which point, I will bring the money to you here, and take the kouool."

Azahad nodded her agreement and Srod Yaorn rose to leave, pulling a gilded viper-mask from beneath his cloak. As he did so, a thick-bodied, muscular man with reddish hair and a broad, wind-burned face approached the collector, standing in his path. Azahad bristled and scowled at the fellow, who shot her a lascivious smile.

"Lord Yaorn, remain a moment!" the man said quickly, in a throaty voice. About his neck was a collar bearing a medallion of the League of Couriers. "I have here a recently-unearthed artifact of great strangeness, for your inspection—given to me two days ago, by a dying vezulnut-gatherer in a valley to the north! He claimed to have found it in a buried tomb, uncovered by a landslide..." He raised a bag in one hand and began to pull at the drawstrings; Srod Yaorn raised a hand in dismissal.

"Hold your item until next week, Bolderge—I have made a purchase from this lady. Besides, I find it more than probable that the death of the item's previous owner did not take place without some assistance from you…To purchase such an ill-gained object would not be equilibrating for one's own net of being."

Bolderge shrugged. "He was bitten by tambens — he withered on the spot. I answered his plea for relief, and he gave me the thing in a hasty fashion, for he was in a rush to die. I do not know its function, but with his last breath he whispered that it was not a thing to be trifled with — that in fact it had somehow led to his meeting with the tambens. Since I am ignorant of its nature, I am asking only twenty-two murtils…"

"As I said, I have already made a purchase from Azahad Zuzirco. Meet with me next week, and —"

"What did she sell you?" Bolderge interrupted, looking at Azahad with a suggestive leer. Pulsifer made note of the shortsword hanging at the man's belt, a weapon of high quality with a well-worn, leather-wrapped handle. Srod Yaorn indicated the jar.

"A living kouool, and a much-coveted specimen. Now, I must depart; I will see you, Azahad, tomorrow evening. Good night." The collector moved around the heavy man and maneuvered between tables, chairs, and patrons.

He reached the door and was gone. Bolderge seated himself at the table, glancing at Pulsifer as if for the first time.

"Hello, Azahad." Bolderge picked up the jar, turning it before his eyes. "I see nothing but a length of bleached intestine — surely you do not perpetrate a hoax upon the collector!"

Azahad fixed him with a hateful gaze. "The kouool is genuine, you pig. More so, I imagine, than whatever you have to offer Srod Yaorn."

Bolderge laughed, and put the jar down. "I carry an ancient object of uncommon origin — an aura of latent power surrounds it. When did you capture the kouool?"

"Last night, on the Ridgeward Road. Calim, here, is a witness to the validity of my claim as to the thing's nature. Now, why don't you leave? You know I despise the sight and smell of you!"

"On the Ridgeward Road," Bolderge repeated, ignoring her taunt. "You captured it whilst in transit for the League! Aha. It's a shame that

Yaorn has departed — he will be interested to hear that you are not qualified to sell the thing."

Despite her bold front, Azahad was obviously unsettled. "What do you mean? The deal has been made!"

Bolderge laughed — seemingly unperturbed, Pulsifer reached for the wine-jug as the man replied.

"According to the tenth article, eighth by-law of the League Charter, anything acquired by a driver for purposes of resale, during the course of a league-assignment, is at once in dispute of ownership. The degree of the dispute is generally in proportion to the standing guild-debt of the driver. You owe five murtils — to be exempt from this particular by-law, you must owe only one. The kouool therefore rightfully belongs to the League, and is not yours to sell —"

He rose with a laugh, and Azahad assaulted him with a stream of curses, tears in her eyes. Pulsifer raised his voice to be heard over hers.

"You also are of the League of Couriers; what, then, is the status of your merchandise in regard to these by-laws?"

Bolderge glared at him belligerently. "That is not a concern of yours, and if you were not a stranger to Yawamris, you would know better than to question me! But my debt is less than one murtil, so I am permitted to involve myself in a bit of private enterprise." He bowed to Azahad. "I regrettably leave you, beautiful lady, but you know at what price my silence is to be bought. I do not understand your reluctance! Your preferred occupation is well-known! My room is two doors down from yours, beside the landing. I will see you tonight!"

With another bark of coarse laughter, he left; Azahad hung her head, and Pulsifer poured them both some more wine.

"Do not be disheartened, Azahad! Bolderge is a buffoon. Your sale to the collector will take place!"

Azahad wiped away tears with the back of her hand. "He will not have what he desires — that is mine to share, and won't be taken!" She looked at him, and smiled suddenly. "Let's go upstairs, and discuss it."

An hour later, Pulsifer lay beside her on the bed, her slow, even breathing telling him that she had fallen asleep. He no longer wondered what her former ambition had been, for she had shown him adequate examples of her craft.

Apparently she needed a considerable sum of money to open an establishment of physical pleasure of her own, in Kraberkrast…He sighed, nudged her slightly to wake her, and after further exercise they fell asleep together.

Pulsifer awoke after midnight. The inn was quiet; one drunken voice sang weakly, somewhere downstairs. The two lamps in the room had guttered and gone out, and the flames in the fireplace were chillingly low. Rising without awakening Azahad, he put fresh wood on the fire and then dressed, the thought of perhaps taking refuge in her planned house of gratification bringing a smile to his lips; taking up his sword, he unbolted the door and went silently into the dark hall, drawing it shut as quietly. Then he went to the room of Bolderge.

Utilizing a piece of jointed wire from one of his pouches, he put it to the use for which it was designed, drawing the inner bolt from its socket from outside. Carefully and soundlessly he withdrew the device — opening the door, he slipped within.

Lamps burned more brightly, here. Pulsifer closed the door and approached the snoring form of Bolderge, who sprawled beneath a heap of blankets. First he meddled with the man's sword and scabbard; then he took from a pocket the purse he had stolen earlier in the evening. He had already removed all the money. He opened Bolderge's belt-pouch and placed the folded purse within; moving in a crouch, he then went to the man's heap of personal belongings, untying the bag in which Bolderge kept his piece of sorcerous merchandise.

He withdrew his hand, a cold, metallic object in his grasp. He examined it for an instant in the dim light. It was a rectangular box of brassy metal, about a foot long, and etched with hundreds of tiny glyphs. Pulsifer stuck it beneath his loosened pouch-belt, retied the bag after placing a scrap of firewood in it, and left the room as soundlessly as he had entered. It took ten additional seconds to shoot the bolt from the outside. Bolderge never stirred.

Smiling, he returned to Azahad's room, hid the metal box, and was soon in bed beside her, already anticipating the morning with eagerness.

Sunlight streamed through the window, for Pulsifer had opened the shutters. He prodded a groaning Azahad Zuzirco from bed, poured some hot Kalsurridin rac-rac, which he had already fetched, down her throat, and threw her clothes at her.

"Get dressed, Azahad—this day you shall be rid of the miscreant Bolderge once and for all! Your future as a businesswoman will be secured, and you will do me a small turn in recompense!"

She looked at him with a mixture of incredulity and suspicion. "I thought that the Bending Thunder would prove too much for you—it not only loosened your joints, but your mind as well! What do you prattle about?"

Pulsifer twisted one of his curled moustaches. "My mind and body are both limber by nature, and the position you mention was less than a knucklecracking. But I tell you this—guarantee a place in your establishment where I might sojourn in leisure for a month or two, and dominion over Bolderge is inevitable!"

She nodded with an eager smile. "Make the dream a reality, and you will stay a year, if you wish! What must I do?"

"Wait until Bolderge comes down for breakfast; then go to the watchpost on the corner and summon a constable. I will delay Bolderge until you arrive, and we shall see if his wits match his bluster!"

They went to the taproom, where bustling servants served trethleber-rycakes, sausage, and gruel. They began their breakfast—when they had nearly finished, Bolderge came down, and Pulsifer nudged Azahad to leave.

Bolderge sat across the room from Pulsifer, who smiled and waved in a friendly fashion; Bolderge frowned threateningly, and motioned for Pulsifer to attend to his own meal. The teamster stuffed a huge piece of cake in his mouth, and Pulsifer winced in disgust.

Soon Azahad returned, accompanied by a tall, steely-eyed man in a grey uniform and cloak. She led him to Pulsifer's side; Bolderge was so engrossed in his meal that he noticed neither her, nor her companion. Azahad indicated the guardsman to Pulsifer.

"Calim, this is Captain Fakness—he is constable of this entire side of the city."

"The pleasure is mine, Captain!" Pulsifer motioned for him to sit, but Fakness stood stiffly, glaring.

"What do you want? Why did you not come in and file a report? This is not an accepted procedure —" He scanned Pulsifer with cold grey eyes. "You're new to Yawamris, aren't you? I would remember a roguish wag such as yourself—"

"My appearance is irrelevant!" Pulsifer interjected, with a note of indignation. "I had you summoned to apprehend a thief! The big man, there, stretching his jaws in such a grotesque manner! Last night I saw him jostle a rotund little fellow, and thought to glimpse him lifting a money-pouch; my suspicions were not confirmed until this morning, however! See how he wears my own good sword, taken from my room during the night! Within the scabbard you will find a dented rinket which I carry for luck, charmed for me by a witch of Nishar! Verify the coin's presence, and you will doubtless find other articles of question-able origin upon his person!"

Fakness studied Bolderge with a serious expression. "A purse was reported stolen from this vicinity, yesterday evening—you are certain the sword is yours? A man's reputation is at risk!"

"I stake my own reputation upon it!"

Fakness looked grimly at Pulsifer.

"You do, indeed. Very well." He strode across the room, to stand before Bolderge, who looked up in surprise. Fakness held out his hand; the other people in the room looked on with interest.

"Fellow, hand to me your scabbarded sword for examination, in the name of the council of Mage-Regents!"

"What unabashed stupidity is this?" Bolderge blurted. "I am guilty of no crime!"

"That has yet to be determined," Fakness said. "The sword!"

Reluctantly Bolderge unbuckled his sword-belt and handed it to the captain; Fakness unsheathed the weapon, then turned the scabbard on end, depositing a copper coin on the tabletop. Bolderge looked on in confusion.

"Aha, Your iniquity is revealed!" Fakness set the sword on the table behind him, out of the reach of Bolderge, and drew his own weapon. "Be so kind as to empty your own pouch, and the bag at your side… Make haste!"

"This is an unwarranted assault upon my integrity!" Bolderge sput-tered. "I am Bolderge Grallko, a man renowned for honesty in all dealings!"

Fakness motioned with his sword; grumbling, Bolderge complied. The emptied purse fell from his pouch and onto the table, along with a few coins; Fakness picked it up on the tip of his blade.

"Purple velvet, with red stitching! Bolderge Grallko, you are under arrest! Empty now the bulky bag!"

A stupefied look was on the courier's face, and he did as he was told without protest. The piece of firewood fell onto the table with a thud — Bolderge let out a bellow of rage. People nearby moved away, intimidated by his vein-swollen, contorted expression.

"I've been robbed! Plundered by magic! This is the work of thieving yelshin imps! I'm innocent —"

"You will be given a hearing," Fakness said with a tight-lipped smile, "Then you will go to the mines! But do not blame the yelshin before the magistrate, or it will go harder for you! Death is less pleasant than a miner's lot!"

Bolderge looked about rapidly, like an animal searching for freedom from a hunter's snare — he sighted a grinning Pulsifer and Azahad, and threw himself across the room toward them with an inarticulate cry.

Moving swiftly, Fakness brought down his iron sword-pommel upon the back of Bolderge's skull. Blood spurted and Bolderge Grallko fell like a tree, splintering chairs against the floor.

Fakness sheathed both his own blade and the shortsword, handing the latter to Pulsifer. "Here is your weapon — do not forget your lucky coin. It certainly proved its good fortune for you today."

"I will retrieve it, never fear," Pulsifer agreed, scooping up the rinket.

Fakness pulled a cord from his belt and tied Bolderge's hands behind his back; then he took him by the legs and dragged him, face-down, out the door and into the street.

Pulsifer buckled the sword-belt and the scabbarded weapon about his own waist, then he and Azahad finished their breakfast. Afterward they journeyed out into the morning, for he now had a fat purse to spend.

Two hours later, he wandered the streets of Yawamris alone. Azahad had gone to the League Depot, for the invoicing of her latest load of freight and missives. Pulsifer assumed that she also went to retrieve the bowl of the sorceress Dacaleevish from her valise, and sign it in as well — but the fact that she had taken the bowl with her after their arrival rather than inventorying it, aroused his suspicions. The bowl, whatever its properties, would fetch a high price in many a clandestine market.

Pulsifer now wore a felt jerkin of blue-and-red plaid, over which he sported a warm blue jacket. His blue linen breeches were new as well, as were his black boots, which sported ornate silver buckles. Upon his back was a rolled bundle, comprised of a set of quilted traveler's clothes, complete with wedge-shaped overboots and a head-encasing *kabeyui*, for the days were growing ever-colder as the Warming drew to a close. In the bundle was also a small toiletry-kit, with razors, scissors, needles, and thread — his appearance was something that, despite his hunted state, he could not bear to neglect. About his waist, the short-sword rode upon a new sword-belt, designed to place the weapon at his right side so that he could draw it lefthanded.

Above this was his pouch-belt, from which there hung a long knife in a red sheath, and a sturdy flask already filled with water. His old clothes were in a trash-heap behind the haberdashery, and he had enough money in his pouch to purchase exactly one tankard of beer at the Mournful Lute. With his expensive garments and accoutrements he felt certain that the pressgangs, assuming him to be a person of consequence, would not molest him.

He walked along a curving street, which spiraled down a building-clustered hill near the western flank of Mt. Yawamris. Occasionally the ground beneath his feet rumbled and trembled, and the volcano belched ash into the azure sky; but a prevailing southerly wind dissipated the murk almost immediately, to the obvious relief of the black-garbed ash-sweepers who leaned on their brooms, talking garrulously with one another. After browsing in various shops and studying the configuration of the city from the hillside, he set off for the Mournful Lute. At the bottom of the declivity he came upon the eastward edge of three extensive caravanserai, which dominated this part of the town with their hundred-acre tracts of supply-houses, outfitters, stables and depots; apparently a caravan of great-wheeled, ostentatious cars, pulled by giant, hornless wubbers and broad-backed girth-horses, had just arrived.

A monstrous cloud of yellow dust half a mile long announced its coming. Pulsifer crouched down behind a crumbling stone embankment to watch the passengers disembark, wary of the lance-bearing guards which paced the cars on the backs of warm-blooded, reptilian durdelains, which were swift and ferocious mounts.

The wind at his back was chill. He searched the aristocratic figures for an easy mark, someone who could be easily followed, a dangling pouch which might be effortlessly slit. Some of the passengers wore masks; others, leisurely of attitude, did not. Aesthetes, Councilors, Warrior-Philosophers, varieties of Lord Merchants — even a few who were evidently Collectors — all of these upper denizens of society were present. Pulsifer knew their types well, from long acquaintance — once he had been their roguish darling, now with typical fickleness, they persecuted him with the power afforded them by their positions! The only manner of aristocrat he did not see represented in the bustle was a Mage or Sorceress; even though he saw no one that he personally knew, he kept out of sight nevertheless. His description had been quite wellspread among the Eight Upper Classes.

He stroked his long jaw thoughtfully as a large yellow car, drawn by red-eyed wubbers, moved slowly toward the platform of disembarkation. It was elegantly covered in gold-studded frieze work, and floral arrangements of crystal and polished onyx. The back half of the car had apparently been modified for the transport of freight. Pulsifer squinted — there was something uncomfortably familiar about the Hawk Motif emblazoned in green on the side of the car. It nagged at him but he could not place it, and his unease was not alleviated when many men rushed forward, armed with long-hafted stunners; these unpleasant instruments glowed with magical force at their bulbous tips. He slunk closer to better view the scene.

The ten men, stout fellows all, gathered along the edges of the platform, flanking the walkway. Two other men unbolted the door. The armed workers tensed as the huge door to the car creaked, and slid open…

A large whiteness quivered into view; curious passersby backed away with gasps and oaths, as a thigh some five feet in circumference was thrust from the dimness of the interior. This limb was followed by its associate, and the form they carried — an eight-foot-high humanoid form composed of massive folds and rolls of flesh, weighing probably well over a thousand pounds. Pulsifer started back, his stomach reacting with a sharp pang.

Someone in the crowd screamed, and the squarish head of the somomorph turned angrily toward the sound. Unlike most of its kind, this lumbering monster was not entirely hairless — long locks of raven blackness poured upon its hammy shoulders. The somomorph moved with a strange, femininely-swaying gait, and an attitude of arrogant dignity — even from the considerable distance between them, Pulsifer caught a glimpse of the thing's vividly-blue eyes. He choked back an urge to retch.

He knew in an instant that they were the eyes of Erhis Sulshaine, daughter of the Lord Collector, Moilerve; she had once been his lover, and was considered by many to have been the most beautiful and desirable of human women. But that was prior to her integration with a monstrous somomorph, the result of the magic of a mercurial djinni…

So shocked was Pulsifer by the sight of his transformed, erstwhile love that he hardly noticed the man behind her grotesque form — a slightly-built man with a shaven, tattooed pate, who wore red robes embroidered with his green hawk-crest. This was Moilerve, her father and a man of unequalled influence. He bore in his hand a rod of control, from which ran two narrow straps, fastened to the shoulders of his unhuman child.

For once Pulsifer was immobilized with shock and surprise. Other than for a brief glimpse, he had not seen Erhis since her transmutation, and the memory of her proud beauty was horribly mirrored in the movements and bearing of the thing on the platform. He watched with a stunned enthrallment as the somomorph boomed down the walkway, the thick timbers of which groaned audibly, with Moilerve Sulshaine close behind. The pair vanished into an opened warehouse door with the ten men behind them, and Pulsifer shook his head in wonderment.

Where and how had Moilerve found his daughter? And what were they doing in Yawamris? His attention was again drawn to the door of the car.

Another figure stepped forth onto the platform — Pulsifer felt a surge of terror, and almost bolted.

The young man who provoked this reaction was tall and slender, dressed in black pantaloons and shirt, a purple vest, and a long black roquelaire. His pale face was youthfully handsome and clean-shaven; he was dark of hair, of eye, and of expression. Upon his shoulder there crouched a mauve-colored, scaled and beaked creature, with the feet of a falcon and a vaguely simian form — this was a hijret, a small supernatural being of baleful potency, from one of the netherworlds within the Earth. Its reptilian eyes darted about with a bird-like quickness.

Pulsifer jerked back behind the wall, his heartbeat drumming in his ears, his mouth dry and bitter. The young man was none other than the mage Morskured Montath, who was, in spite of his youth, possibly the most powerful wizard of Teumdoth — even mages such as Porvul Shuk and Ongliath the Red did not challenge this claim. It was said that Montath was already ranked Tremulator, Effectuator, and Fulminator, and could very well have skills which would make him an Equilibriator, a manipulator of all-governing Equilibrium itself! He was also the sworn foe of Calim Pulsifer, for not only had he been deceived on numerous occasions by the Velvet Knife, but he and his familiar were petrified for over a year in Moilerve's Chamber of Ossifications, by Pulsifer's hand. Dissatisfied with apologies, the wizard still nursed grudges against him.

Despite his fear, Pulsifer risked another glance. Montath and his familiar were not to be seen. Glancing about and upward with unpleasant expectations, he decided to hasten to the Mournful Lute; the hijret Firkui was both phenomenally prescient, and malevolently vindictive. He rushed half-stooped beside the wall of the embankment, recalling stories he'd heard of Montath's ever-growing power — of his citadel Krikenvaxi, in Phontyque, built of stones with the mage's screaming enemies embedded in them, and raised in the span of a single night by unseen hands. It was also said that Montath privately ignored the rules of polite society, taking as he wished those women who pleased him, regardless of their station, for his seraglio deep within the citadel — and none gainsaid him.

He cursed. He had no intention of becoming part of the wizard's masonry! He rushed down an alleyway between warehouses, beyond which he saw a street he thought to recognize. As he went by an opened door, he slowed to avoid a collision with two laborers who were man-handling crates into the alley. Passing them with a friendly nod, he caught a fragment of their conversation as he went by.

"— somomorph? They say it's his daughter! He brought her to Yawamris for to try an' restore 'er girlish form, would yer believe it?"

"That mage-boy, with that hijret on 'is shoulder! Th' little devil looked at me — I swear it made my bones hurt! Bad luck for Yawamris, that creature is!"

The other man laughed. "Yer scared of yer own shadder, you are! That wizard boy is a mean devil himself, though, from what I hear… He come here to help the old collecter shed the somomorph poundage from his baby's bones! Har!"

Somewhat enlightened by this bit of discussion, Pulsifer sidled by and hurried away. By the time he reached the street on which the Mournful Lute was located, he had already decided to leave Yawamris immediately. He stepped suddenly into a shadowed doorway, staring at the two figures coming out of the inn some fifty yards away.

Captain Fakness and the teamster Bolderge stood before the entrance to the Mournful Lute; frustration was etched on the latter's broad face. A portly gentleman, the inn's proprietor, stepped out as well — Fakness said something to him, and he nodded eagerly and went back inside. The constable and Bolderge turned away from Pulsifer and headed for the nearest watchpost, vanishing over the crest of the hill; Pulsifer went back the way he had come.

He circled until he was behind the Mournful Lute; here there were heaps of rubbish, a stenchy pool where chamberpots were emptied, and a storehouse belonging to the inn. Quickly he located Azahad's room, and, making certain that no one was in sight, he applied his expertise to the task at hand. Soon he stood upon the second-story ledge. The shutter was ajar, and the window was raised an inch. He lay on his belly, one leg hanging in air, and peered through the sooty glass.

A figure sat on the bed — he brushed away a bit of the dust from the window with one finger. Azahad Zuzirco, facing the door, had her reinforcer in her hand. Apparently she was frightened by the presence of Bolderge…A red gleam leapt from the ring on her finger. Thinking that he had been detected, Pulsifer started to open the window and clamber into the room—there came a knock at the door, and Azahad jumped. Pulsifer pulled away from the window, listening.

Azahad's voice was without a quaver. "Come in—it's not locked." Pulsifer heard the door open and close, the sound of a man's heavy booted tread.

"Bolderge has agreed to press no charges against you, for the time being." The voice was that of Captain Fakness! Pulsifer's lip twisted in disappointment. "Of course, I could still guarantee a lifetime of misery for you in the miner's brothels; but since you came forth with the truth, I will be magnanimous. If Bolderge's property is recovered, he says he will not dispute your business dealing with Srod Yaorn—but he wants to speak with you privately, before making a final decision about swearing a lawsuit against you…He says to tell you that further negotiations may be necessary between you."

"What of the reward? Am I still eligible?" Her voice was almost pleading.

"If the man is indeed Pulsifer, you will receive a sizeable amount of gold—less the fines for your misrepresentations. The amount of these fines depends on whether or not we recover the incendiary bowl he stole from your wagon; Mistress Murlda is quite upset. If he is not Pulsifer, you will have to be satisfied with my gratitude for assisting in the capture of a felon; we shall have to find another way, however, of settling your account."

"He is Pulsifer, I am sure of it! He is left-handed, and he fits the description that the League issued to its drivers! I also saw a placard, bearing his likeness, in Nishar! But I assert my claim to Moilerve's reward—this is a matter separate from my own misdemeanors!"

Fakness laughed. "Yes, he does look like the rogue, doesn't he? Your assertiveness is admirable, Azahad; you are beautiful, as well. For the consideration of a few nights' companionship, I could certify your claims and perhaps cancel your fines…"

"I am certain we can work something out," Azahad purred, in a silken voice.

"Good! Then I'll be going. Pulsifer may soon return. Immobilize him with your reinforcer when he enters the room — Master Selch will send for me when the rascal enters the inn. I would put men here, but the Council of Mage-Regents has issued an order of greater precedence, also dealing with the needs of the Lord Collector Moilerve. He and his somomorph daughter are at the School of Pharmacological Thaumaturgy; I am required to watch the Lady Sulshaine and take all available men with me. Sometimes her somomorph nature overrides her human restraint."

"I must leave the room only briefly, this evening, to conclude my business with Srod Yaorn. I will carry the reinforcer at all times, be assured! Pulsifer will not escape its flux!"

"Very well — Good Luck to you, Azahad." Pulsifer heard the sound of the captain's footsteps, then the opening and closing of the door. He backed away from the window and climbed onto the rooftop, where he hid in a hollow between two chimneys, his face set in a hard scowl of resentment and anger.

He was again surrounded by enemies, and treacherous acquaintances! The callous opportunism of Azahad Zuzirco stung him in a particularly painful manner. Although he had helped her by incapacitating the kouool and outwitting Bolderge Grallko, she apparently held no gratitude for him, and in fact had betrayed him for the sake of most selfish motivations! It was obvious that she intended to not only turn him over to the authorities for the reward on his head, but to also implicate him as the thief of a valuable object she herself had taken — surely planning to sell it at a later date! The depth of her iniquity, however, did not enrage him so much as his own gullibility, for it was evident that she had intended to do these things from the first moment she met him!

He fumed, as the sun slowly sank from its zenith and into the afternoon.

She knew who he was — he would make certain that she never forgot! An occasional blast of cold, roof-wandering wind blew into his cranny as he plotted, his chin on his fists, his elbows on his knees.

The sun finally vanished behind the mountains, and the temperature plummeted as evening fell. Pulsifer habitually muttered a curse against the oncoming Winter, and stood up on the sloping roof, adjusting his swordbelt and bedroll. He could no longer stay outside, without donning his traveler's clothes — cumbersome gear for inching along the ledge below! He moved to the edge of the roof, stared warily at the empty alleyway between the inn and its storehouse, and then lowered himself to the ledge.

Moving with swift and sure balance, he moved to Azahad's window; again he peered within. Lamps burned brightly inside, illuminating the room before his gaze and rendering him invisible from the interior. He was acutely aware of his limned form, as it might be viewed by anyone passing by below.

Azahad lay on the bed, dozing. Close by her hand was the reinforcer; on her other hand, the proximity-ring gleamed brightly for five or six seconds, sensing Pulsifer's presence. He tried the window; finding it now closed and locked, he mumbled one of a few minor opening charms he knew, and slid a flat and pliable tool beneath, to attack the latch.

He knew not if it were by virtue of the cantrip or his skill, but the latch turned with a click. Azahad moved, but did not wake; gingerly opening the window, he slipped into the room, hoping that the cold air would not instantly arouse her.

She didn't stir. Closing the window, he went to the bedside, took her weapon and shoved it beneath the back of his belt; then he stood staring at her in indecision for half a minute. Despite his anger, he could not help but admire her vigorous beauty. Finally he sighed, drew his sword, and tickled her throat with its tip.

Her eyes shot wide, focusing immediately on the blade before her face.

For a second her hand groped for her missing reinforcer — then she grew still and glared at him. He bent swiftly and kissed her on the forehead.

"Hello, Azahad — it is so pleasant to find you waiting for me in bed! But I have come to inform you of my imminent departure, for I fear that our dalliance is at an end. This evening you will not venture downstairs to complete your transaction with Srod Yaorn — he will have to come to you."

She was livid with hatred. "You are truly the despicable Pulsifer, despoiler of the dreams and efforts of others! I can see why the name of the Uncursable One is now a curse among mages and collectors alike —"

Pulsifer shrugged, still smiling. "I find their attention flattering. Do not forget that I am also the Velvet Knife, foremost strategist of Teumdoth! You should have considered this, before plotting my betrayal —"

Her tone became plaintive. "You are destined to be apprehended by the Brotherhood — I merely sought to hasten the unavoidable! My life's ambition is to provide a service to lonely and anxious men, and in this sense I am working toward the restoration of a multitude of Equilibriums! Do you not see that the burden of many soul-debts would be lessened by assisting my cause? Only for this reason did I seek the reward on you!"

"Your unselfishness moves me to admiration — but the money you were to receive for the kouool will ease my soul aplenty. When someone arrives with the message that the collector awaits you below, you will summon him here, to your room…"

She pouted sullenly. "I refuse to assist you in robbing me of money I have rightfully earned!"

"Very well. I made the capture of the creature possible; I can likewise provide it with an opportunity for escape. Perhaps if the jar were left open, with you tied to the bed beside it —"

She made a wry face. "I have been hasty in my refusal. Surely you deserve some recompense for the trouble I have caused you!"

"Indeed. Now, be still while I tie you — these sheets will do. Do not force me to render you senseless! I am a gentleman by nature, and dislike striking a woman, even when I am left with no alternative!"

She eyed him dubiously as he bound her arms and legs with strips of the sheet. Next he fastened her upper body to the bedposts at the headboard with one long strip, wrapped twice about her torso. She sat immobilized, her face crestfallen.

Pulsifer stood back to inspect his handiwork; then he took his sword from where it leaned against the foot of the bed, and resheathed it.

"I must say that I have never seen you look more lovely! Now, be silent, for I've matters to attend to! If you cry or scream, I will fill your mouth with the jar containing the boneless ghoul. Do you understand?"

She nodded, tears of rage in her eyes. He searched the room quickly, taking out the kouool-jar and setting it upon the nightstand. The creature fluttered like a coiled mass of feathery gills. From a place beneath the floorboard underneath the chamberpot, he retrieved the sigil-covered casket he had taken from Bolderge. He held it in one hand, inspecting it, wondering as to its purpose.

He drew a finger along one line of glyphs, and a tingling sensation ran from his fingertip and up his arm. He poked it in various places, but nothing happened. Finally he pressed two glyphs simultaneously, and a chatter as of distant voices burst from the box for an instant.

Startled, he drew his fingers away, and with a growl of impatience, pressed a different pair of symbols. A low, sonorous moan rolled forth from the casket, to terminate in a single phrase:

"What is your question?"

Pulsifer jumped. "With whom am I speaking?" he asked suspiciously.

"I am called Dacdull, the Interlocutor. Is that your question? Please strive for clarity of meaning."

Pulsifer pursed his lips cautiously. "I am the owner of the object in which you dwell. Describe the identity and function of the box." As he spoke, he held it away from himself, lest he be inundated with dangerous energies.

Despite her own situation, Azahad watched with fascination.

"You hold the cask of Sranophaez, Archimage of Sonda. The cask contains fifty-two thousand entities, reduced to the dimensions of midges. The entities — my brethren — were extracted from the essences of dead deities, each of these discovered in sundry grottoes of the Upper Cavern Realms by Sranophaez, over the course of two hundred and twelve years. Any combination of two of the symbols summons a specific group of deity-mites, if the manual action is accompanied by a simple summons, and each group performs a distinct service."

Pulsifer grinned. "What are these services?"

The voice called Dacdull paused before replying. *"If you will consult the Booklet of Manipulative Instruction, your needs will be met more expediently. It is simply-indexed for the most basic comprehension —"*

"I am not a simpleton!" Pulsifer angrily replied. "The book has been lost for centuries! Sranophaez and Sonda have been frozen beneath northern ice for seven thousand years! You will perform the function of directory, Dacdull—"

"*This I cannot do; I am the Interlocutor. I instruct as to the protocol of function, but do not act as tabulator of contents. If you desire a service, select a pair of glyphs and summon their attendants—but be warned! This may prove hazardous without the Booklet! Once summoned, a group of attendants must perform its service, and will not return to the cask until this is done! Nor may any glyph-combination be invoked more than once in a fortnight, in the interest of maintaining a balanced world-state. I am the only exception to this regulation—I am always ready to serve you.*"

"I see." Pulsifer seated himself on the bed. "My fingers have slipped— which glyphs summoned the Interlocutor?"

"*I respond to the broken reed and gaping clam.*"

"And what is the appropriate vocal summons for the others?"

"*Anything constituting a call on your part—to summon me, you made an impatient sound in your throat. But 'Come Forth' will usually suffice.*"

"Excellent!" Pulsifer exclaimed in a friendly tone. "You have performed your function well, Interlocutor; the information you have passed to me is concise. You are dismissed."

The box was silent. Pulsifer twisted and slipped it into the tight roll of clothing on his back, a grin of satisfaction on his lean, wolfish face. Azahad cleared her throat.

"You are indeed crafty, Pulsifer—I see now how you have survived the anger of the Eight Upper Classes! You are handsome, and accomplished in lovemaking, as well as resourceful! I regret my betrayal, and see the error of my deceptive and short-sighted ways! Untie me, take me with you—I can lead you safely out of Yawamris, along roads known to few!"

He looked her sidelong. "Your words carry scant sincerity for me, Azahad; but I will consider it, contingent upon how well you cooperate with my requests!"

"My helpfulness will be exemplary! Instruct me, and judge my performance!"

"Listen then to my instruction, and earn leniency." He began to speak to her lowly, and she listened with an earnest expression.

An hour later he sat before the fire, looking occasionally at Azahad Zuzirco. They did not speak, for he had nothing more to say to her, and she had been instructed again to silence. He reached behind his back and pulled forth the reinforcer. Her eyes grew large.

"How do I operate this device?"

She shook her head. "It is inoperable in your hands, for it is attuned specifically to the activity of my own nervous system. It could be retuned to work for another, but that is a technical matter of which I know nothing, since I am not a sorceress trained in such things. After attunement by Weldren the Mage-Weaponeer, it took two months for me to master its many functions. It is pointless for you to even consider using it; your position seems to call for immediate resources of protective force. I recommend that you consult the talking box."

"Your own position hardly qualifies you as a competent advisor," Pulsifer retorted. "There is surely a basic maneuver to unleash the energy of the reinforcer?"

"A snap of the wrist, and a squeeze to the handle. Attitude of head and hands, sometimes a tenseness of buttocks, are necessary as well. But in a hand other than mine, the burst of magical energy would be directionless, uncontrolled—"

"I am not unfamiliar with similar devices," Pulsifer interjected. "I will keep the reinforcer, as well as this." He rose and moved swiftly to her side, to yank the proximity-ring from her thumb. It fit his middle finger snugly. She opened her mouth to protest, and the stone flashed a bright red. He motioned her to silence as someone knocked at the door. The knock was repeated, and he waved for her to answer. She raised her voice calmly, without a quaver.

"Who is it?"

A dry impatient voice echoed in the hall. "It is I, Srod Yaorn. I have been waiting half an hour—Why do you delay? Are you coming to the door, or do I take my money and go home?"

Pulsifer nodded at her, and Azahad called: "I'm coming; one moment."

Pulsifer unbolted the door, cracked it to peer out—then he jerked it open with one hand, pulling the snake-masked collector into the room with his other. Srod Yaorn gave a squawk of protest, then Pulsifer struck him on the jaw, shattering his thin lacquered mask. The collector slid to the floor, and Pulsifer closed the door on an empty hall.

Searching the sprawled collector, he at last pulled forth a fat money-purse. He tied the man with the rest of the torn sheet, and, removing the mask, he stuffed a knot of cloth in his mouth. Srod Yaorn would sleep for a while, he was sure — Azahad smiled conspiratorially.

"You have more than enough money, now, thanks to my assistance — take me with you, and we can depart together! I will change my name, to avoid retributive curses, and we will use the kouool again and again, to lure collectors into situations identical to this! I know of hidden passes in the Thuradin Mountains that will see us in Kalsurridin in four days! I will help you escape Fakness, and the grasp of the aristocrats — and do not forget the warm comforts with which I can ease the cold passing of many nights!"

"I prefer the bracing company of the ever-present Chill," Pulsifer replied. "It would neither slide a knife into my back while I slept, nor carry word of my whereabouts to my enemies! You are lucky that I do not give you to the kouool, Azahad; be satisfied with your lot."

Her face twisted with hatred. He gagged her also, and going to her shagreen valise, he emptied its contents onto the floor. He pulled forth the wooden box containing the glistening bowl, and taking the vessel out, he placed it back into the valise; he put the chamberpot into the box. He also put the kouool and Yaorn's purse into the bag, and after a moment of contortion, the Cask of Sranophaez as well. He turned to Azahad with a smile of triumph.

A rattle at the window sent his hand flying to his sword-hilt. He went to it to listen, and the ring on his right hand gleamed a brilliant yellow. He stepped back. The wind moaned through the back-alley; the hairs on his neck and forearms rose upon tingling flesh. The light dimmed from the ring, and the sensation of presence passed. He hastened in his preparations, removing his back roll and donning the warm, many-creased and pocketed overclothes on top of his other outfit. Next he buckled on his sword and pouch-belt, then fastened the valise to his back, where buckles, leathern straps, and adjustable thongs were plentiful for fastening gear. The reinforcer he slipped into a pocket; Azahad watched through tear-filled eyes, thrashing occasionally against her restraints.

Blowing Azahad a kiss, he fastened the hood and mask of his kabeyui over his features, and pulled on his gloves. It was late enough in the Warming season to warrant wearing the mask when going out of doors at night — but it could still raise suspicion, especially in town. Nevertheless, he didn't want an alert citizen to see at his face, not since the authorities were aware of his presence. Waving goodbye to the struggling Azahad, he stepped over Srod Yaorn and out into the hall, avoiding the window as an exit for fear of whatever supernatural denizen of the ancient, frozen Earth might be lurking outside. He drew the door shut behind him.

The noise from the taproom of the Mournful Lute was far from mournful; it rolled up the hallway in babbling waves, loud and boisterous. Pulsifer strode quickly and with a swagger of confidence along the hall and down the stair, scarcely drawing a glance from the mostly lower-caste crowd. A white-haired odalisque from Ibret danced the Rite of Sogypillak the Fertile upon a tabletop, while a troubadour sang a song about dagger-toothed Cucumerin, a sorcerous stallion fed on human flesh, mount of the ancient mage-huntsman Iskiruen. Another man played a seven-stringed rebec in one corner; Pulsifer edged past the yelling forms of the audience, and moved toward the door.

Selch the innkeeper sat near the entrance, conversing with a robed and hooded man; leaning beside the door, his beefy arms crossed, stood Bolderge.

He surveyed the room with the manner of a guard-dog. Pulsifer veered in the direction opposite that in which Bolderge gazed, intending to slip past him — this drew the courier's attention, and Bolderge stepped in his path with a grin.

The thick man pulled forth a long-bladed knife, disdaining the use of the reinforcer hanging at his belt. "Stand, you dog — draw the sword you stole, and attempt to save your miserable life!"

As if by the stilling command of an Effectuator, the room grew quiet, for a fight was entertainment cherished by the low-born masses of frozen Teumdoth. Pulsifer felt every eye upon him — suddenly Selch jumped to his feet, crying out in a cracking voice.

"It is he! It is the rogue Pulsifer! Set upon him!"

"No, he is mine!" Bolderge roared. He lunged at Pulsifer, thrusting at his midsection with the knife — Pulsifer twisted, kicked the rushing Bolderge in his groin, and took advantage of the moment to draw his sword. He parried the next thrust without difficulty, and with a certain nonplussed, graceful style.

"I am Pulsifer, you lumpen!" he cried, "Master of all martial and manly arts! I won't be stopped by an oaf such as you! Move away from the door, or die!"

"Kill me, then!" the red-faced Bolderge sputtered. He attacked anew, slashing with abandon, and Pulsifer was momentarily driven back. The darkrobed man by the door rose, and threw back his hood — a whorl of green fire sparked and whistled about his head and shoulders, and an eerie hum filled the air.

Their quarrel forgotten, Pulsifer and Bolderge halted in fear. Morskured Montath smiled a suave and merciless smile. At his belt Pulsifer recognized the sword Lendyljunct, a sentient blade with black hilts and a red-gemmed pommel; the wizard's voice was as cold as the high plateaus of the glacier Senemene.

"Pulsifer is mine to punish. There is a disequilibrium between us which surpasses this petty squabble! Step back, fellow — lower your blade. Do not move, Pulsifer." He raised his hand and snapped his fingers, creating a spark of green-gold light which danced in the air. "Firkui, Attend!"

The spark darted and grew, becoming a two-foot-long, luminous form, then a scaled, beaked, anthropomorphic creature of disturbing aspect. Firkui the hijret hovered beside Montath, then alighted on the mage's shoulder. The hijret hiccoughed, flushing from mauve to purple and back to mauve; despite its beak, it grinned at the back-stepping Pulsifer.

"It has been long since last we encountered one another, Pulsifer," Montath said, motioning with one hand. By unseen agency, a table slid to block Pulsifer's retreat. "Two years since you left me immobilized among Moilerve's statuary, with only my thoughts, and Firkui, for company. Of course, I could thank you — my powers of concentration, the potencies inculcated in me by a year's isolation and the hate which burned in me, have actually increased my efficacy! But surely you have heard of my growing power — my effectiveness you will discover in due time. You remember Firkui? It was he who flushed you from the egress of the upstairs window. He remembers you well, and has informed me that he will relish renewing the acquaintanceship between you. Ah, do not be foolish — be so kind as to relinquish your weapon."

"Montath!" Pulsifer exclaimed in a jolly voice, as he carefully slid his sword into its scabbard. "See, I am your friend! Could I not have destroyed you while you were ossified, if I had so wished? A knife-point through one eye would have done the trick — but I did not kill you! I sincerely believed that a brief period of contemplation would restore your rationality, and make you aware of the extreme severity of your proposed actions against me! Allow me to depart in peace, and I shall always hold you in the highest regard, as a man of good judgment and level temperament! We have been friends in the past — allow the harmony between us to continue!"

The fat Selch quivered with excitement. "Paralyze him, before he flees! I hereby set forth my claim to the reward, since he is captured in my inn!"

"Your claim is noted," Montath said, still watching Pulsifer. "However, if he tries to escape, I will be forced to unleash a tremulation. Immobilization would entail identifying him by name or form, and due to his powerful buffer against curses, the effectuation might be reflected back at me. But if he flees, I will loose a blast which will reduce him to atoms."

Bolderge slumped against the wall, awed by the presence of the wizard and his familiar, and obviously wishing to remove himself from one about to be struck with energies. Pulsifer tensed, unsure of what to do, and Montath spoke to him again.

"You must be brought to account for your incogitant misdeeds. I would immediately wrap you in mists of acid gas, or introduce a menstruating vesp into your visceral cavity, but you must first make amends for actions perpetrated against others. Moilerve and his unfortunate daughter, and the wizards Pog Trimmanax and Howmish Kaalmale come to mind; in fact, Erhis is being brought here at this moment, to renew the closeness which once existed between you.

Tatimoi Murlda also has plans for you, in the slag-pits beneath the volcano. What a popular fellow you are! You have so many appointments! Come, accompany me outside — do not be recalcitrant, or I will deal harshly with you now instead of later."

Captain Fakness rose from another table, doffing the broad-brimmed hat he'd worn to conceal his features. In his hand was his sword. "I am here to inspire cooperation; please do as Sir Montath requests of you." Blade leveled, he moved toward Pulsifer, who began to shake with adrenaline and fear. Montath turned to whisper to Firkui — the hijret transfixed Pulsifer with a stare that he felt, like the stomach-turning sensation of standing suddenly at the brink of a yawning pit. The creature rose, hovering, to halt before him; reaching out with scrawny arms and clawed fingers, it unbuckled the mask-portion of his kabeyui, dropping it to flap like a leathern beard at his chin. The hijret motioned for Pulsifer to follow and drifted toward the door, which Montath indicated with a smile and an accommodating gesture. He had no choice but to move forward — behind him, the unoccupied table moved along on walking legs, and the patrons of the inn murmured excitedly.

Bolderge spoke up timorously. "Most humble pardon, Lord Mage — but this man has property of mine other than my sword, an item of great potential value to me. Before you remove him, might you not return this thing to me? I ask only because I am a poor and hardworking man, and food for my family is at risk —"

Montath made a hand-motion, and both the hijret and Pulsifer halted. The wizard glared into his prisoner's eyes. "Yet another disproportionate act! Do you have an item belonging to this man?"

Pulsifer shrugged. "All items on my person are mine, by the impersonal Law of Equilibration. The world deals unjustly with me, and I extract recompense! But take the thing, if you wish; it is useless, as far as I can tell. It is hidden in a glass container, in the valise at my back. The container, however, is mine — in the interest of rightful balances you will return it to me!"

"If anything, I shall deal fairly with you in terms of Equilibrium!" Montath's face was stern. "Firkui — find the container and remove its contents; then return the container to Pulsifer's bag of plunder. We shall strip from him things other than his stolen belongings, at a later time — the skin from his body, the nerves from his spine."

The hijret darted to Pulsifer's back. He did not move as the mage's familiar opened the valise at the top and dug into the bag. In a second he heard it hiccough, then it was before him and moving toward Bolderge with the kouool-jar in its two-handed grasp. Its fingers worked at the catch of the lid.

Bolderge's mouth dropped open as his eyes locked on the jar. "But that isn't my —"

The watching patrons yelped in surprise as the lid popped off the jar, as if propelled by great pressure. Firkui squawked like a duck. A long, green-white stream of arching protoplasm sprang from the jar in the startled hijret's grip, to land unerringly in Bolderge's gaping mouth. The kouool filled the cavity for an instant, then with a gurgle it was gone down the teamster's throat.

Bolderge fell in upon himself like a deflated bladder; the snapping of bones was plainly heard. Montath leapt to the collapsing man's side, one hand raised, a spell upon his lips.

Pulsifer shoved a hand into his pocket and pulled forth the reinforcer.

Firkui turned, and flew at him like an angry hornet — he snapped the reinforcer like a whip, squeezing the handle with all his strength. A hot sizzle and white brilliance filled the air, and he was racked with a burning, muscle-jerking energy, which filled his head with excruciating, red-orange light.

Purely by reflex he released the device, and was thrust away by a blast of force as it left his hand.

He fell back against the table and over, to tumble to the floor. His hand closed on the leg of a stool and he pulled himself up, lights still dancing before his eyes. Something which burned like a miniature comet shot about the room at incredible speed, and screams of terror, issuing from floor-hugging patrons, filled the air. Half-crouching, Pulsifer looked about desperately for a path to freedom.

The comet shot past with a whine — he saw that the coruscating, fire-wrapped head was the agonized, squirming Firkui, which hissed like a boiling cauldron — the tail was the uncontrolled reinforcer, a white-hot fork of screeching force. Between these two glowing components was a blazing band of rushing energies, moving in ceaseless waves from the reinforcer, to the hijret, then back to the reinforcer; beneath the flailing hijret leapt Morskured Montath, a blue net of woven power sprouting from his fingertips and stretched between his outspread arms. Nodes of red, blue, and yellow light issued from his mouth and nostrils as he shouted potent Words, and tankards and bottles around the room exploded at the sound of them.

Fakness rose from the floor, where he had been thrown by his nearness to the reinforcer's initial blast. His sword was gone, but he came at Pulsifer barehanded, his face grimly purposeful. Swinging his upper body as he rose, Pulsifer hit the constable between the eyes with the oaken stool. Fakness fell, and did not rise again. Pulsifer ran for the door.

On the floor beside the portal, a quivering metamorphosis was taking place alongside the broken, white-clean bones of Bolderge. A mound of flesh was rapidly forming itself into a nude twin of the devoured courier — the kouool sat up, opened its eyes, and slapped its hands against its chest. Seeing Pulsifer, it smiled.

"Not yet," it said, in its stolen voice, "but another time. My gratitude to you will consist of ripping out your heart — but I must rest, before I begin the great Hunt." It sprang upright and bolted out the door — after a backward glance at the still-chanting Montath and lowering Firkui, Pulsifer followed it into the night.

The stars gleamed coldly above, eyes of the frozen wind which twisted down the street. The naked figure of a man, capering and dancing joyfully, vanished over the westward hill, going in the direction of the caravanserai; Pulsifer ran to the east. As he went, the tumult of the activities in the Mournful Lute followed his footfalls into the street, as did Montath's ear-aching runes.

He looked back. The Mournful Lute was burning with eerie green flames, and customers poured into the street. A pudgy figure he thought to be Master Selch fell to the cobblestones, and was stepped upon repeatedly by more nimble individuals. He glimpsed Azahad Zuzirco, a scrap of sheet still about her ankle, stumbling from the flickering doorway. Over the hill there lurched a huge and shambling shape, pale as pack-ice — it seemed to fill the road with its largeness, and around it there swarmed a dozen men, each holding a taut rope bound to its monstrous form.

The somomorph Erhis stopped, as if studying the fracas below. Beside her the dwarfed figure of Moilerve seemed to gesticulate beseechingly — apparently aroused by the hysteria of the scene, the composite of woman and wildland mutation first swayed back and forth ponderously, then began to strain against its tethers. With a sudden wrench it pulled free, and its captors were sent sprawling or scrambled to get out of its path. It rumbled like an avalanche of flesh toward the crowd at the bottom of the hill. A croaking roar rang between the buildings, and the words were clear:

"Pulsifer, My Love — I am here! Here!"

The subject of this declaration stretched his long legs and ran, as the somomorph plowed into the press of smaller bodies; screams of agony lent him even greater speed. He did not stop running until he was astride a stolen, black-scaled durdelain, and swiftly departing the city for the mountains to the north; behind him, green-burning Yawamris shook with a blight of confusion and carnage.

On distant hills, tall, silent parsennocs gazed wonderingly at the glow.

Part Two

An Icy Weave

Chapter 1

A Jaunt in the Forests

The Warming had died, before Winter's rage. Now the midday air was bitterly cold; the nine months of deadly, flesh-crystallizing Chill had begun in earnest. Bundled in his layered traveler's clothes, Pulsifer scrambled up an ice-slickened rise, the steam of his exertions pouring from the mouth-slit of his rime-crusted kabeyui. He paused, catching his breath as he scanned both the skies above, and the vista below. Yawamris was a month behind him, but pursuit was not.

Before him the bannis-weed-covered plain known as the Yablast Shakal abruptly terminated about four miles away, at a high, dark wall of green foliage; this stretched as far as he could see to the north, south, and east. On their charts, cartographers marked this expanse as the Forests of Iskiruen, named for the long-dead archimage of the defunct Perfidic faction who, a thousand years before, had indiscriminately hunted ochdeviants, human beings, and other creatures through its thickets and glades. It was said that the ghosts of his victims still wandered the murk beneath hoary hardwoods and stupendous conifers. More fleshly dangers were abundant in its largely unknown depths, but Pulsifer found himself viewing it with relief, eager to risk its uncertain perils rather than the distinct ones which had hunted him across the plain.

His hardy durdelain, a vigorous biped, had not succumbed to the frozen rigors of the open steppe—but a huge pride of jinmonanders had proved too much for his sharp-toothed mount. The twitching beast had been dragged into a burrow, where, considering the season, it was probably paralyzed with poisons and left as fodder for unhatched young; Pulsifer had narrowly avoided becoming a meal or worse for the faceless, wattle-necked adults, by leaping onto a chunk of ice in a rushing, frigid stream.

At the present, the night-roaming jinmonanders of a week past were not the source of his apprehension. He watched the leaden skies as he slid down the hill, for this morning he had seen the questing silhouettes of many predatory fottermees, cruising like giant kites above the plain. Their carnivorous inclinations were bothersome enough, but their seemingly-organized flight-patterns, as well as their numbers, spoke of sorcerous influence upon their behavior. Fottermees were solitary creatures, large and ravenous, each beast typically territorial and dominating a wide area. More than likely the lizard-like birds were under the influence of Morskured Montath and his hijret, if the wizard's familiar had survived the unharnessed power of the reinforcer.

Pulsifer began to run briskly, despite his hunger and fatigue. Once beneath the trees, he might find a secluded place, build a shelter, and live apart from other human beings for a while, particularly those of the Eight Upper Classes!

But he knew that this was but a fancy—the forest would be too dangerous for a solitary wanderer. He would have to find a place of temporary refuge among woodsfolk, or obtain a guide and companion...The grey, brown, and purplish blades of bannis waved urgently before him, as if imploring him to haste. He sped up, knowing that a variety of food would be found in the forests, for the bitter taste of life-sustaining bannis-weed, which he despised above all other foodstuffs, still coated his dry tongue. Without his predacious, swift-footed mount, he had been required to bring down his own game, a difficulty on the open plain.

He'd thought of using the Cask of Sranophaez in an attempt to acquire a meal—but he remembered the warning of the voice in the box, as to the noncancelable nature of the summoned entities, before a task had been given them. Also his caution was inspired by the episode with the reinforcer, which he now knew could very well have destroyed him rather than securing his freedom. He decided to procure his meals by the tedious and traditional manner of hunting, and gathering edible tidbits as he went.

The trees grew comfortingly near. His harsh breath, pounding feet, and the rough swishing of the frost-coated grasses were the only sounds to be heard. Suddenly his stomach lurched as a large black shadow, winged of shape, swept over and past him. He glanced up — above him there circled a fottermee of the yellow-winged variety, its beakful of jutting teeth glittering in the brief glow of a stray sunbeam as it wheeled in his direction. It swept down with astonishing speed.

A fear-inspired burst of energy shot from his brain to his feet and legs. The dark depths of the forest loomed — there was a rush of air and Pulsifer ducked, as the eight-hundred pound predator swooped near. He was struck a glancing blow on the shoulder as the fottermee missed its mark, but the force of it sent him tumbling head over heels beneath the nearest outlying trees. The fottermee pulled up, circling for another attack; scrambling to his feet, he sprinted across an open area and toward the safety of the thicker trees. He darted beneath the wide-stretched, icicle-hung limbs of a thistleoak — there was a high-pitched cry as the fottermee hit the ground, sending out gusts of air from its leathery wings, and waddled rapidly toward him. He threw himself behind another tree, drawing his shortsword, and chopped at its snapping head, which was the size of that of a horse, with a beak two feet long and as big around as his thigh. The head pulled back on its feathered, scaly neck; Pulsifer plunged through a thicket of brambles, and away.

Behind him the creature flapped its wings ineffectually, unable to follow him into the close thicknesses of the outlying hardwoods. He stopped to look back at it — it peered with an air of unusual intelligence beneath the trees, apparently unable to see him in the gloom. His pulse pounded in his ears; the fottermee paused in its neck-weaving movements as though in reflection. Its beak opened, and its voice was that of a beast, twisted by magic to form screeching words in the humantongue.

"I will have you yet, O most frumious of scoundrels! The undeniable attractions which regulate the webs of interpersonal interaction will eventually bring you into my hands! Equilibrium will yet see you as my prisoner in Krikenvaxi! You may have gone to ground, but I will flush you from hiding if I must overturn every tree in the Forests of Iskiruen, or blast each withered root!"

Montath's message still echoing among the boles, the fottermee turned, spread its great wings, and took flight. The noise of its departure was soon swallowed by the rustle and creak of the trees. Pulsifer unbuckled the mask of his kabeyui, leaving his hood on to protect his head. He bit his lip until it almost burst — his temporary refuge had become a certain prison! He could not leave the forest now — Montath would surely soon be in close pursuit. Of course, the forests covered hundreds upon hundreds of square miles, territories seldom-traveled, or completely unexplored; surely this offered a diversity of terrain in which to hide. Dangers here, however, as anywhere outside of a city, would be too numerous to begin to name.

For a few minutes he sat sulking upon a fallen limb, while thick-pelted squirrels chattered above him — then the memory of Morskured Montath's hijret familiar, capable of swift movement from one point to another, jolted him into action. Hastily he rose to his feet, sheathed his sword, and set out in a direction he judged to be northeastward, toward the woodland's heart. The thought of the demonic Firkui continued to lend vigor to his limbs. He passed through glades surrounded by tall, gently-moving trees, blanketed in frost and stillness; he skirted waterways where he spied the splashings of undines and the spoor of giant weasels. Surprising a grouse, he leapt on it from behind a tree, and stuffed its carcass into the valise on his back.

For hours through the afternoon he walked, finding that the Forests of Iskiruen were more densely inhabited than any wild place he had ventured into before. Three times he saw the speckled nymphs called sylebers lying languidly on stones and logs, basking in diluted sunlight with their arms outstretched. Their ample feminine charms were well-displayed. He nodded politely to them and hurried past, not caring to arouse either their friendly or less-friendly passions. Next he saw a herd of tuftdeer, stalked by a grey bear; he hid behind a tree until the bear was gone. Later in the afternoon he almost stumbled over a meditating, man-like nust, its spiked back bent, its head tucked beneath a bushy black tail; he passed it by without incident. Finally, shortly before dark, he strode beneath a fir-tree of enormous size. In the deep shadows of its boughs perched a sleeping prainquel, part man, part owl, part something else. It had not yet risen for the evening's hunt, and he hurried away from its vicinity, searching desperately for a place to pass the night.

Above the trees the day still lingered; beneath the canopy, gloom was deep. He moved through the more thickly-grown areas of the wood, avoiding trails and clearings, lest he come upon a parsennoc or other darkling — or a nocturnal predator of natural pedigree, a-prowl and hungry. At length he halted where a giant hardwood lay on its side, recently uprooted by a massive force. It was partially raised above the humus by the thick stubs of its once-proud limbs. Against one side of it was a copse of close-grown larches, overlooking a water-scored ravine — these provided a veritable wooden wall.

He bent and went cautiously into the niche between fallen tree and copse, worming along a narrow passage until he found himself in a triangular opening between the bent, half-crushed larches and the toppled giant. Above was a roof of tangled and broken branches, clean of ice; there was only one entrance, and on all sides was an abundant supply of fall-shattered firewood.

Digging a shallow pit with his gloved hands, he gathered some wood, took out his tinderbox, and set to work.

Soon he had a blaze leaping between the darkness of the narrow opening and himself. Even if his den were discovered by a darkling or other predator, the flames would keep him safe — except, perhaps, from hostile human beings. He roasted the grouse on a larch spit, burying its inedible parts and then cleansing his gloves with water from his flask. While his supper cooked, he stuffed mossy loam into the larger crevices between larches, to minimize the escape of his fire's light and keep out the wind. The smoke was broken and dissipated by the branches above, and his niche grew quickly warmer, though still chill.

He sighed, thankful that he had found a place to pass the night mostly hidden from inimical eyes, and away from the stupendous cold which would already surround his tiny den. While afoot on the steppe, he had been forced to dig shallow shelters in hillsides and flatter terrain, painstakingly tearing through the permafrost with his hands, knife, and even his sword.

He devoured the grouse quickly, relishing the nutty, wild flavor, then he buried the bones as he had its entrails. He sat close by the fire, warming his face and ungloved hands, picking his teeth with his knife-point. The ring he'd taken from Azahad Zuzirco reflected the light dully. He heard the frigid wind moaning through the forest, setting limbs to rattling like bones, and conifer-boughs to muttering. Placing the valise beside him, he began going through its contents as he often had before.

First he pulled out the purse he'd taken from Srod Yaorn, emptying its contents into his palm. Fourteen pieces of gold glittered in the firelight. He scowled — there would be no spending them in this wilderness! Putting the pouchful of coins back in the valise, he took out the golden bowl, admiring the relief-work which spiraled about it. Depicted were many male and female figures, some in poses of subjection; others, with wavy lines issuing from their mouths, probably represented rune-speaking mages. Often repeated was the figure and sometimes the enlarged head of an ugly dwarf, flames rolling from his mouth and lightnings leaping from his eyes.

Pulsifer stared into the bowl, fascinated by its shimmering, blue-grey inner surface. If he could but sell it! He resolved that, as soon as he won free of his current predicament, he would do just that. It was surely a valuable relic...

The fire popped violently, and a small shower of tiny coals fell. He cursed as he flailed about to beat them from his clothing, flinging the bowl to one side. A fragment of coal, glowing lambently, landed in the bottom of it, and he darted to remove it before it marred the dish's finish...

The bowl shook violently, emanating a distant rumble. Pulsifer pulled away as it filled with a red-hot light. The proximity-ring flashed yellow, blue, then yellow again, as if in indecision. The niche filled with stifling heat as a golden fog formed in the bowl, to solidify into a quaking magma which threatened to overflow the container. The lava lumped, swirled, and lumped again, to become the coal-eyed face of the dwarfish being shown on the vessel's exterior. Its eyes rolled about, until they looked on the cringing Pulsifer. The being in the bowl opened its mouth — the toothless interior had the look of a vast molten cavern. Waves of heat poured from it as the entity spoke, its voice stentorian:

"SHIGANDURE IS HERE. STATE YOUR NEED, SO THAT I MIGHT RETURN TO TLEOCAUZUALC. COME, DO NOT WAVER! MY TIME IS PRECIOUS — THE FABRIC WEAKENS WITH EACH AMPLIFICATION!"

Placing his hands on his shaking knees, Pulsifer quickly regained his composure. "To waste your time was not the purpose of this summoning; to question you is!"

"WHO ARE YOU? WHERE IS THE WITCH DACALEEVISH? I AM NO ORACLE —"

"I am the current owner of the bowl in which you reside," Pulsifer replied. "But I ask the questions." As he spoke to the thing, he noticed that several dry twigs rested against the outer surface of the bowl; the wood should have at least begun to smolder. With the incredible heat generated by the bowl-being, the vessel itself should have melted into a puddle of slag! A beetle crawled from beneath a twig, ran onto the side of the bowl, and sat preening its antennae. Pulsifer appreciated the awesome sorcery at work, as he addressed Shigandure again with a lofty air.

"Dacaleevish transferred the bowl to me as a token of her affection; she told me that you would provide instruction as to your purpose. For what reason are you so imprisoned? What are the services you provide for a summoner? From whence do you come? This information is essential, if we are to work well together."

"I AM NOT A PRISONER! I AM SHIGANDURE, THE IMMOLATOR, AND BINDING FORCE OF THE VERTEX OF TLEOCAUZUALC! WITH THE SUBJECTS OF MY SUZERAINITY, I HOLD INTACT ONE VERTEX OF ONE OF THE INFINITUDE OF NESTED TESSERACTS, A PROGRESSION OF UNIVERSES WHICH EXPANDS IN MANY DIRECTIONS FROM THIS ONE. I RESPONDED TO YOUR SUMMONS OF HEAT, BY TRAVELING ALONG THE VERTICES TO THIS SOFTER WORLD. BY A RECENT PACT WITH THE HUMAN MAGE MELGEONE, I BRING DEVASTATION OR IGNITION AT THE REQUEST OF WHOEVER BEARS THE BOWL. THE STUFF OF MY BEING, OF MY REALM, IS IN THIS PLACE AKIN TO THAT WHICH YOU CALL FLAME —"

Pulsifer swallowed dryly. He realized that he spoke with a demiurge, an autonomous being with its origins upon another plane of reality. Such entities had been utilized a few times in millennia past, by human and ochdeviant wizards, in their ravaging wars with one another — and legends spoke of nothing but massive destruction left by the release of such beings. They were even more unpredictable than supernatural agents of the Earth — the djinn, vriodoms, and other demons of inner concentricities — or the demons from other dimensions which were sometimes held in thralldom by mages. The 'recent pact' Shigandure mentioned was ancient in human terms — Melgeone the Savant was a mythical archimage, dead six thousand years. Pulsifer's stomach tightened painfully with fear and excitement — here was a weapon with which to fight Montath and other vengeful mages!

It took a conscious effort to keep the excitement from his voice. "How do I direct you to unleash your power in this world?"

"I REQUIRE AN EXACT PAYMENT FOR ANY SERVICE PERFORMED — A HUMAN LIFE IS THE USUAL FEE, ALTHOUGH I HAVE OFTEN ACCEPTED OCHDEVIANTS, VRIODOMS, AND OTHER POTENT ESSENCES. BY AGREEMENT I TAKE NONE OF THOSE HUMAN BEINGS TERMED 'MAGES,' HOWEVER. SWIFTLY, NOW, STATE YOUR NEED, SO THAT I MIGHT PREPARE; ACTION IN YOUR CRAMPED QUOIN OF SPACETIME REQUIRES PAINSTAKING CONCENTRATION, LEST THE WHOLE PLACE BE BLASTED. THIS IN TURN COULD DESTROY THE INTEGRITY OF THE ENTIRE TESSERACT-STRUCTURE, AND ENTROPY WOULD RULE AGAIN. EVEN NOW, THE WORKERS CLAMOR FOR MY RETURN! THE VERTEX SWAYS — HASTEN WITH YOUR REQUEST!"

Pulsifer made a diffident gesture with one hand. He had no human life but his own; not only would he be reluctant to relinquish it to the demiurge, but if the being would not assault a mage, Shigandure was useless. "Return to your realm — I merely wished to make your acquaintance! You will not be summoned again until you are needed."

The face of the demiurge swelled and reddened, small lightnings arching with cracklings and hissings from his features.

"YOU HAVE THREATENED THE STABILITY OF THE POLYVERSAL STRUCTURE FOR THE SAKE OF A WHIM?" he roared. *"IF NOT FOR THE NECESSITY OF MY SWIFT RETURN TO TLEOCAUZUALC, I WOULD TAKE YOU AS A MEAGER RECOMPENSE FOR MY WASTED TIME! WHEN NEXT YOU CALL ME FORTH, HAVE BOTH A PURPOSE AND MY*

*PAYMENT AT HAND! IF NOT, YOUR ESSENCE WILL BE SPLICED INTO
THE CONDUITS OF THE VERTEX!"*

Like a falling pastry, the face of Shigandure collapsed — the interior
of the bowl bubbled for a few seconds, then again assumed its customary luster.

Sweating and shaking, Pulsifer reached out and touched the bowl
with a fingertip; it was metallically cool to the touch. He hastily shoved
it back into the valise — nor did he take out the Cask of Sranophaez and
toy with it, as he had earlier thought of doing.

Now the hidden den was almost uncomfortably warm. With a start,
he noticed that both his face and the backs of his hands were reddened
and tender, as if they had been exposed to near-scalding water. With a
grumbled oath, he wished he had been able to win the bowl-entity's
goodwill, perhaps by explaining the accidental nature of the summons;
but it was doubtful that the demiurge was sympathetic to human error.
For a second he considered taking the bowl from the bag and burying it
in the loam; but its sale to the right clandestine buyer would fetch funds
to finance his own relocation! Some members of the Brotherhood
and Collectors, as well as many renegade or independent mages and
scholars, might still be willing to deal with the Velvet Knife if the
transaction were not revealed. He bundled up tight next to the fire,
facing the opening with his back to the wall of leaning larches, thinking
that he would keep the vessel until such time as he could arrange a
meeting with a potential buyer — but he did not think that he would
summon the redoubtable Shigandure again.

The night wind whistled through the treetops. His hood, mask and
gloves on, Pulsifer slept, waking often to refuel the fire and listen to
the night. Branches rattled, the wind soughed and cried; flodgets and
goatsuckers cooed and twittered. Despite the constant fire, the air in
the niche was cold once more; beyond its influence, the night would
be deadly of temperature indeed. When he slept, he did not dream,
but the darkness was haunted by fleeting images — the wrathful eyes
of Montath, the laughing, enticing mouth of the Erhis Sulshaine he
had known, the hovering threat called Firkui — these pictures and
others shot from black emptiness to fill his slumbering mind with
consternation and distress.

Finally he jerked awake once more. In his head rang faintly the roar of a mamonlex, the laugh of a djinni. The fire was disconcertingly low; the night was strangely quiet. Somewhere, an eppelero howled, shattering the ice-cold stillness. He sat up quickly, snapped some branches, and tossed them on the begging flames. The fire crackled eagerly upward, and in the darkness beyond the entrance to the hollow, something drew back with a clatter of chitinous legs.

Pulsifer unsheathed his sword with a steely rasp. Using one of the longer branches as a torch, he gripped and held it high. Tiny reflections of the light were thrown back from hundreds of convex lenses as the talycent bent low to peer into the niche. Its jet-black, human features were twisted into an unreadable smile, its compound, insect-like eyes were inscrutable. Beneath its human trunk, a many-legged, pauropodian body filled the passage with a segmented bulk. It whistled lowly, and Pulsifer was not certain if the sound were the result of a conscious act, or an exhalation of darkling breath.

For minutes they regarded each other, neither moving nor speaking. At length Pulsifer heaved a peevish sigh.

"Why do you wait? Surely you have some purpose in lingering — if the sun catches you, your husk will house the carrion-weasels by tomorrow evening."

"My patience is rewarded," the creature replied dryly. Its voice was sophisticated of accent, a dark baritone in which lurked both humor and malice. "I waited for the sound of your voice, so that I might absorb your manner of speech, tone, and inflection. Your appearance strikes a familiar chord, but you wear a mask — ahhh, I know you now! My people will marvel to learn that you are still alive…"

"We've never met, I'm sure," Pulsifer replied. After the devious parsennocs, the abstruse talycents were the night roamers he feared most. "Nor do I care to know you more intimately! I recommend that you rapidly depart, for the sun is coming and the black freeze retreats."

"The Collective Recollection holds much of you in its prism — but after all our observations of your activities, we are not certain of your true name. You have gone by so many… If you will give it to me, a corner of our knowledge will grow more complete."

Pulsifer shrugged. Due to his uncursable state, he did not fear to reveal his name to a thing of darkness. "I am called Pulsifer, by friends and foes alike. I am a wanderer, dispossessed by the uncaring flow of life. There, you have your piece of information for the talycent-mosaic! Now, leave me to greet the day."

The talycent spread black arms with an oily sheen to them, leaning against the fallen oak and the clustered larches. It lowered its gruesome head even more, as if it would enter the hollow, but the fire kept it back. "Your worries are groundless; the flesh of surface folk is a dish I scarcely savor, anymore. However, a prainquel is still hunting a mile to the west, and three parsennocs eat a living man in a cave two miles to the southeast. But you have provided me with information, and I am compelled to offer you one gem from the hoard of the things which my kind know — but ask quickly, for as you say, the night ends soon."

Unstrapping his kabeyui, Pulsifer bared his face. "This is surely a well-used talycent trick. I am no simple farmer — no darkling gift is worth having!"

The talycent smiled. "As a gesture of my honesty, I tell you this — my kind are incapable of uttering falsehoods. Acquiring and dispensing knowledge, the search for inherent truths, are our foremost purposes and reasons for existing. I will also tell you something else; a djinni out of Calambriel came shuddering up from the innermost depths of the Earth, to speak with our Queen about the Reascension of the infallible Pammoth. The name of Pulsifer, called Winter's Ender by the ifrit, was mentioned as well — only now do we have a definite face to fit to your name. The gifts given you by Pammoth the Singularity were also discussed; one boon you used wisely; one you dispensed foolishly; another, you do not yet know, though it is ever with you. But ask your question, and be swift!"

Pulsifer stirred the fire with his torch, filling the air with flitting sparks. The talycent stepped back from the cloud of golden specks.

"Your claim of compulsive honesty is shrewdly improbable, for it could easily be a lie. But I see that you wish to impart to me the nature of Pammoth's alleged final boon, and I admit that my curiosity is aroused. Yet the gift has not made itself manifest, and since its nature is not of my asking, I am content to wait until it becomes evident of its own accord. I will pose to you a query more suited to my immediate needs, which is: Where are the nearest dwellings of human beings, and what are the names, dispositions, and occupations of the inhabitants?"

The talycent made a clicking noise that might have been laughter. "You avoid the meaningful, insist upon the utilitarian! You will not reconsider your choice of question? Very well! Two and one-half miles eastward is the habitation of Jabroal Glispert, a human wizard of questionable effectiveness. With him lives the witchlet Sinfe, a woman of ravenous appetites — she will like you. Farther to the north is a tribe of blade-wielding bandits, who prey upon other men and women; they call themselves the Ycravern. Rascals such as you they feed to their sled-whippets…Fierce pygmies called Sheft are ever about, though their humanity may be debatable. At many locations throughout the wood, often moving, are various human souls — tinkers, traders, hermits, musers, a poet, and several madmen. All of these dwell, or pass often within, a twenty-mile radius of this spot. Also Diostans the werewolf roams the wood by night, but he has no established homeplace — he generally hugs the trails and wider roads where couriers and caravans occasionally pass. There is your answer, as concise as I might make it; now, I must go. My flesh burns with day's nearness — Farewell, Pulsifer."

The talycent backed into the darkness with a frightening lack of noise.

Pulsifer heaped fuel on the fire, creating a terrific blaze to last until dawn, and sat facing the flames. The wind whimpered as night retreated; day-birds woke with twitters and began to sing. The air grew light with a grey-green radiance, as the sun's first long rays slanted through the trees to send shadows racing westward. The forest was filled with a watery murkiness of atmosphere.

He warmed himself well, sitting until the sun was up; then, ignoring the rumblings of his belly, he gathered his things, strapped on his mask, and after a minute of stretching, he set out toward the greenly-glowing east. He moved through the wood with energetic strides. Icicles sparkled in the new light, and the frost-coated floor of the forest crunched under his feet. The mistiness rapidly dissipated, leaving the air astonishingly clear; awakened sprites which might have fit in his hand flitted between the trees. He took a deep breath of the bracing air — This was how it felt to be alive! Let his enemies and detractors grind their teeth — Pulsifer still lived! He laughed aloud.

At length he came to a large open area, dominated by great firs along its eastern edge. In the center of the clearing was a pillar-like conglomeration of skeletal remains, bound together with bits of wire; he counted the bones of at least thirty different types of creatures. It was an impressive display of someone's power. The base was made of the jawless skulls of parsennocs, their triple rows of upper teeth biting the frozen earth; the central body was embedded with bones from humans, olangs or maldergs, tambens, and other beings. The pillar's crown was the two-foot wide skull of a malderg-ogre — in its jaws was the skull of a man, and from between the grinning teeth of this unfortunate remnant, a placard hung on a golden chain. It read:

TRESPASSERS BE WARNED!

Beyond this Column begins the domain of
Jabroal Glispert, Mage, Renegade, Independent.

Consider my Power! Consider my Words!
Unless invited, Return whence you came!

After a moment's hesitation, he stepped past the horrific signpost and crossed the clearing. Passing through a wide band of trees, he moved toward another glade, for he now heard a lilting, feminine song.

Bending low, he crept through the furze until he drew near the glade. An icy mist still clung in tatters here, and the air was very still. In the center of the clearing there was a woman, bundled in robes of ermine and duglouge fur; on her head was a fur hat, from beneath which poured a brilliant cascade of thick, red-gold hair. The tresses fell almost to her ankles. Her face was wide at the cheekbones, narrow at the chin, and her mouth was red and full, puffing a wreath of breath. Although her hands were concealed in a fur muff, she did not even seem to be carrying a mask — he was glad she did not. To his appreciative eye, she was the most exquisite woman he had ever seen. Even the former semblance worn by Erhis Sulshaine paled beside this mixture of ice and flame.

He squatted behind a pine, watching as if entranced as she sang a wordless song, moving in a slow, swirling dance about the clearing. Upon her robes glittered green, yellow and blue gems in flashing, spiral and jagged patterns; suddenly an entire pattern shifted and changed, and another. Startled, he realized that swarms of deadly, inch-long zyphen-wasps, a type of insect vigorous even in the coldest season, formed living sigils upon her robes. As she sang, the sigils flowed into new configurations, and entire pieces of the pattern took wing and shot into the forest — these soon returned, or were replaced by newcomers from the trees.

Behind his mask, Pulsifer smiled. This could only be Sinfe, the Witch.

Now she held up a slender hand, and it filled with crawling, buzzing insects.

She watched them attentively as they moved, her green eyes flashing — then she brushed her hand against her clothing, and they were absorbed by the patterns there. She pirouetted a final time, then her attendants rose in a glimmering cloud, to dart with an angry collective hum toward Pulsifer.

As they fell on him in fury, he raised a gloved hand to keep them from crawling through the eye- and mouth-slits of his mask. But their stingers could not penetrate his thick outer clothing of leathern and woolen pads, much less the compressed felt and down liners beneath. He swatted at them with his other hand, crushing them by the dozens, and the red-haired enchantress ran toward him, screaming.

"Don't crush them! Stop! Stop, I say!" She sang a high, trilling note, and the cloud of wasps dispersed into the trees. Pulsifer stood with one hand on his swordhilt.

"I merely defended myself!" he angrily exclaimed. "You had no right to set your asinine insects upon me!"

"Watch your impertinent tongue!" she rejoined. "I am Sinfe the Sorceress, and due to your indifference to the warning-post which you obviously ignored, you are under my jurisdiction! My action was quite justified! You have interrupted a daily ritual, and rendered hopeless for today the summoning of the Great Braconid Mother! I also thought you one of the Ycravern men, who come occasionally to spy on me in order to feed their lusts!"

"It is evident why they risk the stinging death," Pulsifer smoothly said, his tone changing. "Your beauty is a surprising delight in this wildland! But I saw no warning — I am simply a traveler who has lost his way! Direct me to the nearest place where I might find a friendly roof and walls, and I shall be on my way out of your territory."

The anger faded from her face. "Our misunderstanding is forgotten, for the sake of the harmony we all seek. I apologize for my hasty assault, of both wasps and words! As I said, I am Sinfe. You are...?"

He unfastened his mask and pushed back his hood. "I suppose I am a vagabond. Call me whatever you wish." He smiled.

She returned the smile willingly, and he was dazzled by it. "The name Handsome comes to mind. But I will call you Trespasser, if you are name-leery. As for the shelter you seek, I believe I can offer that to you for a few days... in exchange for a service."

"To your service I am hereby pledged," he replied, bowing; she laughed. "Come along, then. I'll find you some breakfast, and a warm chair by the fire."

They set off toward the east, and a heavily-wooded ridge. A narrow column of smoke rose into the air from an unseen source. As they went, Pulsifer wondered as to the reception he would receive from the wizard Jabroal — he was apparently not of the Brotherhood of Mages, and being a recluse, might not even have heard of the Velvet Knife. He nodded toward the smoke, stroking one of his moustaches with a finger.

"Your home?"

She nodded, and he raised his brows as though surprised. "You dwell alone in the Forests of Iskiruen? Surely a woman as — excuse my candor! — stunning as yourself, would have a partner in life."

"You will meet my husband soon enough," she replied somewhat cryptically. "Here is the path to the cottage; watch the loose stone, there."

She started up the hill and he followed, inwardly cautious, but eager to rest in hiding from his nemesis. Soon the house came into view. It was large, to be described as a cottage. Two stories stood out from the hillside, into which it was apparently built; the low-chimneyed roof was turfed, except on the tower, which had a round tiled roof with sliding apertures, apparently for the purpose of observing the heavens. Other windows of the structure were small and shuttered. The grounds about the building were neither landscaped nor tended, except near an outlying barn, where trees and shrubs looked goat-eaten.

Black spruces grew thickly, casting permanent shadows; a rustic beauty hung over the scene. Sinfe uttered a complex series of guttural syllables at the oaken door — it clicked and opened at her command, and he followed her within. A blaze danced in a large fireplace and the interior of the parlor was warm, the scents of bread, honey, and spices in the air. Small artifacts and devices lined shelves and crannies, as did many hide-bound volumes, their spines stamped in precious metals. To left and right doorways led to other rooms, and to either side of the hearth doors also led away, apparently to chambers carved from the solid rock of the hill. A stair in one corner spiraled up to the floor above.

Pulsifer looked about for Jabroal. He didn't want to anger another mage, but he needed a place to rest, eat well, and think out his next move. He began to unabashedly shed his outer garments and accoutrements, revealing his sweat-soiled, finer clothing beneath. Sinfe watched him with an unmistakably admiring gaze.

"Get out of those things, and I'll clean them for you. You can bathe in the steam room upstairs — I'll bring you a robe and breeches, and slippers for your feet. I'm sure they're sore, with the miles clinging to them…"

He touched his top-most shirt-button hesitantly. "Perhaps I should meet your husband first…"

"Oh, of course." She smiled. "Please come this way." She led him toward the doorway to the left, and passing through some manner of workroom, they entered a library. The walls consisted of shelves, crammed with books and bundled papers; a small fireplace was in one corner. At many spots on the walls, rather than shelves, were the mounted heads of various creatures feared by men. In the middle of the room was a long table, and on this lay a man, all but his head covered with a sheet. At each corner of the table burned a blue-waxed, aromatic candle. Pulsifer looked carefully at the man — he was perhaps sixty years old and rather short, with a receded grey-brown hairline, bushy brown eyebrows, and an enormous, bulbous nose which hung over his upper lip. Judging by his grey pallor, he was also evidently deceased.

Sinfe's eyes were wet. "His name was Jabroal; he was a good man. He turned me from a peasant-girl and into a lady of refinement, teaching me most of what I know of magicking..." She dabbed at the corner of one eye with her sleeve.

Pulsifer looked again at the corpse. "How did he die?"

"He choked on a walnut," she sorrowfully answered. "I was out tending the bees and fish when it happened — I came home to find him in his sanctum, a crumpled book in one hand, and nuts all over the floor. He could not even vocalize a simple spell of dislodgement... Now he is here, surrounded by the books he loved. I will miss his company..." She looked at Pulsifer. "But come with me! I burden you with my grief! We shall clean you up, and get you into something warm and comfortable."

Pulsifer shrugged. "As you wish. Tell me, though, what is the service you desire of me, in exchange for your hospitality? Some hardy labor needing a man's touch?"

"Nothing so strenuous," she replied, leading him from the room by his hand. Despite the nearness of the dead man, her touch sent a thrill up his arm. She seemed unaware of this effect, however.

"I am required by my matrimonial vows to see that his body is tended for four successive nights after his death. Two nights have passed; two remain. If you will watch him tonight, I'll have the strength to do so tomorrow evening. It is crucial that the vow be kept, for he swore that after his death he would return in spirit to the place where his body rested, on one of the four nights. The exact time of the visitation is uncertain, due to unpredictable conditions on the astral plane; he is to leave a message for me regarding his Great Undertaking, his life's work. However, I find myself confused as to my course in life, and my next logical step — do I remain in the forest? Should I venture to the cities I have never seen? Tonight I am expecting a diviner, a close friend of my husband's, and I will consult with him in the tower while the stars are auspicious. A widow must plan with great deliberation..."

Pulsifer nodded uneasily. "I see. But would not his spirit be angered at finding me, and not his wife, in the room with his corpse?"

"You will call me if he appears, and he was a man of charitable personality." She led him up the stair, through two rooms and a hallway, and into a room beneath the hill. Here there was one thick-paned window, set in the rock, through which sunlight poured. The chamber was walled with imported green tiles from Jesbidan, and most of the floor was an elevated wooden platform. Upon this was a large ceramic tub, to which ran pipes suspended from walls and ceiling. Sinfe turned a valve, and water gushed from one pipe and into the tub. She indicated a stack of kindling and firewood in one corner.

"Beneath the raised floor is a heating-device, created by my husband. He claimed that it was equal in ingenuity and performance to the water-warming contrivances of the bath-houses of Phontyque. I do not know the accuracy of this appraisal, but it functions adequately. Stoke it sparingly — it heats the water through conduits in pipe and tub. When the water reaches a certain level, the valve automatically closes."

"I will keep to your directions," Pulsifer assured her.

"Good. Enjoy your bath, Trespasser — leave your clothing outside the door, and I'll bring clean garments." She looked at him appraisingly for an instant, then left. He built a fire as she had directed in the stove beneath the floor, shed his clothes and placed them in the hall, and soon was soaking in a steaming, flesh-soothing tub of water.

The room quickly filled with a heavy steam. He lay in the mist, enjoying the tingle of heat on his weary flesh. He heard the door open and close; the well-curved figure of a woman was outlined against the gleam of the window, sunlight glinting redly in her cloak of hair.

"I've brought you some clothes," Sinfe said. "Your own are quite nice, albeit filthy. The weave of the shirt is particularly good."

He smiled as she stepped nearer. "Thank you. Yours are prettier by far, though — the red-gold of your cape is stunning, and the raised buttons contrast beautifully with the pale stuff you wear! It certainly looks soft; and I must say that it has the finest red trim I have ever seen!"

"This old thing?" She moved even closer. "I've had it ever so long! I'm afraid it's in need of stitching, though — have you a needle handy?"

"Indeed I have! I am always prepared to do handy needlework, for it keeps the Chill from one's flesh! Allow me to rise, and I'll assist you…"

She stood beside the tub. "Take your time — finish your soak! I'll be in the sewing room, down the hall and to the left. Come along when you've finished, though, for I hate to stitch alone."

She descended the platform-steps, and went out the door; Pulsifer hastened to finish his bath.

He passed the day in idleness with the widow Sinfe. Twice he slept.

Outside, a heavy snow began to fall, and evening dropped like a blue shroud on the Forests of Iskiruen.

At length he rose from where he had been sampling the delicacies Sinfe had served to him. With reluctance he looked again at the mounds of sweetmeats he was leaving, not untouched, but certainly not depleted. He went to the door, and she watched him from her seat with a dreamy gaze. "It is nearly time for my vigil to begin," he observed. "Allow me to prepare myself—then I will go at once to my station."

"It is nearly time," Sinfe murmured thoughtfully. "Are you sure that you would not like another nibble of this folded pastry? Darkness is a few minutes off, yet…"

"Your fare is undeniably delectable, particularly the pastry—but I will not shirk my duty!" With a grin he left her, and five minutes later he sat in a high-backed chair beside the laid-out Jabroal. Again Pulsifer wore his own clothing, and both his folded travel-clothes and the valise were close at hand.

If the ghost of Jabroal did return, he wanted to be ready to take his leave of the premises with all dispatch. Despite Sinfe's reassurances, he did not wish to be at the mercy of a spirit which might have been watching his activities throughout the day. He glanced at the man's flaccid proboscis with distaste.

The room grew more chill, and he started a blaze in the fireplace. Then he returned to his chair, where he fought off drowsiness by perusing a copy of *The History of the Zytlime Hegemony*; but he quickly wearied of the repetitive and rather graphic illustrations representing the torture of the Berlix Horde, and the Plague of Dryfiddic Pustules. With a look at his unmoving ward, he returned the volume to its place on the shelf, and took down *Doerrianthic's Guide to Reasonable Persuasion*, which dealt with questions concerning sexual interaction between human beings, and physically compatible beings of various other classifications. This illustrated volume he studied for some time, his eyelids growing heavy, distantly aware that Sinfe moved about and clattered in the parlor, and then the room directly upstairs.

At length he looked up. He couldn't see out of the library very well and the next room was in shadow, but he caught a glimpse of Sinfe's shimmering hair as she busied herself with something. Soon she entered the library, with dark bread, white cheese, and red currants on a platter, along with a bottle of the palate-burning liquor tastaca. She moved a finger beneath the platter's edge, and four telescoping legs descended from the corners; she set the tray before Pulsifer with a swirl of the diaphanous aquamarine robes she now wore. A strand of her hair brushed his face.

"Here is refreshment, in case you grow hungry. Feel free to move about the library, but remember! Stay with Jabroal at all times — do not venture from this room! My guest will arrive soon, and I will be sequestered in clairvoyant consultation for many hours. Do not allow the candles to go out — there are more in the drawer, there."

"And if the ghost appears? How will you hear my call in the observatory?"

Sinfe went to the wall, where the gape-mouthed visage of a voracious grimkel was mounted upon a brass plate. She tugged the grimkel's lolling tongue, and a chiming fugue of bells rang throughout the house.

"This cord will bring me running; now, I must finish preparations. In the morning you can sleep, and later take your leisure as you will." She smiled suggestively, and left — Pulsifer fidgeted with the book he held, rose, and put it back in its slot.

He ate a bit of bread, staring at the necrotic features of the wizard Jabroal. Next, he poked about the room, looking for curios or small items which he might conceal in his pouch-belt. The wind moaned fitfully outside, rattling the closed shutters, and the candles flickered slightly at a draft he could not feel. Something — probably a wind-borne limb — scrabbled momentarily at the shutters, and the horrific image of Montath's hijret sprang into his mind.

He felt increasingly sleepy, so he took another book from the shelf; this time it was a collection of spells, called *Melsion's Compendium of Stolid Effectuations*, bound between covers of jret-leather. He opened it to gaze at the Words of Power scrawled upon the page, but they seemed to writhe, sway, and wriggle, avoiding the capture of his unqualified eye. He quickly wearied of this exercise and tossed the book onto the floor, where it impacted with an almost human grunt of discomfort; he watched the volume sidelong, unsure if he should venture to touch it in order to place it on the shelf again.

Suddenly there came a triple knock at the front door, slow and forceful.

Pulsifer was nearly startled from his seat, for the mental image of the dark-garbed Morskured Montath standing on the stoop had come to him with the sound. He heard Sinfe rapidly descend the stair two rooms away, and his suspicions were aroused — Could she be in league with his enemies? Was he sitting and awaiting his destruction?

Rising, he pulled back to the wall at one side of the doorway, for Sinfe had opened the front door. The sound of wind was accompanied by an icy blast which reached into the library, sending shivers along his skin, and setting the fire to crackling. He heard the door close, and then the low voice of Sinfe, speaking quickly — she was answered by an extremely deep-voiced speaker, but Pulsifer could make out no words of the exchange. There was a sound as of clothing or flesh brushing hard together, then the footsteps of two persons ascending the stair. Pulsifer glanced down as he exhaled in relief.

The ring on his right hand flashed an intense green. Moving away from the door, he bit his lower lip as he thought. Azahad Zuzirco had said that the color green signified the nearness of a darkling, yet despite her witchery, Sinfe was obviously quite human — but her guest was not! Nor would it be a diviner of any sort, for darklings were not renowned for knowledge in arcane matters, with the possible exception of talycents. He shook his head; no talycent ascended a stair on two legs! He drew his sword.

With a look back at the body of Jabroal, he left the library. The house seemed under a spell of silence. He tried the front door — pull as he might, he could not open it. The shutters of a nearby window proved equally adamant before his efforts, nor did any of the lock-forcing charms he knew have any effect. The fire in the parlor snapped; with trepidation, Pulsifer approached the stair, then slowly started up.

The room above was unoccupied; he went to the hall, and it too was empty. He turned to the left, the probable path to the observatory — a muffled noise came from the right. With a ginger thief's step, he moved up the dark hall, toward the boudoir of Sinfe and her departed husband.

The door was ajar. He peered into the room, at the crumpled blankets on the expansive bed. On one bedpost was a long hat of stiffened felt, brimless and hung with scraps of metal. The gleam of naked flesh, the now familiar curve of Sinfe's well-rounded posterior could just be seen. She spoke lowly with someone else, who moved with a rustle of bedclothes.

"I have a man for you, downstairs — he is with my husband."

A rumble of disturbing laughter, soft yet menacing, reached Pulsifer's ears. An unbelievably-deep voice came from the room. "This is good news — I have not eaten since before the sun rose, when my brothers and I dined on a scrawny poet, who screamed bits of verse as he died! An entertaining dish, but nearly meatless...But I long to partake of the flesh of Jabroal!"

"As do I," Sinfe replied. "But Jabroal is not yet dead — I'm sustaining him with candles of zyphen-wax, mixed with a soporific — the other man, too, should soon be sleeping like death. I have not yet found the Cache of Indissolubles, but according to his notes, he only lacked one item from his required list. When I do find them, I will return his soul to his body and allow him to see you before you take him. Then his potential coup of sorcery will be mine, and I will be repaid for the years I've wasted with him!"

The parsennoc, for such it could only be, grunted his approval. "Where have you hidden his essential spirit? If he were to regain it prematurely, the consequences for you, and our offspring, would be unfortunate."

She laughed. "In one corner of the pantry, there is the web of a stilt-legged spider — in the web is a ball of the spider's silk, and in the silk is a silver wasp, immobilized by a drop of the spider's venom. The spider is dead; in her prisoner's thorax resides the soul of Jabroal, wrapped in spite. He goes nowhere."

Pulsifer saw a large, seven-fingered hand, waving expressively.

"Since I was first driven upon the rocks of Krustikus Gorge by the laughing Jabroal, I have longed to shred the flesh from his bones! I desire to consume his drooping nose, surely a potent delicacy, with a passion equal to that procreative urge which drives me to copulate with you — rather than rip out your throat!" The hand caressed her neck roughly. "How hotly the blood rushes beneath your white skin..."

"Your vileness, your hatred of humanity, excites me beyond words!"

Sinfe tossed about in glee, clinching the darkling. Pulsifer caught a glimpse of the parsennoc's heavy, hairless head — its double-pupiled, yellow eyes, the mouthful of bristling teeth, and its rope-muscled jaws. Sinfe pulled the craggy head to her bountiful bosom. "Take me, with your savage gusto — afterward, you can dine on the fool below, while I nurture the seed within me which will grow into replicas of yourself!"

The parsennoc grunted in willingness, heaving his lank, greyish, iron-muscled form atop hers. The sounds of their lust were immediate — Pulsifer backed away along the route he had come, wondering as to the stamina of the darkling, and subsequent duration of its liaison with Sinfe.

As quietly as possible he descended to the first floor. He went directly to the pantry, searching the dark corners and nooks — he found the spider's web, and the ball of silk within it. He removed the ball and placed it in one of the pouches at his belt; then he returned to the library. He extinguished the insidious candles.

Opening his valise, he took out the Cask of Sranophaez. He regarded it for an instant, then selected two of the glyphs and pressed, whispering:

"Come forth!"

A tinkling burst of tiny voices issued from the bronzed cask, followed by a miniature explosion of purple lights. These swirled like a cloud of gnats before his eyes. A voice became dominant over the rest, but was still only faintly audible.

"We are the Proclaimers of Deeds — of what act do you wish to boast, and to whom?"

Pulsifer shook his head. "Return to the box — I have no need of such an announcement."

"An emphatic declaration must be made," the purple wisp insisted.

"*Burden us with an assignment, or we are forced to choose the nearest thinking beings and make to them an announcement of our own choice, in a multitudinous voice.*"

Pulsifer considered. "Which would be?"

"*Your most recent deeds, of course — our release, the removal of the insect from the cobweb, your stealthy eavesdropping upon the pair upstairs. Of course, it would be those you spied upon to whom we would announce these things —*"

"Go at once to the city of Parhimmion, in Jesbidan!" Pulsifer directed, in an irritated whisper. "There is a shopkeeper there called Frudge, with one eye green and one brown. Announce to him that the rascal Pulsifer lives yet but is in peril, and that he might genuflect to his nickel idols for my safety! Now go!"

The lights spiraled and vanished. Pulsifer selected a different pair of sigils.

Yellow-gold light-specks swirled forth. "*We are the Curative Initiators. What infirmity do you wish reversed or eliminated?*"

Pulsifer sighed in exasperation. "Nothing comes to mind. Can you inflict illness as well?"

"*That is the function of another cluster. However, we shall act upon our own initiative — you seem possessed of unhealthily aggressive and convoluted thought-processes, which surely must hinder your ability to function in society. We will soothe and smooth your mind, endowing you with a simpler, more care-free perspective of the tumultuous events in the world around you.*"

"I decline this well-intentioned lobotomy," Pulsifer hastily rejoined. "I have a patient for you — the man on the table, there."

The glittering cloud of deity-mites moved to the table, to hover above the body of the wizard Jabroal. Almost instantly they returned.

"*The man is incomplete — an astral element is missing. We will do our work upon you.*"

"You have been given your assignment!" Pulsifer angrily whispered. "I will soon supply this missing element! Go to the man and await further instruction!"

With a flush into a red hue signifying their reluctance, the deity-mites settled upon the form of Jabroal like glittering motes of ruby dust. Pulsifer heard movement somewhere upstairs — he forcefully pressed two more glyphs. A multi-colored cluster issued from the Cask of Sranophaez.

The voice of the dominant spark, a white-green light, was imperious. *"We are the Enablers of Comprehension — state your need."*

Pulsifer fidgeted with his moustaches. "With what ability might I be 'enabled,' by your power?" Upstairs, floorboards creaked — a drop of sweat rolled down the length of Pulsifer's narrow nose.

"The instantaneous understanding of languages, arcane or other symbology, or obscure references. The level of your comprehension would depend upon the amount of comparative knowledge you already possess. A mage could be given the permanent gift of a dozen extinct tongues, or seventy spells of awesome potency. In your case, we might endow you with the ability to read a single phrase in the dead Yasod-Yomi language, or to comprehend one of the simplest of cause-and-being formulae."

"I choose the latter!" Pulsifer picked up the copy of *Melsion's Compendium*, and flipped it open with one hand. "Select for me a devastating series of runes!"

The lights swirled above the yellow pages. *"The selection must be yours — we will only give you comprehension of it."*

"Worthless fireflies!" Pulsifer muttered, but he scanned the quivering words upon the pages. He indicated a squirming passage with his finger.

"Here! This is my selection!"

"Done," the voice said; the motes formed themselves into a narrow beam of light, reaching from Pulsifer's eye to the pages of the codex. The dancing characters slowed, stilled, then jumped into his mind with skull-aching clarity. The deity-mites vanished.

Pulsifer looked at the book again — all passages other than the one he'd singled out were still unreadable. He went over his selection once more, though it was unnecessary; the caustic syllables were burned into his brain, a red script impressed upon his awareness.

He grinned. The spell was *Lorsulth's Swelling Asphyxiation*, an affliction of the tongue and lymph-glands involving the sylph Lorsulth. He placed the book aside, and the cask back in the valise. The second-story floorboards creaked again, and the tread of a heavy walker echoed down the hall. He heard the parsennoc begin to descend the stair with no attempt at stealth.

He lay down on the floor as though overcome by the narcotic fumes of the extinguished candles, his sword concealed beneath his body, his hand about its hilt. His legs were partially drawn up, as if his knees had buckled. Through slit eyes he watched the doorway. A tall shape wrapped in thick, coarse robes filled the portal — the light of the fire played upon the creature's sallow, vaguely-human features. It looked into the room with a bit of uncertainty, apparently wondering as to the absence of candle-flames, for it was typically cautious and clever.

Tentatively it stepped into the room, its seven-fingered, sharp-nailed hands clenching and unclenching spasmodically, until it saw Pulsifer; it approached its intended victim with a rapid step.

The parsennoc crouched above him — Pulsifer shot out his legs with all his strength, catching it in the groin. Despite its rock-hardness, it took a step back as it exhaled in a gust of surprise and pain, then stumbled over the serving-tray — the image of the runes blotting out his sight, Pulsifer intoned the *Swelling Asphyxiation*.

There was a whoosh, and the parsennoc was thrust back against a bookcase with tremendous force, where it half-collapsed. Books flew noisily to the floor. Pulsifer watched as the air about the darkling's head grew turbulent, and it seemed that he viewed the creature through agitated water.

He scrambled to his feet, holding his weapon before him.

The parsennoc, also, pulled itself erect — its unhinged jaws opened to a terrifying degree, working spastically, and a pale, pink, jerking mass filled the cavity. Its neck bulged at either side, as if pomegranates had been inserted beneath its skin. Its horrible eyes, filled with pain and astonishment, protruded as it strangled — its gaze locked on Pulsifer, and it lunged at him.

Backing away, he struck at its clawing hands with his blade. Fingers fell in the firelight, and reddish ooze spattered. He darted about the table which bore Jabroal Glispert, the stumbling parsennoc after him. It lunged over the table at him, and the red mites glistening upon the inert mage stirred slightly, then resettled. Pulsifer dodged its grasp and grinned maliciously — the parsennoc stumbled, tottered, and fell. The yellow lambency faded from its eyes, and its engorged tongue burst asunder.

Pulsifer prodded it cautiously with his foot — it was most definitely dead.

Sheathing his sword, he grasped it under the armpits and heaved it up with a grunt of effort, for it was heavier than a man of the same dimensions would have been. Its musky, earthen odor filled his nose. He dragged it to the doorway and held it with one arm locked beneath its chin, trying not to look down at its face; with a screech of nails, he pulled the mounted head of a sable panther from the wall with his other hand. Next he hefted the darkling's body — with a savage thrust, he impaled the back of its skull upon the exposed nails. It sagged grotesquely, but did not fall. He raised one of its arms, setting it on a shelf so that it appeared that the creature leaned there rather rakishly.

There was a soft sound from upstairs. Lighting a taper, he relit the candles about Jabroal; then he concealed himself to one side of the dangling parsennoc, flat against the bookshelves. He tugged upon the tongue of the grimkel, and the chiming fugue rang throughout the house. A patter of soft feet answered the summons as Sinfe descended the stair, her voice calling out softly:

"Gortuluk? Is all well, my love?"

Pulsifer replied with an ambiguous grunt; the nude Sinfe entered the room. Smiling, she stepped toward the parsennoc — she screamed in shock at its swollen, lifeless features.

Pulsifer threw himself into the darkling from behind, and it fell upon the witch with its head lolling and lifted arm flailing. Sinfe was slammed against the floor, the wind knocked from her lungs — the parsennoc embraced her with gory arms, its puffed face pressed against hers. Straddling the dead monstrosity, Pulsifer smiled and placed the flat of his knife to her throat.

"Neither spells nor magical motions make, Witch — else you join your lover!" He heaved the parsennoc to one side as he rose, still bent close enough to persuade her with his blade. "Arise and accompany me — do not bolt, for my nerves are on edge and my hand might slip."

She nodded, her face dour. He grabbed a candle from the table and escorted her to the next room, where he rapped her skull with his knife-hilt.

She fell, and he bound her with a tapestry-cord, stuffing a balled strip from a curtain into her mouth to dissuade spell-making; then he set her in a chair with the burning candle close by her nose. Whistling a jaunty tune, he returned to the library.

The mites still clustered upon Jabroal. Pulsifer extinguished the candles again, opened his pouch, and brought forth the ball of silk. Carefully he peeled it open, and daintily picked the silver zyphen-wasp from its embrace, avoiding the protruding stinger. Setting the wasp on a shelf, he cut the stinger from its abdomen and took the insect to the unfeeling wizard. After a second's hesitation, he placed it beneath the mage's drooping nose, and partially inserted it into a nostril.

"Enact your cure, Initiators!" he commanded. "The man's soul is within the thorax of the bug beneath his nose. Its re-integration and his complete recovery are your responsibility!"

The dim lights, now red and yellow, took to the air and coursed toward Jabroal's face; they slid beneath his nose and vanished. A faint hum issued from the wizard's head. Pulsifer took several steps back and watched skeptically.

After two minutes, Jabroal's eyelids fluttered. He moaned, moved, then slowly sat up, wincing. The wasp fell from his nose, and he sneezed.

Yawning, he opened his eyes and looked at Pulsifer — surprise, then confusion, then anger filled his face.

"Who are you? What are you doing in my house?"

With a smile and a wave to indicate the heaped corpse of the parsen-noc, Pulsifer began his story in a casual tone.

Chapter II

Mage and Tinker

"Her treachery still staggers me." Jabroal, in red jerkin and blue breeches, handed Pulsifer a steaming cup of the stimulant beverage rac-rac. Outside the window of the library, morning sunlight glittered on the snow-blanketed hillside. The mage softly sipped from his own cup, a musing expression on his face, his heavy brows like brooding stormclouds above the blue-grey tarns of his eyes. "The last I recall, she served me tastaca; good for you that you drank none of yours! I should have been more careful — she isn't the first woman to fall under the sexual power of a parsennoc. The creatures possess glands which produce powerful scent-lures, perceptible only to women. It is a shame, I suppose, that parsennocs were designed with no females of their own species…"

"That they exist in one gender is blight enough," Pulsifer said. He leaned against the table, upon which the night before had lain the form of the other man. "And Sinfe's wickedness goes beyond mere adultery; her hatred for you, and all mankind, was evident! She spoke with the darkling of her urge to taste your flesh…"

"I'm afraid that is all my fault," Jabroal interjected, shaking his head in self-reproach. "I never should have tempted her with the knowledge of my Great Undertaking, or its nature; I should never have led her into thaumaturgical studies at all. I also should have considered the possibility of sublimated urges beyond her control, which would sooner or later lead her to seek my life. To speak truthfully, Sinfe is not totally of human lineage — she did not have the spiritual strength to resist the darker forces within herself. Her degeneration was the result of primal elements in her soul-mind structure."

"This is as it may be," Pulsifer said, "but what will you do with her now?"

Jabroal grew misty-eyed. "Return her whence she came. Come along, and witness a marvel."

Pulsifer followed him into the parlor, and through one of the portals leading to rooms beneath the hill. They entered a large, stone-walled chamber, well-illuminated with light from hanging glass globes; in response to Pulsifer's query, the mage explained that the light was captured by mirrors from outside and reflected by way of crystalline filaments into the globes. At night, they were filled with the glowing substance orgone, absorbed from the living emanations of the forest during the day. Pulsifer looked at the huge room in amazement — in his lifetime as a thief in the twin Phontyquen cities of Oriaber and Imonber, he had invaded many a private sanctum belonging to a mage or collector. Usually this had been at the behest of another of the same caste. But he had hardly seen such a strange and cluttered workshop before.

The place was crowded with tables and shelves, and braziers, alembics, and other devices were abundantly present. In one corner was a partially dissected, man-sized mufaloon, encased in reddish amber; in another was a glass cube containing water, in which floated strange, jelly-like creatures with semi-human faces. A huge globe in a rotating stand stood in the center of the chamber — upon its surface were etched in detail the outlines of landmasses long-buried beneath world-covering ice. From the ceiling hung a many-harnessed and buckled contraption, having four vespertilian wings of shiny starched taffeta, studded with feathers — loops for arms and legs indicated that it was a device to enable a man to fly of his own power. Beneath their feet was a rug woven of the ears of golden dur-bats. Another door led into a room which Pulsifer could see was crammed with books, and heaped creations of Jabroal's hands and mind; beside the door was a crystal cube some seven feet tall, such as mages and collectors used for the retention of dangerous beings. Within this cage was Sinfe.

She still wore nothing more than her robe of lustrous hair. Her face was twisted with rage, and she screamed silently at them. Pulsifer was unnerved by her unheard attack, but Jabroal reassured him.

"Do not be alarmed, my friend — I have sealed the cube in such a way as to render her spells useless. They can penetrate neither the crystal, nor the layers of sub-particulate force which separate the dimensions."

"A most astonishing place of ideas," Pulsifer observed, taking his eyes off of Sinfe and looking about the room once more. "Surely you are renowned in the Brotherhood —"

"I am not of the Brotherhood!" Jabroal announced, his voice bitter. "They ousted me long ago. In my studies I lean toward concepts which often do not utilize magic, and I seek to control reality without necessarily resorting to the application of sorcerous strength, and compelled spirits. Sometimes wizardry does not blossom in my hands…Things go awry. But I have learned to blend my magical knowledge with the data of my other experiments, and have achieved things the likes of which the other wizards of Teumdoth could neither imagine, nor emulate!" He indicated Sinfe.

"Take Sinfe, for instance; beautiful, is she not? And undeniably of an astounding intelligence. But she is not wholly nature's child, and this is the source of her deadly fickleness."

"What do you mean?" Pulsifer asked; he studied the ravishing Sinfe with appreciation, in spite of his disgust with her love for the parsennoc — there was a quality about her which was inexplicably alluring, and she was still the most incredible woman he had ever seen. Jabroal scratched his drooping nose with a long-nailed finger as he continued.

"Most of the manlike creatures, and other perils, which roam old Teumdoth are of mostly non-human or unnatural extraction. Some originated as the result of the curiosities of mage-experimenters, others as accidents involving the minglings of magical forces, and nature's evolutionary quirkiness. Still others were created by the now-hidden ochdeviants for the purpose of destroying mankind, or by human wizards of the Perfidics for the same reason. Yet others, such as the ochdeviants themselves, are extraterrestrial or intraterrestrial in origin. Our friend the parsennoc had his extraction in an original mix which was well-documented by an insane creator — part demon-cat, with portions reptilian, human, and tundra-wolf; and partly an aquatic, sapient mammal of predacious temperament. A large portion of his spiritual essence was derived from the perpetuities of Cold and Unlight.

The sylebers are barely human, largely elemental, and somewhat molluskan — and so on, for the rest of the unnatural creatures of night and day.

"Due to a bit of a human genetic heritage, many creatures seek to mate with human beings — or must, as in the parsennoc's case. For some this is probably an unconscious urge to regain a lost humanity which they never really had. Sinfe is among their company, to a lesser degree..." He shook his head sadly, then went on. "Sylebers usually reproduce asexually, but as you know, liaisons often occur between the nymphs and men. A man in my employ once impregnated one of several sylebers, which came often to bask in a garden I then kept — after the child was born, the syleber and her sisters caught the father in the forest, tore him apart with their talons, and devoured him. I found the child, completely forgotten and abandoned by its mother, in the wood — due to my ministrations alone, the hybrid lived. The mother-syleber leaned heavily in her elemental urges toward empathy with hymenoptera, and other insects — as does her daughter."

Pulsifer looked again at Sinfe; she did seem to possess the unnaturally glamorous sheen of sylebers and aquatic merileuts.

"Does she know?"

"No — I gave her into the care of a woodcutter and his wife, and she was brought up as a human being. To complicate matters, I fell in love with her after she reached adulthood — and I thought that she loved me in return."

"Perhaps her human percentage does love you," Pulsifer mused, "but her unhuman nature is obviously dominant. Yet many men have known a lesser love."

Jabroal nodded. "This is true. Now, however, I am faced with a choice of unpleasant options — her humanity is tenuous at this point, and definitely frail. In order to preserve her soul, extant and transferable to another plane or incarnation, I would have to put her to death at once. This would not only cause me considerable grief, but the power of her elemental heritage might assure that I instead unleashed a fierce and malevolent ghost, not wholly human, to haunt the forest. On the other hand, I may be able to shift her form and mind, releasing her fractional human soul to course free, and changing the rest into the complete syleber she was meant to be. The latter seems the only reasonable course available, and naturally-conducive to a healthy equipose between us. In all things, a rightful balance should be considered."

As he listened, Pulsifer eyed some valuable stone heads of the Kreshaik period, which looked as though they might fit nicely in his palm. "Your judgment exhibits both wisdom and mercy. When shall this transformation take place?"

Jabroal rubbed his chin as he considered. "Now seems most expedient. Go into the front of the house and amuse yourself as you like. I will come for you when she is finished, and we will talk further about your tenure here." He turned toward the yet-raving Sinfe; Pulsifer inclined his head, closed the door as he left, and returned to the parlor.

For half an hour he sat before the fire, thinking of departing the house of Jabroal; yet the fear of Morskured Montath which urged him to flee, also kept him from wandering into the forest. Shortly after he had told his tale to Jabroal the night before, the wizard had deduced his outlawed status — claiming a right to assistance in the name of Equilibrium, Pulsifer had been startled when the mage had readily offered him both asylum, and employment as a laborer about the grounds. Upon learning that his new guest was the unrepentant criminal Pulsifer, Jabroal had assured him of his own neutrality in the matter between the Velvet Knife and the other mages of Teumdoth, reiterating his desire to help the fugitive in return for Pulsifer having saved his life.

Pulsifer stretched his long legs and smiled. Jabroal was not of the Brotherhood; chances were good that Montath would not bother to inquire here at all, if he even knew of Jabroal's abode. This place offered a fine sanctuary from many enemies, for the winter's duration; and, he reminded himself, he still retained *Lorsulth's Swelling Asphyxiation* —

With a startled oath, he twisted suddenly in his seat. It seemed that something flitted before his sight, stinging his eyes with bright red bursts. He rubbed his eyes with his fists, then shook his head — again, he experienced the painful radiance. A strange tickling began in his neck and throat, and seemed to slowly creep up toward his mouth. His tongue grew numb, and he leapt to his feet with a yell.

At this moment Jabroal entered the room — his face grim, he went directly to Pulsifer's side. "What ails you, Pulsifer? Describe it briefly, and with precision!"

"Bright lights, jagged images on the eye — a swelling sensation in throat and palate!" He gagged. "Shortness of breath is present, as well!"

"Hm." Jabroal guided him back to the chair. "I was astonished by your apparently innate ability to utilize the *Swelling Asphyxiation* — now it appears that your mind is no longer able to compartmentalize it, as it does other conceptualizations. The spell is beyond your mind's ability to restrain, and you seem to be in peril of falling victim to the very effectuation you used against the parsennoc. Well for you that you did not intone *The Sacred Voktmeth Sphincter*, or *Leclendel's Inversional Trapezoid of Pain*; these would have already burst free from your brain! But the sylph Lorsulth is unaware of the situation, for the spell is unvocalized; else he would already be here to end your life! I suppose we should remove the spell from your skull —"

"Then do so!" Pulsifer felt his face growing puffy. "I strangle while you chatter! Extract the cursed spell!"

"Ah, yes — Sorry." Jabroal placed his hands on the sides of Pulsifer's head. He muttered a string of consonantal sounds which leapt from his mouth as blazing blue helixes — red cubic shapes slid from Pulsifer's forehead to meet the blue runes, and both spells vanished with an ear-popping shriek.

Pulsifer fell back in his seat, breath filling his lungs again.

Jabroal rubbed his hands together in satisfaction. "Thus and so. Now, then, come and assist me with the syleber Sinfe; she awaits release into the liberty of the woodland."

Still gulping for air, Pulsifer rose and followed the mage. They reentered the workroom, and he looked at the cube containing Sinfe.

She stood trembling and subdued, like a creature of the wild. At first she looked the same — then Pulsifer realized that her beauty was even more vibrant, her hair even more lustrous than before. Her eyes were whiteless as well, deep pools of shimmering blue-green which contrasted starkly with her snowy skin. But she lacked the speckles, the over-developed buttocks, and the long, pointed ears of a syleber; also, she still had only two breasts, rather than four or six, as the nymphs often did.

"Her human appearance is still inherent," Jabroal explained, "but she is wholly syleber in her interior configuration. Her other line of ancestry left her quite malleable to organic rearrangement." He stared at her wistfully. "She doesn't remember us, of course — she knows nothing of her life here, or as a human being. She will only be happy when she is free." He picked up a jar containing a few ounces of bloody liquid. "I removed the eggs fertilized by the parsennoc — the darklings' scent-signals influence a woman's body to react with multiple ovulation. It was necessary to remove them — otherwise a new and probably terrible mutation would have resulted from their union. Sinfe surely knew that newborn parsennocs rip their way free from their mother's womb, and devour her — but she was so filled with hate that she did not care." He put the jar down, and lifted a blue crystal from the table. "As her humanity expired, I snared her departing soul in this flake of delidrium." He held it before his face, and whispered: "Remember, Sinfe! Remember that I loved you." Tears in his eyes, he crushed the crystal between his fingers, and sparkling powder fell — a silver light with the appearance of a glittering thread twisted up from his fingers, then was gone.

After a moment, he sighed and turned to Pulsifer. "We shall release the creature, now. She is still stunned by her recent metamorphosis, but beware, lest she inadvertently unsheathe her claws! Their poisons work rapidly, leaving one sensate but paralyzed for hours, before death comes. Do not stroke her back or torso as we move her — this would arouse her passion, and as I told you, I lost one servant previously due to such a liaison. If such a thing were to occur, even by accident, she would not rest until she had had physical congress with you. She is totally syleber, now."

"Your advice is taken to heart." Pulsifer joined Jabroal as the wizard dissolved the front pane of the cube; following Jabroal's directions, Pulsifer took her left hand while the mage took her right. Slowly, as if they led a small child, they guided her through the house; like a wondering child she stared at them, and at her surroundings, her lips parted slightly. Pulsifer saw that her teeth were now unbroken white ridges, and her tongue was both speckled, and cloven at the tip.

Guiding her to the front door, they led her outside. Seeing the open, snow-covered woodland, she sprang naked into the frozen drifts, leaping away with the speed and agility of a deer, her hair a flaming cape. Down the hill she went, never slipping or falling — she vanished into a dense thicket of spruce. There was a flash of red-gold tresses, then nothing but the deep-shadowed wood.

Stepping back inside, Jabroal again heaved a solemn sigh and closed the door. He turned to Pulsifer.

"That is done. Now, let us discuss the terms of your stay here, and your duties. I must warn you that the infamy of your activities has even reached my ears, here in seclusion; I will tolerate neither lies nor theft. Keep in mind that your position is based on my gratitude, and my interest in maintaining a healthy interpersonal mesh between us."

Pulsifer spread his hands in a gesture of agreement, and smiled. "My situation is that of an honest but misunderstood man! Like you, maintaining Equilibrium is my primary concern in my dealings with others! But you leap quickly to business — would not a jolt of bold tastaca soothe your injured spirit?"

Jabroal nodded thoughtfully. "An intelligent suggestion! Five bottles rest in the pantry — your first task as my seneschal is to assist me in their rapid consumption! The door is bolted, the fire does its task — I find myself desiring the temporary oblivion of inebriation."

"My own needs are less drastic, but, I, too, would like a drink. In this first assignment, as in all to come, you will find me expedient." With an eager step, Pulsifer went to fetch the bottles of harsh liquor. Jabroal sat on a divan near the door, gazing out a narrow window and at the ice-coated forest.

Days and weeks passed. Pulsifer chafed at the menial and repetitive nature of his duties; never in his life had he worked in such a way, for either livelihood or self-protection. More than once, the demeaning aspect of his situation nearly drove him to leave. But the sight of the dark forest, thick with shadows which Montath might have ensorcelled to seek and grasp him, drove the thought of travel from his mind. Better by far was it to empty the table-scraps into the goat-pen, or scrub the wooden floors of the observatory, than to be captured by his enemy's baleful magic! He bit his lip when he became discontent, and reminded himself of his good fortune.

One morning, Jabroal killed a spying hawk with a whistled Word;

another time he generated an illusion-man of shadow and light, in the likeness of Pulsifer, and sent it running southward through the forest. The mage said that he had detected the heavy presence of a jret or hijret, and he swore that the entity he'd sensed had rushed in pursuit of the flitting, uncatchable shadow-double.

The reclusive mage was not an unkind taskmaster. Pulsifer soon found that Jabroal was usually preoccupied and somewhat absent-minded as well, and rarely noticed the quality of the drudgery done at his request. Pulsifer's efforts lessened appreciably, and he found himself with more time to wander the immediate area around the house, or explore the strange variety of books in the library. The wizard seemed to unceasingly concentrate on his Great Undertaking, the nature of which Pulsifer had not ascertained, and gave scant thought to anything else. He would occasionally be gone for two or three days at a time, to return muttering about talycents and enigmas, caverns beneath the Earth, and a Final Ingredient.

In the morning, generally after an early breakfast, Jabroal would assign Pulsifer his tasks for the day, don thick robes and an insulated leathern badger-mask, and then be gone into the forest for several hours. Usually he rode upon the back of a silver-chested grey bear of enormous size, which awaited him at the edge of the clearing about the house. Before leaving, he would invariably instruct Pulsifer not to enter or tinker with the items in the workroom while he was gone, in that he might accidentally come to great harm. Always Pulsifer assured him that he would do as instructed; always, he went to the door of the workroom, curiosity nagging like an insect in his ear. The thought that this was a test by Jabroal to gauge his trustworthiness kept him from entering the sanctum.

After a time, however, Jabroal ceased these admonishments, apparently assuming that Pulsifer would continue to avoid the workroom as he had requested. Jabroal continued on his daily journeys; the deep, hateful Chill of mid-winter had now settled over the Forests of Iskiruen. One day he stood watching from a window as Jabroal vanished into the dark trees, mounted on the bear; with a snort of disgust, he threw the broom from his hand. For nearly three months he had forced himself into this routine of tedious monotony, and he could take no more — He was Pulsifer! He feared destruction, but he feared insanity and self-loathing to an even greater degree! The fire crackled at his back, enticing him with its warmth; he gazed at the leaden sky, stretched above a world that would be in deep winter for six more months, and thought of the rapid life in distant cities, where people sought desperately after pleasure and joy with fatalistic fervor. There was still much to do, on the old and frozen Earth...

Hastily he gathered his belongings. By now Montath surely searched elsewhere for him! There was an understanding between himself and his host, that he would depart whenever he wished. He filled his valise and the wide pouches inside his traveler's clothes with food from the mage's larder, particularly stuffing the *manathte*, the large pouch beneath the back of his coat. He also appropriated a tight coil of rope and an extra knife, stuffing them into the valise. On the pantry door, he left a note of thanks for the mage; then, bundling up, he started for the door, looking about to be certain that he'd not forgotten anything.

His eyes locked on the passageway leading to the laboratory of the wizard.

For a moment he wavered in indecision — but had he not entered and safely left dangerous places before? Was he not Calim Pulsifer, foremost thief and procurer of guarded objects in the whole of Teumdoth? He strode confidently to the portal and down the short hall to the chamber.

He looked about with keen eyes, his inquisitive sense for valuable items perked and searching. He had been in the sanctum many times to perform some mundane task or other, when Jabroal had been present, so he had an idea of the order in which the seemingly-cluttered contents of the room were arranged. His eyes found a stack of hide-bound parchments — Jabroal's notebooks! Here perhaps was information worth knowing — but not spells, he reminded himself! Still, the theft of knowledge was particularly sweet; it could be taken, carried away in one's skull, and the victim would never know of its pilfering.

He flipped through first one booklet, then another — the obscure or meaningless nouns and phrases left him unsatisfied. Finally, he opened a red libram, its cover worn smooth by constant handling. Scrawled on the page was a note of familiar title:

A SYNOPSIS OF A REVOLUTIONARY ENDEAVOR
IN THE REALM OF EFFECTUATIONS

I, Jabroal Glispert of Mishraen-in-Phontyque, Mage Independent and Unaccepted, for the admiration and wonder of other mages, do write herein a spell which is such that it can never be reconstructed in this continuum, and can be used only once—hence, I write this without fear of plagiarism from lesser minds which fancy themselves of the Brotherhood. The efficacy of this formula, ingredients transformed by thought-inversion into runes, is unsurpassable. I, myself, shall integrate the spell into my being, attaining ultimate mastery over life, death, and all sorcerous comprehensions and phenomena. Mages of the Brotherhood, you will gape at my mastery—but by then I will be visibly ascendant over you! The final ingredient, for which I have long searched, is finally within my reach, and the fruit of twenty-eight years of labor ripens now! I set forth the essence of the Penultimate Postulation, given me through a priori revelation in my youth, a transforming spell of godlike power. As is known, the six Categories of Magehood are these:

1. Tremulator: One commanding the unleashings or harnessings of various elemental or supernatural energies, or entities.
2. Effectuator: One capable of transforming matter or life-forms, and affecting states of being with transitory effect. Conceptualizations, concentrated as runes, are utilized.
3. Fulminator: A caster or architect of Curses, Blights, and Murrains. Elements of the above two categories are often utilized.
4. Inquisitor: A delver of secrets, a diviner, a truth-finder.
5. Initiator: A specialist derived from any of the above categories, practiced in controlling cause and effect relationships of various types.
6. Equilibriator: A specialist derived from the first five categories, expert at applying specific knowledge to the underlying synchronicity called Equilibrium.

Melgeone the savant acquired four of these — some say five. Shiarscurry also had four, and in our own time, there are a few practitioners adept at three. Some say the upstart Morskured Montath has more, but this is so improbable as to warrant dismissal as ludicrous. No human skull can survive the retention of such a burden — until now. I announce a seventh Category, of which I, Jabroal Glispert, shall be the only qualified example: to wit, the Category Encompasser, holding all knowledge and capabilities of the above varieties of Magehood. Never has such an individual existed; and without the integration of the Penultimate Postulation, I would be torn apart if I attempted such comprehension. The following are the elements of the spell, gleaned and gathered over twenty-five year's time:

1. A drop of golden blood from the embryonic viodom Tharsrip, of the concentricity of Rioda;
2. A bubble of potentiating dream-thought, from the Sleeping God Hymakki, passed unsullied up through the sieve of Earth and snared with a net woven of widows' laments, and the breath of day-old infants;
3. The first cry of a freshly-hatched mamonlex;
4. Three drops of milk from a barren cow;
5. The odor of a troll-king's corpse;
6. The membranous laugh of a parsennoc, interwoven with a battlefield breeze;
7. The zig-zag of a thunderbolt;
8. The mummified ring-finger of the conqueror Somnelian Tonx;
9. Four intertwined winds which met at a crossroads;
10. The spittle of a night-mare;
11. A crystalline brain-nodule from an ancient talycent;
12. And, most important, the astral sleeve or essence of the man called Pulsifer, gifted by the Singularity Pammoth with Uncursability, and an Aura of Unaging Physicality (I was informed of his condition by a talycent of Zev Grotto, and am all but certain of the veracity of its information). These gifts are only wasted on a wastrel such as he.

So, these are the elements, the Indissolubles; the last supercedes another, which I could not have likely procured in any event. The rogue Pulsifer wandered into my hands; by using him for this, rather than turning him over to the Brotherhood, two purposes are served. One is the leveling of a disharmonic imbalance between the Brotherhood and myself; the other is the fact that he serves my purpose more easily than if I had still to obtain the soul of one of the frozen demigods of glaciated Genserengue. That was a task I admit having contemplated with dubiousness. Now all but Pulsifer are contained in an impermeable pouch, fashioned of leather from a viodom's wing. At Endyear, when Pammoth's protective layers are weakened a fraction by the influence of the planet Henevolepi, the man Pulsifer will at last serve a worthwhile purpose. His physical shell will perish, but this is a disequilibrium I am willing to create and risk. He saved my life; I saved him from an uncontrolled effectuation — that debt between us is cancelled. I chose to not look at this as murder — in a sense, he will live on within me.

Pulsifer dropped the book with a curse. Everywhere, treachery and deceit! The mage Jabroal extended him tedious hospitality, while plotting to rip away his soul for the sake of a self-gratifying experiment! In a gesture of outrage, he half-drew his sword —

He froze. "Aura of Unaging Physicality?" he said aloud. He picked up the book, found the page, and read the passage again. The words of the talycent in the forest, concerning Pammoth's final boon, rang in his ears. An exuberance swept through him and he rushed to a dusty mirror to examine his rakish features.

He detected no difference in his appearance, but only two years had passed since his meeting with Pammoth. An unaging state was not immortality in the truest sense, but it was certainly a condition which all human beings, from the lowliest of beggars, to the most high-born member of the Eight Upper Classes, had dreamt of at one time or another! If one guarded one's life well, it could be maintained for an incredible length of time…

Pulsifer hooted with joy, smiting his hands together. Clenching his teeth in a strong white grin, he tore the page from the book and set about searching for another thing. At last he found it, hidden behind a pot of greenish liquid — a black leather bag which he'd often seen Jabroal clutching tightly as he departed on his forays, but not during the last few weeks. Apparently the brain-nodule of a talycent was a recent acquisition. Pulsifer untied the cord which held it closed, and peered within.

A jumble of round and jagged shapes, of various hues and flashing intensities, met his eyes. He closed the bag, and thrust the Indissolubles of the Penultimate Postulation into one of his inner pockets. Then, putting on his mask and hood, he departed the house of Jabroal, his mood jolly despite the danger of Jabroal's wrath, or the forlorn howling of the wind in the trees. The rush of blood through his limbs felt new and electric, and he strode through the forest with a song, the horrid coldness not yet penetrating the seams of his clothing at all.

Still, he went in a direction opposite that taken earlier by Jabroal the Mage.

Late in the afternoon, Pulsifer paused for breath atop a craggy knoll where few trees grew. Bones aching with exertion and somewhat numb with cold in spite of his thick garments, he looked back toward the southeast. He had no idea of the exact location of Jabroal's home, but the mage would soon be discovering his disappearance and his theft. The forest stretched away in all directions, a tossing green sea foam-tipped with snow; the sky was a glaring bowl of blue-white color. Flexing his gloved fingers, he searched the vastness above for fottermees, or indeed for any flighted creatures which might carry tales.

A rock scraped behind him —

He whirled, whipping out his sword. A black-furred nust stumbled back in surprise, a cudgel of gnarled wood in its grasp. Its ugly face seemed that of a shriveled child; the dirty, matted beard which hung from beneath its chin trailed the ground beneath its feet. It scrambled frantically upon its own tail and beard, then lost its balance and tumbled down the other side of the hill.

Pulsifer came after it with a cruel laugh.

The dwarfish creature was finally brought to a painful halt, its beard entangled in a twisted tree. It hung with its feet ten inches from the ground, grasping desperately at the limb beyond its reach, writhing, swinging, and snorting as its kind were known to do. It seemed unable to extricate itself—

Pulsifer approached it with another laugh of amusement, and it grew still, watching him with one terrified eye as it faced the sky.

He sheathed his sword and unstrapped his kabeyui, grinning. Arms crossed, he leaned against the contorted stuntwillow. "You seek to harm me, little one? What wrong have I done you? I may just leave you hanging, for the wood-tambens to torment and devour—"

"Do as you wish," the nust grumbled. "I am powerless to stop you. However, you will lose valuable information as the price of your revenge..."

"Speak and I may not kill you! First, tell me why you sought to waylay me!"

The nust's face was red with strain. "Release me first, and I will tell you all—"

"What? And have you vanish like a leaping hare? I think not. Speak, or you hang here 'till you're coated with the embrace of the night's ice-fog."

"Huuu! You are in command of the situation! Dur-bats flit through the forest, and water-spirits babble in stream and brook! Jabroal the Mage searches for one such as you, offering great reward! Indeed, many beings look for you now. The wood is a-whisper with tales of a young man, a wizard of terrifying potency..."

"I thought as much. What is your name?"

"Cholct. You are the man called Pulsifer, are you not? As I said, another man looks for you as well..."

"I am Pulsifer. Tell me, Cholct, are there any other men in the vicinity, to your knowledge? Speak quickly, or I desert you dangling!"

"Beneath this hill, a parsennoc dwells—he may have captives, I do not know. A tinker camps beyond the eastern ridge; a band of Ycravern are but a mile away eastward, smithying weapons, repairing skis, and shoeing horses. Yesterday, a caravan of men was destroyed by Sheft, ten miles south. Prisoners were taken. Now, help me to the ground! It longs for the touch of my feet!"

"I cannot comply with your request." Pulsifer shook his head with a sympathetic expression. "Your kind are notoriously filled with spite and rancor. You would seal my destruction —"

"You promised!"

"I said I would not kill you — I keep my word. The night will soon come, and wrap frozen arms about you. I am not responsible for the weather! Nor am I to blame for your present position. I leave you to contemplate the self-centeredness which brought you to this situation, and I depart with no ill-will toward you —"

"My Curse upon you!" the nust screamed, flopping in rage as Pulsifer turned away and started down the hill. "Run fast, but to no avail — the death-curse of one of the nust-folk will burst your skull —"

There was a loud, wet pop. Pulsifer turned to look at the brain-ooz-ing, hanging corpse of the nust; its own curse had been reflected back upon it. He shrugged — at least it would not freeze to death. Quickly he left the vicinity of the parsennoc's den, before evening could fall about him.

As darkness settled beneath the trees he neared the camp of the tinker. Moving stealthily, he positioned himself on the ridge above the leaping fire.

Below, several men moved about in the gloom; a shaggy wubber snorted near a dilapidated wagon. One man was bent and elderly, his hands gnarled by work and age; the others were young, large, and thick-bearded, of savage demeanor. Their faces were brutal within their hoods. Swords, axes, and knives bristled from their bulky, fur-clad forms, and being of low or barbaric caste, neither the tinker nor the Ycravern were masked.

The bandits haggled with the old tinker, their words carrying clearly in the cold evening air. It seemed that they were on an errand for their womenfolk, and could not agree over the price of mending which the old man had done on some pots and pans. Their leader argued loudly, his words laced with threats; the tinker shook his head obstinately with a curt reply. The bandit raised a gauntleted fist, and the tinker shrugged fatalistically. The leader of the robbers viciously struck him to the ground.

Pulsifer unfastened his mask, then eased down the slope and entered the camp, just as the Ycravern were raiding the wagon and stuffing food, tools, and utensils into large, coarse-woven sacks. The old man lay moaning on the ground near the fire. At first Pulsifer went unnoticed, as he seated himself by the fire, unbuckled the attachments at the tops of his shoulders, and removed the valise from his back-harness. He then took out the golden bowl, which he placed in his lap. Next he took out a hunk of greenish cheese, and a bottle of tastaca. One of the bandits glanced over at him, and the man's jaw fell open in astonishment.

The bandit threw aside his booty-sack and cried out in an incredulous voice. "An imbecile! A traveler! A victim! Look, he begs for death! See the gleam of the gold he holds!"

The leader of their band drew a long, broad-bladed sword. His steely blue eyes flashed fiercely beneath black brows. "Valyati will warm me for a month, when I bring her such a gift! Man, I know you not, but if you would live another minute, surrender me that bowl!"

Pulsifer took a pull at the bottle of tastaca, smacked his lips, and set it aside. His expression was exaggeratedly confused. "Bowl? What Bowl?"

The tall bandit grew livid. "Do you mock me? I am Nanoki Ru, the most feared freebooter of the Forests! My spoken name causes the mightiest to tremble! Are you addled? No matter—your arrogance tells me that your head is ripe for splitting…"

He approached Pulsifer with a heavy tread. Pulsifer poked idly at the fire with a stick, half-smiling. The other Ycravern men began to close in as well, grinning bloodthirstily. Nanoki stopped across the fire from Pulsifer, and raised his sword.

Pulling the twig from the flames, Pulsifer thrust its burning tip into the bowl he held in one hand. The interior of the bowl began to glow ominously.

Nanoki stepped back, sudden fear on his face. "A mage! Pardon, Sir Mage!" He lowered his eyes respectfully, and his sword as well, and his companions moved uneasily away. The tinker moaned, but did not rise.

With a hissing metallic screech, the white-hot face of Shigandure the Immolator rose from the bowl. His voice was like thunder between the hills.

"PRESUMPTUOUS AND UNBALANCED ONE! I WARNED YOU AS TO WHAT WOULD OCCUR—"

"Your price is met, and overly so!" Pulsifer cried, thrusting the tilted bowl toward the bandits. "Take the men you see standing, and you are also paid for your earlier inconvenience at my hands! I offer this out of a spirit of gratitude!"

With a roar Shigandure shot from the bowl — as he passed over the fire, a blazing, stocky shape, he took most of the flames with him, a shadow of fire at his heels. On legs of scarlet heat, his presence was a brilliant beacon — golden lightning arched from his outspread arms and opened mouth, to leap like tentacles and wrap about the forms of the seven bandits. The Ycravern instantly became wraiths of twisting ashes. The demiurge turned, a horrid dwarf from the guts of a sun, and looked at the shaking Pulsifer.

In a second, Shigandure elongated himself into an arch of fire-stuff, landing in the bowl in Pulsifer's quivering hands — the force of the entity's return knocked him back two feet and onto his back, but he did not drop the bowl, which he now held above himself. Shigandure's face glared down at him, radiating a painful heat. Pulsifer turned his own face away.

"THE PRICE IS PAID, AND YOUR ACCOUNT IS SETTLED! NEW WORKERS WRITHE AT THEIR TASKS! WHAT DO YOU ASK OF ME?"

"Your service is performed in this instance!" Pulsifer gasped, closing his eyes to protect them from being melted. "Return whence you came!"

With a wry twist of its mouth, the face of the demiurge retreated and vanished into the glimmering bowl. Pulsifer staggered erect, holding the bowl in one hand. The ancient tinker stirred with a cry of pain; he was scrawny, with a shock of reddish-grey hair.

Pulsifer went to his side, and the old man looked at him in confusion.

"Where is Nanoki? Where is the robber Prewj? Who are you?"

"The bandits are dead — their extortion will threaten you no more. I am your friend, and your new companion. Have you a place in your wagon where I might be concealed?"

Wearing an unsure expression, the man nodded. "Aye. I am Glemmet, a tinker. You are — ?"

"I am Pulsifer. I have been called the Velvet Knife."

Again Glemmet moaned. "I was better off with the friendship of the Ycravern! Not only are you an outlaw, but you will bring both bandits' and mages' wrath upon me as well! Depart, and I will not mention our meeting!"

Pulsifer shook his head. "This is not reasonable reciprocation on your part, Glemmet! I possibly saved not only your wares, but your life! Assist me in crossing the Forests, and not only will we be at counterpoise, but two murtils of gold will find your palm!"

Glemmet sat up, his face canny with a haggler's cleverness. "Two murtils, you say? Have you perhaps three — ?"

"Two is the offer — do not forget my recent assistance! Nanoki and his curs could have cost you life or livelihood! Be appreciative of my generosity!"

Glemmet reached for the fur cap which had been knocked from his head by Nanoki's blow. "My ears freeze — let us go to the fire, and discuss our bargain in greater detail. I must soon erect the firefence about the camp. Darklings already scent on us." He looked up sidewise at Pulsifer. "Unless you would vanquish nightwalkers as you did the Ycravern —"

Pulsifer laughed. "Let us erect the fence! That which helped me against the bandits is more unpredictable than all the horrors of the night!"

Soon a circle of spiraling, perforated tubing was uncoiled about the campsite. Filling the oil-reservoir and lighting the many wicks which protruded from the tube, they were quickly surrounded by a thousand points of light. The wind blasted fiercely through the hollow, and the flames flickered; beneath the protective branches of a nearby bush, a quail twittered nervously.

Glemmet invited Pulsifer to join him in a meal of wild roots and roasted pikas. The rodents were somewhat gamey, having hung from the rear of the tinker's wagon for three days; Pulsifer nibbled at them with disgust, planning to later break out some of the food he had taken from Jabroal's chateau. As they ate, the old man spoke to him with easy familiarity, shreds of half-chewed rodent from his nearly-toothless mouth.

"You'll have to stay in the wagon, most of the time — the Sheft-dwarfs are hunting for you, at the command of a dark wizard who seems to have terrified them into his service. They're a scary bunch themselves, the Sheft — expert torturers, you know, and worshippers of the demon Rewelquian. I'll not stand by you if you're discovered by them; I draw my pension with the Warming, guild-willing! I intend to live to receive it!"

"Concealment is my foremost consideration," Pulsifer agreed. "Allow me along as a hidden passenger, that's all I ask. A few weeks of confinement are not beyond my capacities; just see me to the Peldrain River, and the gold you receive will cushion you in your retirement."

Glemmet guffawed. "You set a brisk pace! But the paths through the forest are winding and perilous — to stray from them and into the deeper thicknesses would be stupid and suicidal. I'm afraid you'll have to trudge along with me on my customary route. Three months will be good time."

Pulsifer grumbled in agreement. Glemmet didn't seem to notice his guest's dissatisfaction, but launched into an account of his many years in the Forests of Iskiruen, obviously eager for some casual conversation. Pulsifer barely listened as he searched the darkness about them for movement — fearing that Jabroal, or worse, Morskured Montath, might come upon them, he excused himself abruptly and had Glemmet show him to a place of rest in the wagon, beside the stove.

Glemmet soon joined him, locked the door, then lit a small fire in the stove. An occasional gust of air through the narrow ventilation-slits made the flames flicker, and Pulsifer huddled more tightly in his corner. As he fell asleep, he heard Glemmet talking lowly, apparently to himself.

Outside, the wubber snorted in the cold, and pawed the frozen ground.

Chapter III

Passage Found

Twelve days passed in bouncing procession. During the afternoon of Pulsifer's first day with Glemmet, the tinker reported seeing a bat-winged, man-like figure riding the upper air like a night-flying prainquel, or a demonic viodom. Pulsifer knew that the old man could only have seen Jabroal Glispert, in his winged harness. Now he found himself sore and irritable from cramped confinement, and the lurching of the creaking wagon along forest paths. The going was slow, for the wubber paused often to nibble foliage from evergreens as they went. Three times, Pulsifer's proximity-ring had alerted them to dangers near at hand — a club-wielding olang, hairy and huge, was driven away by the threat of torches; parsennocs were similarly dissuaded from violence; and a pit-full of slithering grunds was bypassed at the last moment. They had stopped upon five occasions for purposes of business — once in a dell near an Ycravern village, twice for hermits of unkempt appearance and dubious employment, one time among a colony of aborigines who lived in tree-top huts, and most recently at a settlement of the Sheft.

Pulsifer had peered through the grimy windows on either side of the wagon, while Glemmet mended pots and kettles for the pygmies. The Sheft men and women were hardly distinguishable from one another due to their similar apparels of bulky, hodge-podge furs; their faces were round, their features pinched, their teeth filed to wicked points. He thought that their voices where maddeningly high and shrill, sounding like the chitterings of hyraxes, and was relieved when the wagon pulled away from the hole-covered hill, upon which they teemed like umber ants. As they left, Pulsifer sighted four halfburned cars from the caravan mentioned by the nust, in the process of being broken into firewood and usable sections. There was no sign of the occupants of the train — Pulsifer had rubbed his chin thoughtfully. How had primitive minikins like the Sheft taken a well-armed convoy such as that?

They trundled onward, the forest growing ever denser and darker as they neared its heart, the trees massive and menacing. On several occasions they came upon circles of standing stones, around which the ground seemed welltrodden; huddled in his heavy outer clothing, Glemmet would snap the reins to hasten the wagon away from these sites, muttering uneasily about Eldest Magic. The Sheft-hill was now a day behind them, and dim sunlight fell in feeble shafts upon the frozen forest, setting the trees faintly aglitter. They were enroute to a small trading-camp, where Glemmet would barter wares and services for food, oil, and other essentials. Deciding to risk exposure in daylight for the sake of some fresh air, Pulsifer donned his travel-wear and opened the hatch at the front of the wagon, clambering out onto the elevated bench beside Glemmet. The tinker's traveler's clothes were battered, and torn in places, and his peeling ovoid mask was unbuckled, but he did not seem excessively uncomfortable. He looked at his emerging passenger curiously, but said nothing. Pulsifer bared his own face to chill wind and warming sun.

A plan for escape had formed in his mind. When he parted company with Glemmet at the swift-flowing Peldrain, he would stow away on a barge or other vessel and ride the mile-wide river southward; coming ashore at Pegres, he would follow the river until it vanished in a swirling maelstrom beneath the glacier Paruthais. He then intended to skirt the glacier until he could cross its most narrow stretch, and find hidden sanctuary in the nation of Ibret. There was the maze-avenued city of Aggaram, a topsy-turvy metropolis where he had heard a man could lose himself forever — a den of pariahs, thieves, and expatriates. The genius of his plan filled him with exultation — even Montath would never find him there!

The wagon swayed, the wubber plodded stoically. The trees were covered with fresh-fallen snow. They came to a rickety bridge spanning a half-frozen, rocky runnel; looking down as they passed over, Pulsifer saw the slender, hairless forms of merileuts slip from the banks and into the sparkling water. They fluttered and turned like fish beneath the surface, changing color as was their fashion.

The rattling wagon rumbled up a rise covered with a frosted pelt of spruce saplings and furze. The vehicle crested the hill, and fir-boughs swished as nine or ten sylebers, and as many deer, were flushed from their place of repose beside the trail. By startled reflex, the woman-like creatures scattered in many directions, their exaggerated feminine attributes bouncing; one, seemingly a beautiful, red-haired human woman, fled westward. The two men had only a glimpse of the syleber Sinfe as she was swallowed by afternoon shadows, and Glemmet exclaimed at the sight of her. Pulsifer stated that he himself had seen only sylebers, and that a woman had not been with them. Glemmet argued, and Pulsifer shrugged.

Late in the afternoon they approached a small vale, its depths blue and black with shadow. Pulsifer detected a defensible prominence along the farther side, and the glimmer of a frozen waterfall beside the bluff. He pointed this out to Glemmet as a potential campsite, but the tinker halted the wagon, gazed at the site, and shook his head.

"That would not be safe — we'll camp here by the road, and cross the valley in the morning."

Pulsifer looked at the road — since several trails had converged to create it about five miles back, it looked well-traveled. Such a road would be a likely place for his enemies to search for him...Again, he pointed at the bluff.

"It seems to me that yonder bluff is the wisest choice for a campsite. The road is worn by many feet, and our chances of encountering one of my persecutors is increased by the length of our stay on it — or beside it."

Glemmet creased his face obstinately. "You know nothing of the forests — you are a creature of the cities. Under the trees, reaching like fingers toward the surface, are said to be many cavities of the Upper Cavern Realms, such as Zev Grotto and Lunkin Karst. The limestone hereabouts is supposedly five miles deep. In Zev Grotto dwell talycents and vampires, and also grunds the length of a tall fir's height.

Somewhere in the depths of Lunkin Karst, in a turreted manse of chalcedony, dreams the ochdeviant Kreeisfu Kwae, a creator of man-killing abominations — or so rumor maintains. Also near the surface world are the caverns haunted by the ghosts of Perfidic wizards, and some say the buried giant Rewelquian, the demon worshipped by the pain-loving Sheft. Encounters with all of these are to be avoided. The vale before us is said to be one of the few locations concealing entrances to the hellish grottoes — therefore, we will cross the hollow in the morning, and be on our way."

Pulsifer made an uncaring gesture with one hand, and began to climb down from the wagon. "As you wish. I prefer to camp on the bluff, however."

He pointed to a tree beside the road, freshly scarred with jagged tears in the solid wood. "Observe the claw-marks of a rutting byrex — thus do the great cats mark their territory. Even a city-born fool such as myself knows this. Also, I detect the distinct sulphurous odor of a night-roaming grimkel; this carnivore, too, must have its lair close at hand. Our oil is low, and the flamefence will not burn throughout the night. I have a quick sword-arm, as well as a means of magical protection which made short work of the Ycravern, and I also possess the entity-sensing ring. But be so kind as to reach into the wagon and hand down my bag, and perhaps we shall meet up in the morning."

Glemmet chewed his weathered lip. "Hm. Perhaps the crag would better serve as a campsite. Just you keep your articles of sorcery handy, and your nerves alert." Clicking his tongue, he snapped the reins. Pulsifer reseated himself as the wagon lurched forward.

Down into the vale they went, and as they left the direct rays of the sun, the intensity of the cold caused them to put on their masks. Pulsifer tightened the fastenings of his clothing and buckled straps on his gloves, then placed one hand on his swordhilt, for his sense of unease increased as they descended into the gloom. The floor of the vale was thickly-forested in some areas, sparsely-wooded in others. Over everything hung a heavy stillness. They forded a shallow stream which, at one time as a glacier, and later as a young, broad river, had carved the vale from mountains which were now rocky hills. Twice they passed ominous moraines of granite, and in the side of one of these was a black hole, from which issued a moaning wind. Glemmet gestured wordlessly at the cave as they bumped past. Nearing the bluff, they passed through a thick and dismal band of woods — Pulsifer was startled by a giant, hunched, and reaching shape poised over the trail, but it was only an ancient conifer, bent and blasted by time and the elements.

By the time they reached the top of the bluff, they looked back at a dim, setting sun. Snow was falling lightly. They hurriedly set up camp beneath a large, solitary spruce, placing the wagon to the north side of the firepit, to keep off the flesh-killing northern wind. Around this they erected and tied down the flamefence, and Pulsifer gathered a plentiful supply of resinous branches, as well as the ice-shattered limbs of a dead sabelende.

The fire was large and hot. They cooked their dinner in the open and night came down. Pulsifer shared with Glemmet the last of the sausage and cheese he had appropriated from Jabroal's cupboard; then, lighting the wicks of the flamefence and setting the oil-valve on low, Glemmet rolled out the bedding and insulated pads for his wubber. He secured the animal beside the wagon, out of the wind and close enough to the blazing fire to absorb some warmth from it. The wubber rolled its eyes fearfully but did not shy away from the flames, for it had felt such heat on many nights. Glemmet brought it a bucket of grain and fir-needles, and then joined Pulsifer in the winter-repelling wagon.

Pulsifer had a blaze going in the stove. Rubbing his bare hands together, he sat quietly in thought, dreaming of fortunes won and lost, of women he'd known and some he had yet to know, of the vagaries of fate, and Pammoth's final gift. What reason, other than gratitude, could have moved the Singularity to endow him with a condition such as that he had discovered? A small gift did his 'Unaging Physicality' seem, if he were doomed to spend his days as a vagabond and fugitive! The perse-cution of the Brotherhood of Mages, of the Collectors of Knowledge, would never let him rest — not so long as Morskured Montath and Moilerve Sulshaine lived! If Montath were, as rumor had it, a mage with the potential to rival the greatest wizards of previous centuries, then he, too, could live for several hundred years! It was evident that the young sorcerer would not rest until Pulsifer was destroyed…

And now he had Jabroal to contend with as well! He snarled an expletive and struck his fist on his knee, interrupting the chattering Glemmet, who was relating an anecdote of a fight he'd once witnessed between a malderg and a swarm of tambens. Misunderstanding Pulsifer's action, Glemmet glowered sulkily and did not resume his tale; he re-hung some tinware which had fallen, and moved to his own pallet near the rear of the wagon. Soon he was snoring resonantly.

The stove-fire crackled with begging flames. Pulsifer opened the door of the stove with a stick and tossed in some lengths of wood. Looking out the window, he could see that the wicks of the flamefence still burned, the long flames flickering in the wind, but not going out. They were only extinguishable by water, or shutting off the flow of oil, and the latter would soon occur due to the lowness of the fuel-supply. Eyeing the darkness uneasily, he went back to the stove and roasted some nuts in a long-handled pan. The aroma filled the wagon.

As he ate he scowled at the unfairness of his predicament. There was only one solution — he would have to avoid and eventually neutralize those who sought to do him harm! Particularly did Montath come to mind. Perhaps the awesome spell he had stolen from Jabroal, or some of its ingredients, could be turned into an offensive effectuation to use against the young mage! But at the present, Pulsifer was not only wary of spells — he was without guidance in their application or uses. He looked at Glemmet; the other man was deep in a stupefied sleep. Opening his valise, Pulsifer glanced at the bag containing the Penultimate Postulation, then took out the Cask of Sranophaez. He pressed the glyphs of Dacdull the Interlocutor.

The voice of Dacdull rang in the stillness. *"What is your question?"*

Glemmet grumbled in his sleep, but did not awaken. Pulsifer hissed.

"Speak more quietly, Dacdull! My question is this — you can in no wise act as a directory to the functions of the cask?"

"This is the way of things."

Pulsifer knit his brow in thought. "So. Tell me this, Interlocutor — how do you spend your time when you are not called forth to converse? Do you chat with your fellows in the cask?"

"I experience the timeless peace of oblivion, the unthinking rest from which Sranophaez took and bound me."

"Which of the two states do you prefer?"

There was a pause. Then Dacdull said: *"Oblivion is my ideal. I am an incomplete fraction of my former self. I am only a memory. By the decree of Time, I should sleep forever."*

Pulsifer nodded. "You are dismissed."

The cask was silent; Dacdull was quiescent. Pulsifer pressed the sigils of Dacdull again.

The voice of Dacdull issued from the cask. *"What is your question?"*

Pulsifer said nothing, but pressed the glyphs yet again.

"What is your question?"

Pulsifer pressed again.

"What is your question?" There was an unmistakable note of aggravation in Dacdull's tone — although a dead memory, it was not beyond emotional responses. Pulsifer pressed again.

Now the Interlocutor's voice was clearly angered. *"What is your question?"*

Pulsifer smiled. "You have said that you can not serve as a guide to the mysteries of the cask — is this due to the design of Sranophaez, or your own wish to not be bothered unduly? I tell you this, Dacdull — I can arrange for you to be summoned in this manner, every second of every day. In fact, I have nothing better to occupy my time."

Dacdull's voice was resentful. *"Upon occasion I may by coincidence have knowledge of certain glyph-combinations, and their attendants. But I must tell you that if I am overly-invoked, I will grow incompliant to all questioning."*

Pulsifer held the cask closer, for Glemmet flailed about. "Good. I will ask no more than once or twice daily — both my peace of mind and yours shall be satisfied. Now, which glyphs summon a cluster of spies?"

For several seconds, Dacdull did not reply. *"If I were to tell you that eye and wave-bladed knife were the symbols you sought, I would be disobedient to the directives of Sranophaez — so I will not impart this information to you."*

"I understand. Nor would you tell me the symbols to call makers of curses?"

"I cannot. The crow and toad you must discover for yourself. Now, may I return to nonexistence? The world pains me with its harsh pretensions of space and form!"

"You are philosophical! Yes, you are dismissed."

"*As you wish.*"

Dacdull was gone; Pulsifer sat memorizing the combinations which had been imparted to him. At last he pressed the eye and knife, speaking a soft command.

A familiar tinkling filled the air. A faint voice issued from a swirl of golden mites.

"*We are the Furtive Observers. Which do you require — espionage, reconnaissance, or exploration?*"

Pulsifer lowered his voice to a whisper. "I would know the whereabouts and activities of the wizard Morskured Montath, and his repulsive hijret familiar! I would also know the same about the wizard Jabroal Glispert. Go!"

The mites swirled and were gone. After ten or twelve seconds they returned.

"*Morskured Montath is sixty miles to the southwest, a guest in the village of predacious pygmies. A hijret haunts the night near the wizard, perched in a lightning-blasted oak. Jabroal Glispert is in Zev Grotto, conversing with talycents near their lair. Jabroal has no hijret. Our report is completed, and we depart —*"

"Wait!" Pulsifer said. "I must know also of the circumstances of a Lord Collector Moilerve —"

"*Summon us again in a fortnight — our energies are spent, the task is done.*" The swirls returned to the cask. After a moment's reflection, Pulsifer pressed the toad and raven symbols.

"Come forth!" His command was a whisper.

A blackish cluster of mites appeared, difficult to see. A glistening blue mote flashed into prominence in their midst.

"*We are the Fulminator Cluster. What are the natures of the curses you desire, and upon whom are the banes to be enforced?*"

Pulsifer considered. "Are your fulminations effective against even mages of high degree?"

"*Without knowing of whom you speak, this is unanswerable. Also we must know the curse you have in mind — most imaginable wanions are within our capabilities. Our effectiveness is generally potent.*"

Pulsifer bit his lip, his face a mask of indecision. "If your curse should somehow fail, would its origin be detectable by the intended victim? I do not wish to be found by my enemies…"

"This also is unanswerable. However, in regard to a Mage First-Degree, or Uttermost, caution is recommended. Either a curse of the greatest magnitude, or of the most trivial nature, would be most likely to succeed — the first in case of attempting the subject's total destruction, the second for purposes of revenge, without rousing suspicion. Inconsequential difficulties are often not suspect, but are viewed as misfortunes."

Pulsifer gnawed at his knuckle as he considered the possibilities. The degree of Montath's power was unguessable, but it was almost certainly beyond the Brotherhood's conventional measurements. A major assault would be risky. Smiting the hijret Firkui was definitely out of the question — an elemental being such as that was too dangerous to trifle with. Jabroal, also, was not a sorcerer in the traditional sense. Pulsifer addressed the Fulminators again.

"What would occur if I were to decide that I did not wish to make use of your services?"

"We are required to act — the nearest human beings would suffer a fate of our choosing."

"I thought as much. Very well! My companion deserves better. In a village to the southwest is a sorcerer named Montath — he deserves constant indigestion, and stubborn infestations of lice, fleas, and other parasites. Jabroal Glispert, in Zev Grotto, might do nicely with chronic forgetfulness and confusion. As for the Lord Collector Moilerve — wherever he may be — destruction of his personal property, sexual dysfunction, and severe hemorrhoids will combine to shake his self-confidence and destroy his nerve. There is your assignment!"

The deity-mites vanished on their errands. Pulsifer looked at Glemmet, who now slept with his head thrown back and his mouth open; then he ate a handful of nuts while he waited. After a few minutes the cluster of dark particles reappeared in the air before him. The voice was a rusty whisper.

"The curses have been set in motion. The wizard Montath ate the food of the Sheft, and was shown to a heap of rushes for his bed — this will allay any suspicions he may have tomorrow when his conditions become evident, for food and bedding will serve as catalysts for the fulminations. Jabroal

forgets the queries he puts to a talycent even as the words leave his lips. Moilerve's mansion topples, the inhabitants of his menageries roam free while his artifacts crumble, and the stress of these things has already served to prepare his mind-body structure for the physical infirmities. We return to the cask."

The dark cluster disappeared. Pulsifer placed the cask in the bulky valise and lay back beneath the warm blanket given him by Glemmet, his travelclothes still on. A terrible chill persistently seeped into the wagon, and he kept his gloves and kabeyui near at hand. He chuckled as he fell asleep.

Sometime during the night he half-woke, thinking to have heard a rattle at the window-latch; there was no other sound, and even the keen-sensed wubber outside was silent. Remembering his ring he glanced at it, but it was lifeless; rolling over, he was haunted by the feeling that its gleam had awakened him. He fell into slumber once more.

The morning was announced by the hysterical screaming of the tinker, outside the wagon. Fumbling for his sword, Pulsifer eased toward the door at the wagon's rear with his hastily-grasped belongings under one arm, prepared to fight or flee if the Sheft had followed and found him. He opened the door — Glemmet's oaths rang in the frosted stillness, but there was no other sound. Sliding cautiously to the ground, Pulsifer crept around the tree and gazed at the campsite.

Glemmet hopped and wheeled as he yelled in a fit of rage, bits of his breath following his movements. Before him was a heap of stark white bones, and pieces of the wubber's long, shaggy pelt were strewn about, mixed with shredded scraps of padding. The flamefence on this side was trampled into the ground, by enormous feet of an unguessable spoor. Broad, flat tracks filled the campsite, and the barrel which had been emptied of its last drops of oil had also been crushed by the intruder's tread.

Spying the shivering Pulsifer, Glemmet raised his fists in a gesture of extreme indignation.

"Idiot! Malcontent! I told you this valley was not safe! I am doomed, thanks to your selfishness! Without Reeshra, the wagon is unmovable! Without my wagon and its wares, my years of effort are for nothing! My retirement will be delayed a year, or two! And the parsennocs will appropriate my wares, so I am obligated to melt the wagon and its contents into a pile of slag, to prevent its misuse! Then we will have to walk through over one hundred miles of woodlands! May you not survive the journey, for you are a carbuncle on the arse of humanity! I am accursed by my association with you, brief though it has been! Depart from me, O left-handed fiend in human guise —"

"Calm yourself!" Pulsifer angrily exclaimed. "This can in no manner be attributed to me, and I protest your accusing tone! Instead I blame your lack of foresight, in that you carried an insufficient supply of oil for the fence! I still maintain that the roadside would have been a foolish location for a campsite! As for your expenses, I am sympathetic to your plight, and am willing to advance you one murtil of gold for the transportation and lodging you have provided to me thus far. Continue to guide me through the forests, and another two pieces will be yours, as well as one more, as recompense for this inconvenience — but this is no admission by me of responsibility for your misfortune!"

Glemmet's face twitched. "I do not believe that you intend to pay me — I don't think you have any money at all! You have duped me from the moment we met —"

Pulsifer opened one of the compartments of the pouchbelt about his waist, and drew forth two murtils of the fourteen he had taken in Yawamris from the collector, Srod Yaorn.

"Here is half of the promised fee — enough to more than pay off the debt you owe the guild for the wagon and wares. Now, let us return to the warmth of the wagon — you can gather the monies you've accrued already on this journey, and your other things. I myself am freezing!"

Glemmet grudgingly took the coins from Pulsifer's hand, and they went into the wagon again. They started a large fire in the stove to warm themselves while they prepared for their walk, and also ate some breakfast; Pulsifer warmed his traveler's clothes near the fire, then slipped them on again over his other clothing. He secured his hood and mask into place, and fastened on his snow-striding overboots above his other pair. Again he buckled the valise into the looped straps on his back. Glemmet watched him with a despondent face, as he methodically prepared a pack for himself. His own outerwear was old, but well-oiled and in good enough repair for the journey. The old man gathered his coins and trinkets, put them in a bag, and then into his pack along with some food, a knife, and utensils. He strapped on an ancient swordbelt and a shortsword in a battered scabbard, and gestured as to his readiness to depart. Pulsifer nodded, and they stepped out again.

Glemmet halted beside the wagon. "Wait — we must create a blaze of extreme hotness, and destroy what we leave behind."

Pulsifer shook his head. "Who will know, if we do not? We don't have the time. The trading outpost is two days' walk —"

"Three."

"Three. Our situation is not of pleasant outlook, for whatever killed the wubber may return and hunt us. We should leave this valley with all haste."

Glemmet reluctantly nodded, and they set out. They headed back down the trail they had come up, for to the east was a sheer, unclimbable cliff. As they descended the trail it grew convoluted and rough, strangely narrow at times and not as they remembered it — after twenty minutes of walking, it led around a knoll, and they came to a large, relatively clear area.

Before them was an enormous fir, and a ramshackle wagon.

Glemmet shook his head. "We took a wrong turn on the trail — we're on the other side of the bluff! Let's try it again." His voice was falsely assured.

"I was about to make the same suggestion," Pulsifer agreed. "Be alert for the branching we missed before!" They crossed the bluff, passed their abandoned campsite, and started down the trail again. They found a path they hadn't noticed before, and took it; after half an hour of walking along a mostly overgrown trail, they came to a small hill. They glanced at one another, and stepped around it.

The tree and wagon were there, just as before.

"Magic!" Glemmet yelled. "A witch or ochdeviant torments us for pleasure! Let us return backways along the route we just took, and confound the spell!"

Pulsifer waved a hand in disgust. "A useless exercise. We would wander the hexed path until night fell — obviously we would be easy prey along the darkened trails. Let us better spend our time by gathering a large supply of firewood, and wait for our captor to be revealed."

Glemmet nodded. "At least there is food in the wagon — we will not hunger before we die. The water-barrel is full as well." They trudged back to the camp.

Throughout the day they ventured with axes to the edges of the bluff, gathering wood. By the afternoon they had accumulated a great amount of fuel, and had begun fashioning some of the saplings into sharpened stakes.

These they embedded in the ground about their campsite, concealing them with heaps of brush. Fires were kindled to either side of the wagon, and also in the stove within.

With dismal anticipation the two men watched from the fire nearest the tree, as night settled over the valley. The western sky was a frigid burgundy, the color of the ancient wines found in the crypts of Parhimmion. Pulsifer sat as near the flames as he could tolerate, for the flesh-aching Chill had utterly invaded their tiny kraal. He and Glemmet both bared their faces to the soothing heat of the flames, and Pulsifer watched dispassionately while the tinker prepared gruel for supper. The tinker's guest did not think of food, but desperately ran plans for escape through his mind. Calling forth Shigandure would not be wise, for the bowl entity, after destroying whatever held them on the bluff, would require one of them for his wage; Pulsifer needed his life, and a guide through the thickest portions of the forests, which were still ahead. Using the Cask of Sranophaez was also pointless, for the night before he had invoked both the Fulminators and Furtive Observers; the former might have provided defense, the latter could possibly have uncovered a route to freedom. Fuming inwardly at his haste of the previous night, he rose with a curse and stamped toward the wagon; he returned to the fireside, carrying the Cask of Sranophaez in one hand.

Glemmet looked at the cask inquisitively. "What is that box? An ill-gotten possession, no doubt! The metal is interesting, though—perhaps an alloy of titanium and virtulien, or greel. I would like to examine it, if I may."

"Are you never silent?" Pulsifer snapped. "The cask is a valuable and magically-potent relic, dangerous to any but one adept at its use. Be still while I seek information to assist us. Dacdull!"

He pressed two symbols. The voice of Dacdull rolled forth, and Glemmet nearly dropped the long-handled pan he held.

"What is your question?"

Holding the cask at arm's length, Pulsifer's face was a picture of studious concentration. "I hesitate to ask of you a pair of sigils, to summon a swarm of counter-conjurers, since I know that you will not reply. You will not assist me, will you, Interlocutor?"

"Indeed not. Lightning and mandrake are two symbols of which I may not speak. Ask another question, and perhaps I might be of some use to you."

"Thank you, no," Pulsifer refused. "As ever, you are recalcitrant. Return to the oblivion of the box!"

"As you wish." Dacdull was gone; Glemmet gaped as, with a command, Pulsifer activated the box again. A green and red cloud of lights danced forth.

"We are the Reflective Tremulators. State your need."

Pulsifer's voice rose with excitement. "We are held captive by a confusing glamour, a trap created by an unknown enemy! Find the spell's source, turn it back upon its maker, and allow us to leave this black valley!"

"We go." The mites vanished. Glemmet opened his mouth to speak, but Pulsifer silenced him with a stern look. A flodget cooed in the tree.

The cluster returned, with a tinkle like small voices laughing.

"The spell is not of a type to be cancelled or reversed. It is an extension of Will, composed in part of the life-force of that which would destroy you. It is in effect unalterable, except by the physical death of the being whose will maintains it. This entity is somewhat elemental, somewhat earthly — it will be difficult to slay."

"Can you not kill this being?"

"That is not our function — our realm is strictly that of sorcerous rebuttals. Assign us another task —"

"Of course," Pulsifer sighed. "Choose at random a wizard of the Brotherhood of Mages who currently works magic, and reflect his own spell back upon him. Then you may return to the cask."

The swirl disappeared again. Glemmet shook his head. "You are unqualified to operate an object such as that — the wrath of legitimate wizards will eventually find you! You have learned nothing helpful, and you trample upon the established codes of behavior by which all castes live…"

Pulsifer snorted scornfully. "I seek to save our lives; you dare complain? Prepare the gruel and keep your thoughts to yourself!"

The old man scowled angrily but said nothing more. After a minute, the green and red cluster of deity-mites returned, to dance like sparks above the flames.

"Vipprol the Equilibriator, of Mishraen-in-Phontyque, has been stricken with a Brazen Rigor of his own making. The spell was directed against his rebellious apprentice, a youth called Grestel Flijian. Our task is done, and we return to the confinement of Sranophaez."

The mites were gone. Pulsifer looked at the box for a moment, then rose and returned it to the valise in the wagon. He rejoined Glemmet, and they ate bowls of the watery porridge, shuddering at the wind at their backs. They neither spoke to nor looked at each other. Stoking the fires well, they soon retired to the wagon to wait out the night.

An hour dragged past, as they sat with travel-clothes and gear on, prepared for flight. Looking out the windows periodically, they saw the ever-diminishing flames of the fires leaping in the wind, and a deep, somber darkness beyond the blazes' light. Pulsifer had removed his gloves and again sat eating roasted nuts, his sword close at hand.

Grumbling, Glemmet rose, pulled on his hood and mask, and crawled through the small frontward hatch. Watching from the window, Pulsifer saw the tinker re-stoke the fires on each side of the wagon. Next Glemmet stood near the evergreen, and surveyed the barrier of brush and brambles they had constructed. He returned to the wagon — as the old man clambered up onto the bench and opened the hatch, the ring on Pulsifer's finger flashed blue, then green, then blue again.

Springing forward with a yell, Pulsifer yanked Glemmet into the wagon as a tremendous snapping sound was heard. Glemmet sprawled with a cry of pain amid pots, pans, and metal scraps; Pulsifer slammed and bolted the hatch, then leapt to the south-facing window.

Outside, something huge was bursting through the barricade. The sharpened poles snapped ineffectually against an indistinct grey-brown hide.

Pulsifer glimpsed a towering, broad, long-armed form — then it retreated again into the darkness. A palpable silence fell.

The tinker groaned as he pushed himself to a sitting position;

Pulsifer remained at the window. Without a word, Glemmet went to the other and watched the night on the northward side of the wagon.

Pulsifer's ring flashed, went out, flashed again. With deliberate regularity the thing beyond the barricade drew nearer, then pulled away from the vicinity of the large blazes. After many minutes of this, the ring ceased to detect any nearby presence.

Scanning the darkness fearfully, Pulsifer shook his head. "It's gone — temporarily, I'm sure. I suggest that we draw lots, to decide which of us is to go out and lead it away. The other can then attempt to foil the spell it has laid on this place, while its attention is diverted."

Beneath his kabeyui, Glemmet laughed ruefully. "Hah! The greatest scoundrel of the modern age seeks to draw me into a game of chance, with our lives as the stakes! No, thank you; I will await the monster's return with you."

"As you wish." Pulsifer made a flippant gesture. "We shall both die, then." He returned to his place by the stove and began cracking nuts once more. Glemmet moved back and forth between the windows, peering out of each in turn; at last he sat down at the rear of the wagon, unstrapped his mask, and resentfully glared at his companion.

His own face expressionless, Pulsifer continued eating; but his mind was racing. His abdomen quivered in fright, and his stomach reacted to their plight with sharp, insistent pangs. Once, as he cracked a nut, he thought to hear the sound distantly echoed in the wilderness outside, but he wasn't certain, so he said nothing.

Glemmet began to nod, scarcely able to fight away sleep — Pulsifer, too, felt a deep drowsiness coming on. He slumped back — his ring flashed blue again and he bolted upright, freed from the unnatural sleepiness. "Glemmet, awaken! The creature returns!"

Glemmet jumped up and went to one window as Pulsifer went to the other.

"I see nothing! Your excitability is the result of a guilty conscience! The night is quiet —"

A loud whistling sound rang out, as something large passed over the barricade, to land with a ground-shaking thud atop the fire nearest the tree. A hiss filled the night. Pulsifer had a glimpse of flames flickering beneath a great slab of ice, probably broken from the waterfall they had seen from across the vale — under the slab, the flames struggled for an instant, then were gone. Almost immediately there was a second thud on the other side of the wagon, and Glemmet yelled in dismay.

Outside darkness was complete in the vale, beneath moonless skies. Again silence reigned. Pulsifer turned to the tinker.

"Perhaps we can placate it — gather all the food!"

Glemmet shrugged, and made a small heap of various edibles. "This is the food we have. Offer it if you wish."

Pulsifer examined the pile with a dour expression. "One of us would provide greater nutrition. Are you sure this is all?"

Glemmet made a wry face, sighed, and knelt. Activating a hidden spring, he released a section of the floor and pulled it up. Reaching into the cache, he pulled out a hefty smoked ham, which he deposited on the floor. He grinned sheepishly at Pulsifer.

"Emergency provisions. I saw no need in informing you of it — we would have had to leave it behind anyway —"

Both men were suddenly flung to the floor, as the wagon was rocked by a powerful blow. The rear door buckled and broke, and a gigantic four-fingered hand, at the end of a stupendous arm seemingly made of rough and pitted wood, was thrust into the wagon; it groped with hairy, limb-like fingers. After several seconds of banging the walls above a dodging Pulsifer, the hand locked around the leg of Glemmet — screaming and flailing, the twisting tinker was jerked into the night outside.

The sounds of his pleading wails rapidly faded as the invader retreated into the wood. Pulsifer dug himself out from beneath fallen metalware and shook violently with a rush of fright and relief. He went to the shattered door and gazed out into the night; then realizing that he probably hadn't much time, he rushed to the stove and set to work.

Gathering jagged metal scraps and rounded ingots of brass, copper, and iron, he set them in an iron container, in the heart of the stove's flames. While these heated, he drew his knife and carefully carved a hollow in the ham; this he laced likewise with sharp bits of metal debris. Returning to watch the heating metal, he waited.

After half an hour he heard a crunching sound, as the thing returned along the trail. The fire had been a hot one, and the pan was aglow with molten and red-hot metals. Shoveling in a few coals, Pulsifer removed the pan with a pair of tongs, and slipped the container into the ham. Almost instantly the mouthwatering scent of cooking meat filled the air, along with a sizzling sound; he plugged the hole with the meat he had carved from the middle, and shoved the ham out onto the platform at the wagon's rear. Putting his gloves on, he waited. He hardly breathed as he heard a gigantic tread outside.

The creature crunched up to the wagon — looking out, he saw its legs, like grey tree trunks. Glemmet's blood glistened where it ran down the front of the thing. It paused for a second, unmoving as it considered the offering — then a monstrous hand grasped the ham, lifting it swiftly out of sight. A stentorian gulp was heard.

Sword in hand, Pulsifer waited with a most uneasy anticipation. The thing bent to peer within the wagon. Its face was a lunacy of rough, ape-like features of flesh, and woody coniferous branches. It opened its mouth to reveal a gullet like the hollow of a tree — Suddenly it straightened, swaying as it silently screamed. Pulsifer did not wait to study its next action — he scrambled for the hatch at the front, and slid out. Hitting the ground, he set off at a flying run.

He shot through the hole which the monster had torn in the barrier.

Nearing the slope of the bluff, he looked back — the glow from the doorway of the wagon revealed an anthropomorphic, tree-like thing some eighteen feet tall digging at its chest, with fingers sporting nails like spades. Its limb-rattling, stump-like head was thrown back in suffering, smoke puffing from its mouth. As he watched it swayed, and fell with a crushing weight on the wagon, sending splintered wood, pots, and kettles flying. Pulsifer continued to watch with satisfaction.

To his horror the thing slowly pulled itself from the shattered wagon; a dark, scraping mound, it began to crawl toward him. Strapping on his kabeyui, and checking the valise on his back with one hand, Pulsifer ran down the trail and into total blackness.

He knew that he would again be doomed to return to the bluff, for the thing still lived — hoping that its sorcery would be weakened by its injuries, he plunged into the wood alongside the path, crashing through the underbrush, and careening painfully from tree to tree as he half-tumbled down the slope.

At last he came to a level area; pausing to listen, he heard nothing but his pulse in his ears, and his coarse, gasping breath. He sheathed his sword and broke some branches from a tree which felt like a spruce; kneeling in the darkness, he fumbled with his fire-kit until he had lit the end of one branch. He held his torch aloft, and gathered a bundle of others to carry beneath his arm as he started moving again. The fire might draw the thing he was fleeing, but without light, he might run into it in the darkness — and it obviously disliked flame, so the torches were his only weapons.

For an hour he half-ran through the wood, his sense of direction completely lost. Eventually he heard the roar of water. Lifting his brand high, he saw that the eastern wall of the valley was before him — this meant that the bluff was behind him. Here there were a broad pool and tumbling stream, and into the pool fell the waterfall, its outermost layers thickly frozen. Twelve feet up were several holes, through some of which running water poured; these had apparently been made by the tree-being when it had ripped away the chunks of ice. Beside the waterfall the rock was sculpted into an irregular wall by the floods of years past; taking a cord from a pocket and binding his bundled torches, he hung them from one of the many straps on his coat and attacked the climb zestfully. Soon he would be out of this vale of death!

He was eight feet up when the snapping of branches and saplings startled him nearly into falling. Clinging precariously with one hand, he looked back with torch high, to see the stooped and groping monstrosity coming toward him, arms outstretched, hands poised to grasp and crush. Its eyes were squinted in agony, its mouth twisted into an unbelievable, face-splitting grimace. Smoke still curled from its oral cavity. Scrabbling at the rock, Pulsifer pulled and pushed himself upward.

The thing rushed forward. Beside Pulsifer's head was a jagged hole in the ice of the waterfall, through which a cool wind blew, entering the eye- and nostril-slits of his mask. Twisting, he flung the torch at the creature — the thing batted at the brand with chair-sized hands, but missed. A second later, its resinous head burst into yellow flame. Pulsifer desperately heaved himself over a ledge of rock and through the hole in the waterfall, empty air before his questing fingers.

He fell ten feet, to crash painfully to a rocky floor. The sound of water filled his ears — on the other side of the translucent shield of water and ice, a giant, staggering figure was ablaze. The cave was filled with an eerie, dancing light.

He looked about. He was indeed in a limestone cave, which descended steeply into the depths of the earth. Here it was somewhat warmer than without. Taking a branch from his bundle, he struck flint to steel and ignited some tinder, and soon had another torch. Rising, he looked back — beyond the ice the wood-ogre still cavorted, slapping at itself to extinguish the flames. It stumbled and fell — there was an enormous splash, and the ice of the waterfall creaked at the backwash. The light from outside was gone.

A heavy blow banged against the ice. Pulsifer turned and descended into a twisting passageway, thankful that it was too small to admit his pursuer. As he rounded a bend he heard another blow, and ice shattering behind him like glass. The face of Glemmet, sad and comical, leapt into his mind — the forest had at last claimed the tinker. Unfastening his mask and letting it hang, he sighed as the passageway branched; a slight wind blew in his face, perhaps proof of another entrance. After a moment's hesitation, he took the leftward path.

Despite the wind, the mixed odor of burning wood and flesh followed him into the blackness of the Underearth.

Part Three

Underwoven

Chapter I

In Warrens Underearth

Pulsifer was lost. Since entering the cave-passage behind the waterfall, he had attempted to follow an elusive air-current, using the smoke of his brands as a guide. Soon, however, he had become aware of the fact that the drafts were multiple, as he passed through tortuous, crawling labyrinths of twisting passage, and lofty caverns lost in blackness. North and south, east and west did not exist; the only directions were up and down, left and right, forward and back. He had no exact idea of the length of time he had wandered the subterranean routes, for time was hard to measure without night and day — but on five occasions he had slept upon elevated niches in the clay and rock.

All that he was certain of was that, despite his efforts to the contrary, he had moved steadily downward. After his underground walk had begun, he eventually grew uncomfortably warm, for the age of ice was far above. Now his outerwear was rolled upon his back, and the valise hung at his left side in a makeshift harness, fashioned from the rope he'd taken from Jabroal's supplies.

After the flaming torch he carried had burned out, he would have one brand left — fortunately he hadn't used them all, since the black recesses had recently begun alternating with larger, phosphorescent areas where water lay in still pools, and layers of a glowing, slightly-quivering substance resembling lichen coated the ceiling, walls, and floors. He'd stepped on one patch of the glowing carpet, and it had emitted a strange sound like lips smacking; he hurried from that chamber, for the rustlings of the lichen-things had increased in their degree of agitation.

Sometimes in the deeper pools and streams he glimpsed movement, and his left hand would jump to his swordhilt. Once a white, eyeless newt some fifteen feet long rose from an inky pool, apparently drawn by his movements — it rushed him with gills fluttering and saw-toothed jaws agape, but he dissuaded it with the hot end of his torch. Periodically it seemed that he sensed distant rumblings, felt more than heard, through miles of stone.

Upon another occasion he passed a natural window in a wall of limestone, where an enormously vast, glowing cavern was revealed — there he saw what looked to be thirty or more nude men and women, their skins transparent as glass after countless generations away from the sun; the details of their musculature and circulatory systems were exposed to view. They toiled with crude tools among patches of puffy brown fungi, while a pair of enigmatic talycents supervised their actions.

Now he seated himself upon a rock, watching the darkness beyond his light as he rested. Perhaps he should have killed Jabroal while he slept, and stayed in the mage's home for the winter's duration! He looked down at himself with disgust — he was caked with mud and viscous clay, some dry, some wet. Supposedly entrances to the underworlds were plentiful enough, in those areas where the inner realms neared the surface; but he had given up seeking assistance from the Cask of Sranophaez. He had used the Furtive Observers only one night before his flight underground — not only had the diminutive entities revealed themselves to be spies, but explorers as well.

Now their services were lost to him for a fortnight! His voice echoing mockingly, he cursed, as he recalled a cluster of deity-mites, the function of which was to assist lost persons — Dacdull had readily 'not' given him their glyphs. To his dismay, these mites had proven to have a single-minded determination to return him to the place where he had first entered the Underearth, and where the maddened creature which had pursued him into the cave might still wait. With an oath of exasperation, Pulsifer had dispatched them to find any lost individual in the forest above, and return him or her to an appropriate place of origin; the cluster had departed, to return only with the information that a bewildered person was being assisted. Upon hearing this, Pulsifer shrugged, put the cask away, and had not used it since.

He was hungry and weary; the last of the food he'd had with him had been consumed many hours before. His arms and legs, his elbows and knees, were intensely sore from bangings, scrapes, and scrambling falls among piles of rock breakdown, and the narrow walls of serpentine passageways. Many times he had come to a dead end, and with great exercise of memory, or perhaps purest luck, had found his way back to a recognizable spot — or at least, to a spot he'd thought to recall. His burglar's nerves had served him well, for he had often chimneyed up and down to continue his journey, climbed like a snow-ape, or walked while squatting for painful lengths of time. When he slept he was haunted by black dreams, which were filled with the sensation of his hands groping along unseen textures of stone and silt, or endless coilings of torchlit tunnels no worse than the waking reality. When he woke to total darkness, he was inevitably disoriented for several seconds.

Now as he sat in the dark, lightly kicking at the wall of the narrow passageway, the monstrous hopelessness of his situation fell on him like a curse of despair.

It was Montath's fault, everything was! Out of unjustified resentment, the young sorcerer had resolved to make the Velvet Knife's continued existence an impossibility! Clenching one fist, Pulsifer ground his teeth in rage. He would refuse to die! Was he not Calim Pulsifer, darling of a thousand women, despoiler of the most sacrosanct treasuries, and a legend well within the span of his own life? With Pammoth's gift of Unagingness, he had the potential to outlive most legends! He would not starve in these wormholes! When next he came upon a living creature, he would kill it and test its edibleness! He rose, determined to move on and circumvent the influence of Morskured Montath upon his life.

He pushed forward, resolved to discover a route back to the surface world. The tunnel he was in began to slope precipitously, and the roof lowered with jagged formations. Great curtains of flowstone encroached into the passageway, and it began to resemble a funnel. After a second of consideration, he turned and went back the way he had come. He didn't want to travel any deeper, or he would undoubtedly be lost forever...

A distant clattering sound reached his ears. He turned back toward the funnel, listening; the noise had come from below. There — he heard it again!

For a moment he hesitated, then moved carefully down the declivity, holding his torch low. The passageway indeed narrowed down to a crawling tube, and he worked his way along on elbows and abdomen, occasionally using his knees. The valise dragging at his right side and the rolled clothing on his back jammed a few times on rocky protrusions, and he had to back up and wriggle around the obstructions. He began to notice a faint radiance like he had seen before, and he extinguished his brand by thrusting it into a streak of the damp clay caked inches deep on his leg.

He eased forward to where the tunnel ended in a hole overlooking another of the enormous caverns, like those he'd seen previously. The same spongy and flattened growths were everywhere, and this grotto seemed to be the largest yet, maybe stretching for miles into dimness. It vanished into an indistinct murk of distance, great flying buttresses and striated columns of stone supporting a vaguely-seen ceiling. Shadows were an inky black, colors almost imperceptible. Something batlike and transparent fluttered past the hole and Pulsifer drew back — just as he did, four undulating black shapes, their forebodies manlike, moved into view on clicking legs. His ring flashed a deep green, for these were darklings averse to the sun.

Pulsifer was surprised — although stories said that talycents gathered in settlements of some sort, it had always been assumed that they were solitary creatures. As far as he knew, never had one been seen in the company of another. These did not speak among themselves, but gestured and moved their insect-eyed heads as if they did; it was apparent that they were conversing on some non-vocal level. They neared the hole from which he spied, and suddenly they stopped, looking about suspiciously. Terrified of their clairvoyant senses, Pulsifer pulled away and buried his face in his arms, thinking of nothing but darkness, of dripping water and hollow stillnesses beneath the earth. After an agonizing ten seconds, he heard them resume their scurrying pace.

He waited until their movements were faint whispers, then eased himself out onto a shelf of rock beneath the hole. Perhaps here was his only opportunity for escape from the Cavern Realms! The talycents were either going to their abode, or to the world above — either way, he would follow them at a distance and eventually find a path to freedom! He slid down twelve feet, glanced about furtively, then hurried after the creatures.

The four talycents came into sight, looking like tiny arthropods against the fantastic size and grandeur of the dimly-lit cavern. Pulsifer thrust his extinguished brand beneath his swordbelt and alongside the other, and drew his sword. He took care to neither step on the lichenous stuff, nor to stray too near the numerous pools and darker passageways in the floor and nearby cavern wall.

For two hours he followed them, hanging back lest he alert them again to his presence. About him, giant mineral flowers and trees of gypsum spread immobile arms — his shoulder brushed the tip of one, and it shattered almost soundlessly, turning to powder as it fell. Occasionally the proximity-ring would flash, announcing the darklings' existence. He slipped like a shadow from cave-formations to boulders, or around hill-sized mounds of rubble where massive sections of the ceiling had fallen to the floor. Finally the opposite side of the cavern came clearly into view — the walls stretched up like those of a bowl, their surfaces weirdly ridged and bubbled, and Pulsifer knew that he must be in Zev Grotto.

The walls of the cavern were covered with a flowing, organic growth of rounded and many-angled structures. Some of them, in the dim light of lanterns, glittered with jarring mixtures of colors. Like a fungal growth half a mile wide and two hundred feet high, a subterranean city of the talycents was revealed to his wondering eyes.

He halted a quarter-mile from the hive-like structure, hunkering low behind a fallen limestone slab of gigantic proportions. The four darklings he'd been following were ever-dwindling as they drew nearer the city. He decided to sit and wait, until he saw one of their kind departing, and follow it to the surface. Judging from the fact that those he'd followed had been returning, he knew that it must be daylight in the world above, so he prepared himself for a long wait. As he sat, the torches beneath his belt jabbed him uncomfortably in the ribs, so he removed them and put them in the dirt-caked travel-bag.

He had been sitting for twenty minutes when he heard feet approaching — he slunk into the recesses beneath an overhanging piece of stone. Fifty yards away and moving toward the city was a talycent, driving before it a docile herd of human laborers, with transparent skins and vacant stares. All of the laborers bore armloads of purplish and brown fungi, and had baskets filled with the substance strapped to their backs. A flash of blue caught his eye, and he craned his neck for a better look — one of the slaves was garbed!

Jabroal Glispert staggered beneath a huge basket, his face filthy, his thick robes dirty and torn. His mask was gone, and his eyes were set resolutely upon the floor of the cavern, for the bruises on his forearms and face attested to the fact that he'd already stumbled and fallen many times. His oversized, flaccid nose swung slightly with his stumbling gait. The talycent prodded him with its long, hardwood staff — the wizard stumbled, increased his pace, and continued to stare in the direction of his feet.

Evidently the curse of the cask-fulminators had weakened the magician's power, allowing his capture! Pulsifer felt a sweet twinge of satisfaction — then the ground moved violently beneath him, and dropping his sword, he was thrown to the stones. Again the ground lurched, and a deep, distant, groaning roar echoed through the cavern. Hands over his head, he looked up — the human slaves careened about, while chunks of stone from the size of peas to boulders rained from the cavern ceiling. A particularly large slab caught his eye as it hurtled downward.

The talycent was crushed like a great black caterpillar, its humanoid section severed from its hind parts and flung free. Globs of yellow liquid spattered. Several of the clear-skinned humans were killed by the same slab.

The talycent lay clawing at the ground and twitching its muscular arms; its posterior was unseen beneath the giant stone. Jabroal also lay face down in the dirt, his basket tumbled over his head and shoulders, completely covering his face.

The rumbles and shiftings lessened in intensity, then stopped. Layered patches of phosphorescent growths quivered with agitated smacking sounds.

The slaves milled about aimlessly, none attempting to seek their freedom; Jabroal did not move. Pulsifer rose, sword again in hand, and approached the group.

Perpetually staring with transparent eyelids, the slaves hopped away from him with nervous gruntings. Jabroal was motionless, and Pulsifer did not approach him. He went instead to examine the talycent.

With a startling motion, the thing lifted itself up on its elbows, and gazed right at him with it fist-sized, compound eyes. Yellow ichor oozed from its mouth, and pooled behind its torn extremities. Pulsifer tensed to run — would the darkling somehow betray him to its brethren in the city? The talycent stared at him for several seconds, then rasped:

"*Man. Classification: Neoglacial, Civilized. Value Rating: Nine on Palanjitte Scale. Genetic Worthiness: Unknown, but in probability considerable.*"

Pulsifer exhaled in relief. The shock of its misfortune had left it insane and almost certainly incapable of causing him any difficulty. The dying darkling continued its rambling observations.

"*Pain: Extreme physical discomfort, primarily localized to area of injury. Disabling and mind-clouding. Cause: Cavern instabilities, stresses, due to writhings of Rewelquian —*"

Pulsifer squatted ten feet away — there was a name he had heard before. Whatever caused the tremor, he wanted to avoid it at all costs. "What is 'Rewelquian'?" he interjected.

The talycent tilted its head to regard him. After a moment, it replied in a slow, didactic tone. "*Rewelquian: Creature of another epoch, of the Phylum of Ancient Titans, also called Draumiank Colossi. Draumiank Colossi: The seven species are Mamonlexes, Pirkests, Gulch Demonics, Sea Lordids, Stridulating Thunderers, Attitudinal Reshi, and Indefinite Hybrids. The Colossi were generated by the energies of unconscious human thought, accumulating and assuming entity-forms over seventy-million years, in various subterranean strata. To begin descriptions, the mamonlex physiology is regulated by an adjustable metabolism, in which —*"

"You digress," Pulsifer interrupted. "What is Rewelquian? A mamonlex? Where does he dwell?"

"*Rewelquian is of the Indefinite Hybrid species, and is the last of his kind. He has been bound in the lower basaltic caverns, twenty miles above the First Layer of Fire, by the ingenuity of the extinct Nole civilization. The Nole: Highly cognitive insectoid omnivores, active in the Bessential and Vaglusian Epochs, three million years past; exterminated by plague. Briefly revived by the power of Pammoth the Singularity, to serve the purposes of the insatiable human miscreant, Calim Pulsifer—"*

"Enough of the Nole!" Pulsifer snapped. "Tell me of the nearest pathway leading to the surface world—a route with few hazards, if you know of such…"

The creature replied instantly. "The Spiral Boreway is but a half-mile toward the—"

Its head slumped, and it slowly sank to the cavern floor. The talycent was dead. Pulsifer yelled in disgust and turned to Jabroal.

The mage was sitting, staring at him with a dazed expression. He rubbed his nose with the back of one hand, confusion only growing in his eyes.

"Ahem. Do I know you, my good fellow?"

Pulsifer nodded and smiled. "Indeed. We are old friends."

Jabroal nodded thoughtfully. "Of course we are! I nearly remember—something. You rescued me from the bondage of the talycents?"

Pulsifer shook his head. The glassy-skinned folk watched their exchange with a dull curiosity. "You were freed by fate, Jabroal. How much do you recall?"

"Jabroal, Jabroal." The wizard wore a perplexed expression. "Yes, I am Jabroal! I remember you—you are my servant, aren't you? Good fellow, faithful fellow!" He looked about. "Ah, Zev Grotto—alas, my thoughts are murky and fraught with inconsistencies! I do feel that this is a dangerous place—we should leave at once!"

"My exact sentiments." Pulsifer helped him to his feet, and cut the strapped basket from his back. "Let us depart for the Spiral Boreway—do you know the shortest route?"

"The name is familiar, but there is no image to fit to it, ah—What is your name?"

Pulsifer paused a second, then sheathed his sword. "I am your friend, called Pulsifer. Come, Master Jabroal, we must go! A city of the talycents broods nearby!" He went to the broken basket, and picked up a chunk of the fungus.

"Is this edible?"

Jabroal nodded. "I think so — I believe the talycents sometimes eat it, and they feed it to their slaves, who are basically of human stock. I'm not sure, but I think I was given some myself…"

Pulsifer began picking the stuff up and cramming it into the valise.

"Good — I'm hungry. Is it flavorful?"

"Quite bitter, with an undertaste of decomposing matter which is very unpleasant."

Pulsifer curled his lip. "My refined palate wearies of such culinary obscenities! Another score to settle with my tormentors, I suppose. Do you think that you would recall a path to the surface, if you were to see one?"

Jabroal shrugged. "I don't know — I recall many things, then they slip away, scattered by an unexplainable confusion. For instance, yonder talycent-hive is called Kahij-Vyreg. As to my identity? I am no longer certain. What did you say my name was?"

Pulsifer sighed. "Jabroal. You are Jabroal. You are something of a minor mage, and you are also my assistant. I am the wandering scholar, Pulsifer, of the Warrior-Philosophers, conducting an epistemological study which is quite beyond your comprehension. I have lost precious time searching for you; do not dally! We must go!"

The mage didn't argue but stumbled after Pulsifer, as he headed away from the city. Pulsifer munched on the fibrous purple stuff, its taste acrid and stomach-turning. After they had walked for a few minutes, they became aware that the human laborers were following them at a distance; Pulsifer shouted at them and they stopped. When he started moving, they began following again like masterless dogs. He picked up a stone and flung it — it struck one fellow, and a dark splotch blossomed beneath the clear skin of his cheek. He recoiled and fell with a cry of pain; the others gathered around him inquisitively. Pulsifer and Jabroal rushed away; looking back, Pulsifer saw one of the pigmentless people hesitantly picking up a stone. Another hefted a rock in each hand — then the wretches were hidden from view by a mound of rubble.

The two men from the upper world moved on, toward a towering column of stone, dimly seen about a mile away. Water poured in a steady stream from a hole in the pillar's side, and a deep echoing roar was faintly audible. After almost two hours of strenuous walking, they came to the column's lower ramparts; the water fell with a metallic sheen and into a hole in the cavern floor nearly a hundred yards in diameter. The cataract disappeared into the blackness of the pit. Pulsifer pointed to a possible path up the column's side, and to an opening free of rushing water, about eighty feet above.

"Perhaps there is our route to the surface." He gestured at the chasm before them. "Here is another path, which would seem an unwise one to attempt..."

Jabroal nodded, his eyes lighting with recognition. "Yes! Three miles below is the Sea of Breel, wherein float the giant slugs Jersh. On the shore of the sea is a dead Nole city, haunted by the ghost of the Perfidic, Pondion Zagresis. Adjoining caverns lead to the Lower Cavern Realms, including the sentient and carnivorous Caverns of Yoch, from which few return. Deceptive tunnels also lead down past the mantle, to first a shell of magma, and then the Inner Concentricities. The latter are the haunts of viodoms, jrets, djinn, and other unpredictable entities — thus it is truly an ill-advised route."

Pulsifer looked at the mage with amazement and caution — if his memory had just returned, he would be a dire threat. He kept the suspicion from his voice. "Ah — Your memory has come back to you! Now we can be leaving quickly —"

Jabroal shook his head with a sorrowful expression. "Only in bits, and apparently only with proddings such as your remark about the pit. In a few minutes, I will have forgotten the gist of this conversation, and come to tears of anguish before I recall it! You must lead us out of this place, so that I might find some method of restoring my mind! It seems that I have some books, somewhere..."

"I will treat you with fairness, never fear." Pulsifer wriggled his shoulders as he readjusted the weight of his tightly-rolled gear. He slid the hanging bag around to his back as well. "Let us begin our climb. Do not grasp at me if you slip! Your dexterity is your own concern! Hopefully, that tunnel may lead to the Spiral Boreway."

"Spiral Boreway? I have never heard of it — do you think it may be a route to the surface?"

Pulsifer heaved a sigh. "I believe so. If only you could recall something simple, such as a spell of transportation!"

Jabroal frowned. "Transportation. Hm. A series of syllables comes to my attention, worming from the fog in my brain. 'Nuegoon's Self-Jettison, Limited Range.' It seems that I am still a mage — but I don't believe the spell would take us to the surface, for we must be at least two miles below the world's skin."

Pulsifer nodded. "We are deep. I do not wish to be lost in an unknown tunnel again, if it is at all avoidable. The spell would most likely deposit us short of the surface." Suddenly he smote a fist in his palm. "Aha! Fast, before you forget the phrase! Transport us to the Spiral Boreway!"

The forgetful sorcerer nodded agreeably. "Yes, at once!" He stepped close to Pulsifer and raised his arms, fingers outspread. As he vocalized the spell, a whooshing sound drowned out his words. Green lights leapt from his fingertips.

With the sound came a blast of wind from the solid rock beneath their feet. Suddenly they were rising on an invisible column of air, at an alarming rate of acceleration. Both men sprawled wildly as they hurtled toward the curved canopy of the cavern ceiling — they threw their hands up with screams of despair as they rushed toward the rock.

The unseen force which held them curved them away from the ceiling, only five or six feet short of impact. They continued to hurtle along, moving up or down as the contours of the ceiling demanded, flying around stalactites of various sizes, twisting and yelling as they went. Now Pulsifer clutched the valise to his chest as if he held the ground. Without warning, they were spun violently, unable to see anything as they hurtled through darkness — then light shone about them again, the force slowed and weakened, and they were dumped roughly onto a smooth, cold surface. With a groan, Pulsifer raised his head.

They were in a large vaulted chamber of bizarre, convoluted design.

Before them was an upward-angled stone ramp, which led through an opening in a polished wall of multi-colored stone — surely this was the entrance to the Spiral Boreway! Pulsifer started to push himself to his feet — the ring on his finger flashed an intense, unwavering green.

Beyond the light of flameless, bluish lamps, there were rustlings in the shadows. Dozens of talycents eased into the light, gazing silently at the visitors to their city.

Wiping his shaking hands on his clothing as he rose, Pulsifer smiled uneasily. The talycents moved in, to welcome the newcomers to Kahij-Vyreg.

Chapter II

Delvings and Deepenings

P ulsifer walked reluctantly before the prodding of talycent staves. He and Jabroal moved through circular tunnels, and large open areas surrounded by swollen structures of an organic appearance. Bulbous lamps emitting an unwavering, heatless, and dim radiance were fastened to walls, over lintels, and even aloft on the vaultings of ceilings. Two silent talycents drove them through the avenues of the city, past other darklings either moving on unguessable errands, standing immobile as if in contemplation, or engaged in peculiar and unfathomable activities. Pulsifer saw one, bearing a platter of freshly-severed, transparent-skinned arms and hands; as the creature moved along, those it passed took bits of human flesh from the platter and fed themselves. Another sat with its multiple legs folded beneath its body, preening its eyes with a prehensile tongue which protruded from its human-looking mouth. Nowhere did the two men see a talycent of female appearance.

The silence was as terrifying as the sights, for none of the creatures spoke, either to one another or to the captives. Pulsifer and Jabroal were taken through the twisting passageways until they were utterly lost from the Spiral Boreway. At length they entered a ramped edifice, within which there was no furniture of any type, and were shone to a dome-shaped cell. There was no door to the room, but the two talycents settled just outside. Pulsifer paced in vexation, and Jabroal, leaning against the wall, sank to the floor wearily.

Pulsifer's belongings had not been taken; the darklings seemed uninterested in examining the contents of the valise, and were totally unconcerned with the sword and knife at his belt. For a brief instant he considered attacking the pair of guards — but to what end? Even if he managed to incapacitate or kill them, the talycent-city was a hive-like maze, and it teemed with the darklings. Pulsifer heaved a sigh of exasperation and moved nearer the entrance to speak with the guards. They regarded him wordlessly.

"Your city is lovely!" he began in a friendly tone. "Perhaps you might arrange a tour for me, so that I can see all its marvels!"

The talycents did not reply. Pulsifer cursed them and turned back to the shadows of the cell.

"Why are you angry?" one of the creatures asked; Pulsifer turned in surprise.

"You did not offer a reply to my statement, either yes or no!" he snapped at the darkling.

The talycent tilted its head, the mannerism of a mantid. "It was a banal statement, scarcely worth notice. Apparently wasted words are a typical result of human conversation. You are an uninvited intruder here, and not a guest. No member of your species has ever before entered this city willingly."

"I came to you out of a sense of Brotherhood, as a fellow think-ing being! My goal was to exchange knowledge, and reach mutual understanding! This may be the threshold of a new era of peaceful coexistence, even cooperation, between our races — but your behav-ior belies any pretensions you may hoist to represent your kind as civilized!"

The talycent smiled. "I might say the same. You are Pulsifer, are you not? Your image is a recent one, and readily brings a flood of informa-tion from the Compilation. As for understanding — we understand you and your kind well enough. There is no chicanery between members of our species; but you are a master of deception among your own kind. Yet if you presume to an attitude of honesty and openness, we can exchange information. Perhaps if you actually impart worthwhile knowledge, the Queen-Mother will exhibit tolerance in her decision regarding your fate."

"Very good!" Pulsifer agreed, thinking that perhaps in this way he might gain his freedom. "I will ask first, if I may." He looked about desperately; the walls of the room were of the same strange material he had seen throughout the city, a porous, multicolored stone with swirls and globs of brilliant, muted, and metallic colors. He laid a finger on the wall. "What is the origin of this stone? Its like is unfamiliar to me."

The talycent's mellow voice held a note of surprise. "You are so ignorant? The stone is called *sescren*; we quarry it from pockets and veins below this level. These were apparently once repositories of discarded materials — garbage, we have decided — from past ages, which have been compressed and transformed by the pressures of the Earth's mantle into metamorphic rock. From fossils found, we have determined that the material was originally human in origin, from a time of your species' over-proliferation. We are not certain, however, if Man as we know him is a recent phenomenon, or if evolution repeats itself. No other creature seems to have plagued the Earth with such persistence." The talycent leaned forward.

"I do not know what to ask you — all queries would seem beyond the scope of your knowledge. Yet I will try ..." It paused as if listening, then raised its head.

"Ah, yes. A question has been given me by another: What is the origin of the enmity which exists between you and all other members of your species?"

Pulsifer shrugged. "Is it not obvious? I am a non-conformist. I refuse the dictates of a society which attempts to stifle my individuality, and this creates resentment and antagonism in others! Consequently, I am forced to defend myself. Does this satisfy you, or whoever created the question?"

The talycent jerked its head strangely. "On the contrary, your answer simply raises more questions. Truth by its nature is singu-lar — it cannot be relative, despite the protestations of mankind. Whose truth is Truth — yours, or your detractors'? Relative truth is a delusion which afflicts your race, sowing discord and confusion. It is at this point impossible to determine if your answer is fact, or baseless opinion."

"What of my status? Am I prisoner, or guest?"

"Two words which are often interchangeable. Any classification you receive will come from your audience with the Queen-Mother."

Pulsifer turned away with a scowl of dissatisfaction. Jabroal gazed at him with wondering eyes, his thick brows raised like a fir-topped ridge.

"Pulsifer! You are Pulsifer! The Singularity Pammoth endowed you with — something! Why can't I remember? I'm terribly sorry! If not for my forgetfulness, we wouldn't be in this predicament! I sense a gross disproportion between us, an unbalancing on my part! The interpersonal net must be askew!"

"An understatement in the uttermost sense." Pulsifer seated himself beside the mage, and took out some of the fungus he'd gathered.

"Here — eat. I'm famished, and we will undoubtedly need our strength if we have an opportunity to run. Can you remember anything about the psychology of talycents, or the personality of their queen?"

Jabroal shook his head. "All is vague. In regard to the darklings, I sense only an alien consciousness, and emotions incomprehensible to human beings. Created by the accursed Perfidics — may their souls burn! — long ago, the original purpose of the talycents is unknown. Of their queen I recall nothing."

Brooding, Pulsifer ate in silence. After three or four hours — it was increasingly hard for him to gauge time in this unchanging environment — the talycents outside abruptly rose and gestured with their hardwood staves.

"You are to come with us — the Queen-Mother awaits the pair of you. Move swiftly as we go, for she must not be kept waiting."

The prisoners grudgingly followed. Again they entered the tilted, curving streets of Kahij-Vyreg; looking up, Pulsifer was startled to see talycents scrambling upside-down across concavities in the city's substructure, like great black cockroaches. The group passed beneath a pitted, bridge-like span, covered with fleshy, purple organisms that resembled flowers, yet swayed of their own volition; dark, pulpy nodules were nestled in their centers. The group entered a vast, plaza-like area from which a few small passages branched away; it was paved with flags of sescren, each one gleaming like a pool of mixed oils in the dim light. Here talycents milled in silent discourse, gesturing with hands and heads as they conversed. The two men looked at the expanse with foreboding — the only sounds were the movements of the many darklings' chitinous legs, and the scraping of their segmented bodies upon the paving stones. More of them poured into the chamber, and it was evident that all the talycents of Kahij-Vyreg would attend this particular audience.

The chamber was rounded, with walls of sescren and polished limestone. Giant panels of milky quartz were on all sides, ranging in shape from ovoid to angular. Fibrous tendrils of the purplish, blossoming growth covered the walls here as well, except over the quartz panels. In the center of the plaza was a triangular pit; looped tendrils twisted in slowly-writhing cables, hanging from the ceiling and into the hole, which seemed filled with the meaty flowers. The two men and their escorts neared the pit; the sound of something massive shifting its weight sent an ominous rustling through the chamber.

The dozens of talycents in the chamber grew still, each turning its head toward the depression. The two escorts urged the men forward with prods of their staves; Pulsifer and the mage approached the hole with trepidation.

Looking down, they gazed upon the Queen-Mother of Kahij-Vyreg.

At first Pulsifer was struck with the impression that he looked down on a giant black vegetable the size of a fallen tree, convoluted like a tuber, and surrounded by mounds of purplish foliage. The purple growths grew out from puckered openings at one end of the thing. The opposite end was buried in the morass. The bulk quivered as if it contained thousands of gallons of liquid beneath the black skin; the pit rustled as hundreds of appendages were seen, dwarfed by the body. The limbs toward the buried end were several-dozen shapely, feminine arms; toward the sprouting posterior, the hundred or more pairs of appendages were long, stick-thin, and insect-like.

Slowly the concealed portion was raised into view, terminating in what seemed a tiny, atrophied member — the two men each drew a sharp breath.

Before them rose the ebony body, from the waist up, of a woman; it was human-looking but for compound eyes which made the head seem small. The Queen-Mother was small-breasted without nipples, smooth and oily-looking as an eel. She examined them with her arms crossed, and her head tilted jerkily from side to side as she regarded them. The juices within her colossal body sloshed noisily.

Pulsifer and Jabroal stepped back involuntarily. The creature raised her foreparts ten feet above them. The growths originating from her rear extremity moved with a gentle susurration, and the entire chamber seemed alive as the purple tendrils writhed on the walls. Pulsifer's legs quivered with fear, and Jabroal gaped wordlessly. Pulsifer beat at his grimed, dirt-caked jerkin and jacket, then bowed gracefully.

"O Wondrous Sovereign of the Watchful Folk—"

"Do not speak!" The body of the Queen-Mother quivered in agitation. She raised one hand. Her voice was cold and unfeminine, strangely resonant. "Your flatteries are meaningless here. I am Tarxicrexi, Mother of Kahij-Vyreg; this in no way qualifies me for the title you bestow, for the centers of talycent-activity are many. I have a number of sisters, and this is but one point in the network which comprises the Collective Recollection."

She eased forward on the bed of her own plant-like organs, looming above them, and continued speaking in a tone filled with condescension. "You are Calim Pulsifer—the effects you initiate and unleash upon the History of this Age are of extreme interest to the purveyors of the Recollection. And you are Jabroal, aren't you? Not an enemy, not a friend, but a self-serving mage, and most recently a laborer. Your fate is unimportant—but I have questions for Pulsifer."

Jabroal said nothing, but his brows were knit like two clashing wooly ibex. He shook slightly. Pulsifer smiled amiably.

"I would deem it an honor to supply you with any information I might have, and then be on my way. I have appointments…"

"Indeed." Tarxicrexi settled back somewhat; the vine-like organs rising from her body moved more energetically. "Direct your eyes to the memory-accessor to your left—scrutinize it for relevancy in accord with my words, answering as you will. It has been altered for the benefit of your sight—tell me if adjustment is required."

Pulsifer looked as directed, toward the far left, curving wall. Pulpy organs trembled, twisted, buckled like crawling worms; a quartzite parallelogram began to glow with a faint pink light. The crowd of talycents in the room froze, as if in concentration; splotches of color, half-formless, began to coalesce into images within the lambent panel.

A life-like picture was presented—a gaunt, fanatically-eyed man with unkempt grey hair and beard was seen, wrapped in crude fur clothing. He huddled before a fire, beneath a rock ledge; beside him squatted a grotesque barbarian woman, covered with tattoos. A scrawny tot grasped at one of her breasts, which had the appearance of a stretched and drained, flapping wineskin. The man was the very picture of self-absorption, lost in thought — he was also Megwurl Lunt, one-time social reformer and the original detractor of Pulsifer. The scene faded away, and the crystal was clear. Tarxicrexi spoke. "This man is known to you, is he not? Although far-removed from humanity's civilized lands, he dreams of your destruction. At one time he was an enormous force for societal change, predictable in history's skein, and adumbrated to us by the Laws of Eventualities — we had expected him, or one like him, for centuries. Utterly unforeseen, you enmeshed him in your own rippling, disequilibrating influence, and he was destroyed. You must be informed that his movement, though extreme, would have with time resulted in improvement for your species — do you regret your actions against him?"

Pulsifer shrugged. "I've lost no sleep. Had he not sought my down-fall, I never would have brought about his own. His sect is now defunct, and I see the world as a better place for it. As a side-effect of my quest for vengeance against him, the world's winter is no longer indefinite — but this you already know. I believe in the maxim of Free Activity — I live my life as I choose, and permit neither philosophers nor others to remold me to their liking."

The Queen of Talycents said nothing; again her parts about the panel moved vigorously, and another scene was depicted. A wild moor-land was shown, beneath an icy blue sky — a monstrously-fat white shape moved, sobbing, with a lumbersome tread. Long black tresses spilled over the somomorph's beefy shoulders as she swayed wretch-edly from side to side.

"As you know, this creature was once a human woman. This obser-vation was retained after the mamonlex walked Phontyque, your doing. It has been heard by us that her condition is also your doing. Do you feel remorse, or justification as with the previous sample? Was she an enemy, or a friend? We understand that this state does not conform to her desired one —"

"It certainly does not!" Pulsifer snarled. Though he was not sure of the reason, the subject irked him. "Her condition is accidental, as much the result of the plots of the first man you showed to me, as actions of my own. Primarily her own carelessness led to her state — that, and a djinni of capricious temperament! She inadvertently brought about the mamonlex's release; taking liberties with my instructions, the djinni altered her form to protect her from the titan! I feel neither remorse, nor justification — she was my lover, when she was human!"

"Your emotional outburst is difficult to gauge," the queen observed. "Feelings of guilt? Sympathy? Persecution? You are a fascinating subject, an anomaly in the rigidly-coded world of human interaction. Tendencies are sensed in your behavior yet are never clearly defined — you have been observed engendering unwarranted destruction, yet you saved the world from the certainty of Hymakki's frozen death. Pammoth booned you — your own kind revile you! I could easily study your physical-psychic emanations and reactions for centuries…"

Pulsifer began to ease back. "I hope I have clarified things for you. Now, if you will kindly show me to the Spiral Boreway, I'll take my leave…"

"But I am not finished." Tarxicrexi reared up several more feet. "I've decided to keep you for further study — you must appreciate the extent of your uniqueness, in that the talycent-folk have always disdained the retention of physical specimens! You will serve a dual and dignified purpose — much can we learn from you, and the last five Fathers rapidly wasted away. Fresh stock is called for, I think — our human workers are not as hardy as once they were."

"What do you mean?" Pulsifer looked at the bulging creature with horror, searching with his peripheral vision for a quick, clear path through the crowd of darklings.

Tarxicrexi rolled her body ponderously, her flesh rippling with waves of interior liquid motion. Through translucent black skin, giant, shadowy organs pushed and rolled against one another. A pale yellow underbelly was revealed, along with three orifices. The Queen-Mother gestured at these.

"Observe the second aperture — there you will be inserted, and pulled into a comfortable and form-fitting cavity. Your sustenance will be provided by sweet secretions; we will converse often, on a mental level made possible by your oneness with me. The vigorous activity of your human seed will replenish the drones of Kahij-Vyreg for an indefinite span, due to your unaging state, and life will be simple and pleasurable for you. I admit that you are also taller and more likely to struggle than the human males of our slave population — physically, this will be more interesting for me. Be pleased! This is the most logical fate for you, a justification of your existence! An honor such as this I've not bestowed on a man of the surface world for a thousand years!"

Pulsifer's guts knotted with terror. Brushing back a strand of his tangled locks, he smiled coyly. "You overestimate my worthiness, kind Queen…"

His eyes darted about, his hand inched toward the bag hanging at his side. Perhaps the cask of Sranophaez could create a brief diversion — he glanced at Jabroal. The wizard observed the exchange between Pulsifer and Tarxicrexi with a mixture of befuddlement and incredulity.

Pulsifer tensed as the talycent to his left approached with its staff outstretched, to persuade him into the pit. The orifice Tarxicrexi had indicated on her underbelly began to gape expectantly —

A heavy shudder swept through the air. Green and white lights exploded soundlessly everywhere, and both talycents and their human prisoners were blinded by the sudden brightness. Unseeing, Pulsifer fell into a running crouch and headed to the right, colliding with the yelling Jabroal; both men tumbled to the floor. The clatter of armored talycent bodies was deafening. Pulsifer rose shakily to one knee, and Jabroal raised his head. The chamber was filled with a golden light and the talycents were slowly falling to the floor. Only their queen seemed unaffected — she loomed like an angered snake, her many limbs moving furiously. She stared behind the two men, a harsh clicking sound issuing from the depths of her body, and Pulsifer glanced back toward the chamber's entrance.

His mouth went dry with fright such as even Tarxicrexi could not inspire.

A man stood in the archway, surrounded by an aura of flapping blue fire. He was black-haired, dressed darkly with a wide cloak which billowed like wings; at his belt was a long sword, a red gem in its pommel. His hair moved as if alive, his upraised hands shone with an orange radiance. His demeanor was both commanding and haughty. Directly above him hovered a mauve scaled being with a bird-like face — a hijret.

Tarxicrexi's voice was a roar. Her body swelled unbelievably, a black cloud. *"Who dares invade my nest? Who dares? Who interrupts the neural flow of this Collective Mind?"*

The young man smiled, without mirth. "I dare. I am Morskured Montath, a mage such as you have never seen, pretty Tarxicrexi." He brought his hands together, and the boom of a thunderclap reverberated throughout the city.

Tarxicrexi thrashed with frightening limberness, a palpable mist rising from her body. The air of the chamber seemed to thrum with her aroused energies.

Pulsifer started to rise, but Jabroal grasped his arm and pulled him to the floor again. "Be still!" the wizard hissed. "My memory may be deficient, but I sense the flux of incredible powers! To rise above our present level is to invite a quick death — I seem to recall admonitions concerning the absorption of fatal essences by the mind-body structure! Keep your head low, and avoid the two of them as best you may!"

"That is my intention!" Pulsifer yelled, clawing at his valise. "We must escape at once — that man is my nemesis! Recall the spell you used previously and transport us to the Spiral Boreway!"

"What spell is that?" Jabroal asked in a surprised tone. "I do not remember a recent spell of any description…"

Pulsifer released the catch of the valise, and groped inside for the Bowl of Immolations — just as his fingers closed upon its cold, curved surface, he recalled the conditions stated by Shigandure. The entity would not take a mage as its payment — but would it destroy one as its required service?

Finding out would be too great a risk, and at any rate, he did not have time to even spark a summoning flame. He removed his hand from the valise and snapped it shut, determined also not to assist Montath by using Shigandure against the talycent-queen. One hand drawing his shortsword, he looked about wildly for a route to freedom, then turned to Jabroal.

"Wring your brain for magical assistance! Surely you can recall something!"

Montath stood as if musing, an elbow propped in one hand, fingers gently cradling his chin. Transfixed, Pulsifer stared as both the hijret and wizard began to move forward. Montath spoke to Tarxicrexi.

"I am surrounded by a reciprocal force of the twelfth degree, darling darkling; attempt no tremulations! My quarrel is not with you, unless you would have it so — I have come for the man Pulsifer, for retributive purposes. Give him to me and I will be gone, leaving your drones as they were. The other man you may keep — he is not of the Brotherhood, and even if he were, I have risen above such obligations as any which might compel me to assist him."

Along the sides of her massive body, Tarxicrexi's many arms moved in an eerie, gesturing dance. "You are in my demesne, wizard — do not issue ultimatums! I am intimidated by neither human magic, nor sub-servient hijrets! I have my own uses for the man called Pulsifer! Insights into the influence of Chaos upon History's flow are to be gleaned from prolonged observation of this man! Be aware that I will not relinquish him without determined resistance!"

Montath still smiled, and glanced at the other two men. "Be still, Pulsifer; your fate is in the balance here." His face twitched, and Pulsifer could see tiny, pale flecks sprinkled throughout the young sorcerer's thick mane of black hair. His skin was covered with irritated splotches. Montath lifted one hand, flicked a louse from his right eyebrow, and grinned at the Velvet Knife.

"Firkui traced you by your use of magic — the curse which you set on me by way of your captive entity-fragments has been exceedingly bothersome! I could have cured myself, but the spell which replenishes the parasites and troubles my stomach is my only link to you, and we've followed its scent ever since we discovered you as its source. I will repay you a millionfold, for this and other affronts you've committed — or perhaps you will spend your years servicing Tarxicrexi, in the event of my defeat. Aside from my own plans for you, I can think of none more fitting than hers; but now, to the matter at hand!"

Firkui began to drift toward the two men, radiating malice; its eyes gleamed with reddish highlights from interior fires. Morskured Montath turned to face the house-sized Tarxicrexi, and the longsword at his side seemed more to leap into his hand than to be drawn from its scabbard. He held the heavy, quivering blade aloft as if it were a feather, to display its four-foot long, rune-covered surface to the creature before him.

"Behold the sword Lendyljunct, forged in Yawamris' deepest fires! The lava of the Sphere of Outer Fire tempered this blade! It cries to me, it cajoles, for darkling lives—yours it will find a succulence of grossest proportions! Through my left arm surge tremulations, trailed by unvoiced effectuations such as you've never known; in my brain, rock-powdering fulminations jostle among themselves to be the first vocalized! Be aware that I am the first mage in twelve centuries to hold four of the six categories under my sway; surrender if you wish, and be spared!"

With a harsh sound like hammer strokes on rock, Tarxicrexi surged forward to loom above Montath. The mists surrounding her began to solidify into tendrils of purplish ectoplasm, much like the growths covering the walls of the chamber. Each newly-formed tentacle was covered with thousands of mouth-like orifices, each one gaping to grasp the flesh of her challenger; the tentacles' bases now sprouted from her giant, segmented body. Montath stood his ground, the blue flames about him brightening intensely.

Firkui neared Pulsifer and Jabroal. Pulsifer tensed, but he did not turn his back on the hijret in order to run. He had previously seen Montath's familiar accomplish frightful things, not the least of which was the swallowing of a living man ten times its own size. Jrets and hijrets were uniformly spiteful, and unfailingly vindictive when harboring grudges; Pulsifer was certain that he had more than inspired this hijret to wrathfulness upon their last encounter. Clawed arms outstretched, the little monster swooped at him with its beaked jaws opened wide.

Tarxicrexi moved, and the air was filled with motion. Firkui was ensnared in a whipping mass of the tapering tentacles, and flung with the speed of an arrow across the chamber—it slammed into the wall with bone-shattering force, and cracked a panel of quartz. Instantly the hijret was covered with the seething, wall-covering extensions of the Queen-Mother, and buried beneath a struggling mound of her tissues. The next instant Montath uttered a Word, and most of the queen's tentacles began to sizzle and dissolve into a dripping ooze.

Bent low, Pulsifer and Jabroal scrambled away from the dueling pair.

The wizard and the darkling-queen were wrapped in opposing cocoons of energies, envelopes of flickering light — Montath's was sharply-angled, of blue and orange flames, and that of Tarxicrexi was a murky, ovoid, red-violet skin of sparks. The fields of magical force pressed against each other, clashing with shrieking contacts which set the other men's teeth on edge.

The two men ran across the chamber and toward a low, dark exit. Suddenly the talycents in the room began to stir, twitching legs and arms — due to the intense concentration he had to maintain as he struggled with Tarxicrexi, Montath's control over her offspring was slipping. The darklings, sluggish and groggy, rose into awareness — one swung its staff at Pulsifer. He dodged and cut its arm off at the elbow, and Jabroal grabbed up the creature's staff and struck another, creating a spray of yellow ichor. They skirted a cluster of several others, and one darkling nearly pulled the valise from its makeshift harness. With a terrific tug, Pulsifer pulled the bag free and sprinted away. The tunnel was near — behind them, the talycents clattered into life.

The chamber filled with a head-splitting roar. Pulsifer and Jabroal looked back to see Montath levitated in a polyhedron of blazing forces, from which he showered down arching tremulations with his one out-spread arm.

Spiraling effectuations poured from his lips. Poised as if weightless in his right hand, the sword Lendyljunct was a-flicker with tiny blue flames.

Tarxicrexi defended herself with a dimming violet shield, its weak-ness a testimony to the power of the young mage, while the talycents in the chamber crowded beneath Montath, attempting to reach him with their staves — those which succeeded in landing a blow on the glowing polyhedron shuddered, and crumbled into black fragments.

Behind Montath's levitated form, another contingent was joining the battle. The huge entrance was filling with the figures of the trans-parent-skinned human chattel of the talycents. They bore their baskets, which now were loaded with stones — as they hefted missiles and began to pelt their darkling masters, Pulsifer and Jabroal ran down the dark, sloping passageway and into a labyrinth of lamp-lit tunnels beneath Kahij-Vyreg. Behind them, echoes laughed mockingly of the battle.

They ran until the noise had faded with distance; finally they came to the last bulbous cresset, stopping short of plunging into darkness. Jabroal grabbed Pulsifer by the arm.

"Several bothersome images surfaced in my mind during that debacle, and as a result I am not certain that you are wholly the friend you claim to be! Who was the furious young archimage? An awesome enemy! He looked somehow familiar…"

Pulling a brand from his bag, Pulsifer began to strike some flints. "I've no time for your questions — where is your sense of gratitude? Go your own way, if you wish, but do not waste my time! One of the combatants will be after us!" The short torch in his grasp blazed up, and he took the other out and thrust it under his belt. Jabroal made no move to leave; sheathing his sword and handing the lit brand to the sullen mage, Pulsifer took out the Cask of Sranophaez. He selected the glyphs of Dacdull the Interlocutor.

While the wondering Jabroal looked on, Pulsifer sorted through a half-dozen clusters of deity-mites at the non-direction of Dacdull. A mirthful wraith was created by one swarm, and sent by an impatient Pulsifer to entertain Tarxicrexi and Montath with its acrobatic maneuvers and droll anecdotes; he was next given the choice of either a six-hundred pound byrex or a white-pus pestilence, to unleash upon an enemy. He had the mites send the tigerish predator to the scene of the battle as well. A magnificent meal was next created, and he instructed Jabroal to gather the food in the gold-embroidered cloth it was spread upon. Two otherwise worthless boons were sent rapidly away; the sixth proved profitable.

Before he could direct the swarm of glittering mites, there came a shrill, distant scream and an audible thud which shook the walls. Tarxicrexi was dead, and Morskured Montath would be the victor. In a sweat of apprehension, Pulsifer unleashed upon the young mage a fulmination particularly reserved for long-winded orators, called *the Stifling Spontaneous Generation;* this insured that whenever the wizard attempted to speak, his words would be choked by the emergence of a furred toad from his throat. Certain that this would slow the mage down for some time if it took effect, he gathered his things again, took the torch from Jabroal, and set off with the older man wheezing to keep up, bundled platters of food hanging from the mage's stolen staff.

The thought of the maddened hijret and its master haunted the both of them into the depths; in an hour, Jabroal had forgotten the entire incident. Pulsifer cursed periodically, for he had not.

Their resinous torches were gone. For hours they stumbled through near-darkness, their path lit only by a small but stubborn flame which they had managed to coax into life at the end of the talycent-staff. The bemused mage carried it gingerly, occasionally depending on assistance from Pulsifer to climb over mounds of breakdown, or to inch along ledges overhanging fathomless chasms. As often as they could they attempted to take upward paths, but they knew that they were still heading downward.

Eventually limestone gave way to the metamorphic rock and basalt of the upper mantle; the tunnels they traveled were fissures, and magma-created, bowel-like tubes of gigantic proportion. The food was gone, having provided two excellent repasts — while moving, they had eaten of dishes such as the finest epicures of Phontyque or Kalsurridin could only dream of experiencing. The ornate cloth had provided the brief-lived head of their hardwood torch, providing the extreme heat which had managed to start the wood to burning. Every so often they found themselves forced to pause, and puff the coal-end of the staff into flame again.

There was no pursuit yet, and Pulsifer wondered if Montath and Tarxicrexi had slain each other — but surely Firkui would have survived! Despite his wonderings, he knew that Montath would be alive. Whenever Jabroal asked him the identity of that which they fled, Pulsifer muttered ambiguous answers. Upon three occasions, the basaltic world around them had quaked violently, and Pulsifer remembered the words of the dying talycent concerning Rewelquian the Colossus.

Each successive body-flinging tremor had been stronger than the one before; fortunately, neither falling debris nor yawning pits had claimed them at these times. For the sake of safety they stayed as near the walls as they could. The air grew cooler, and Pulsifer put on his traveler's clothes, letting the mask dangle from one side of his hood. He fastened the valise into his back-straps, then he and Jabroal each tied an end of the rope about their waists, Pulsifer carrying most of the slack in one hand. Several times he thought of abandoning the treacherous mage, but occasionally Jabroal would seem to recall something about their surroundings, and Pulsifer wanted to hear any clue the man might unwittingly reveal pertaining to a way to the surface.

Once they tottered above a black gulf, where the light of their brand was reflected from the bluish scales of a silent grund, its millipedian body coiled upon a ledge. It began to stir, and they hastened around a bend to avoid its paralyzing gaze. Sometimes they heard rattlings in the darkness, and they would glimpse small, darting beings which fled the light of their torch as if wishing to avoid detection. Finally they came to a great black cavity, and paused at one side of the cavern to rest. Arching his back, Pulsifer stretched his stiff muscles; Jabroal sat on a rock and rubbed his legs. Pulsifer kicked the cavern wall in frustration, and sat down as well.

"There must be a way out of here, and upward! Surely we leave the surface world irretrievably far behind!"

"Indeed we do," the mage replied. "Your words inspire spurts of memory. We are entering the Lower Cavern Realms, a most unpleasant level that underlies the entire surface of the Earth. I think I have only journeyed this deeply in spirit — physical exploration would have been much too dangerous! Luckily these caverns are more stable than those above, being composed of denser materials — the once-floating plates which compose the Earth's shell are static, for the planet's inner configuration changed long ago. I only fear that we will stumble somehow deeper than these regions, perhaps through a gateway leading to the Concentricities; there the density of matter changes, and our bodies would be either as vapor, or most-densely compressed stone!"

Pulsifer looked askance at his companion, wary of the man's fickle memory and his own record in it. "These places we are entering are more hazardous than those through which we've already come?"

"Most assuredly! I am one of the few thinkers to have discovered the exact nature of our senile planet, which is loosely-layered much like an aged onion, a condition quite different from its youthful state. These lower caverns are stunning in their variety; some are filled with fire, others with water, air, or even ice from subverted glacial flows. Below these realms we are coming into are many others — first is the Sphere of Outer Fire, which is an ocean of magma, then the Concentricity of

Riolda, the haunt of jrets, vesps, and the ancient, dreaded viodoms. It is ruled by the demon Salanque, an old, old power. Beneath Riolda is Suuge the High Hells, under the rule of the ifrita dominatrix Lijjelda, a most dislikeable entity. Under Suuge are the Caverns of Damnation, also called the Low Hells, and then the three nested Concentricities of Calambriel, Grome-Urul, and Yurdash. Beneath Yurdash is the midmantle, where, it is rumored, exists the Grotto of Pammoth the Sublime, and beneath that mantle is the Ring of Inner Fire; then comes the inner mantle. In the planet's center — so the djinn report — is sensed a great spherical hollowness, the contents of which are a mystery even to them."

Jabroal's face grew intense. "I mentioned Pammoth — hm. That seems to loosen memories about someone, a person granted boons by that ultracosmic being —"

"Surely a person of no importance," Pulsifer smoothly interrupted, his casual tone belying his desperation to halt the mage's recollection. "We had best be continuing on our lost road. We will not find freedom sitting here, and the talycents, or others, will surely persist in their pursuit."

"We are endangered?" Jabroal asked with genuine surprise. "Talycents, you say! Their methods of execution are often quite painful, due to their inborn curiosity! I recommend that we flee with all haste!"

"An excellent suggestion," Pulsifer rejoined, rolling his eyes with exasperation. "Which direction do you choose?"

Jabroal shrugged. "Only downward, at this point. There are several routes leading from the Lower Cavern Realms to the surface, or so I was told by a parsennoc who claimed to have been lost down here for some time. He answered under an exacting compulsion, and I do not think that he lied. I believe that we should search for these passageways. If we fail to find them, we will meet our end in these depths."

"Search we shall, then," Pulsifer agreed. He rose. "Let's get on with it."

Jabroal stared absently into the blackness. He shot Pulsifer a puzzled look.

"Search for what? Have you lost something?"

"My mind, nearly," Pulsifer grumbled. "Follow me closely — remember the pits we skirted in the last cavern we passed through of this size!"

"Pits?" Jabroal looked about desperately. "We are underground! I sense the pressure of miles of rock above us! Do I dream?" He squinted at Pulsifer. "Who are you, O Phantom of the Dream-Grottoes?"

Pulsifer yanked at the rope impatiently, compelling Jabroal to follow.

"Come along, and give me the torch! You are awake, and I am your friend!"

With a befuddled expression, the mage complied. "I know that I am a person of some consequence — but who? My mind is a porridge of lumpy impressions. You are my friend, you say? Why then do I feel only a hesitant acceptance of your company?"

"Your doubts are the result of your lack of memory — twice I have rescued you from talycents, and even now we are in search of a route to the outer air! Come along and do not waste time! I thirst, and there is the trickle of water from beyond the jagged formation, yonder. Again, be alert for pitfalls!"

Together they rounded the massive pink formation, to find a wide stream with banks of crystal-studded stone. Pulsifer cautioned Jabroal not to step on the thinner shelf-like formations, lest they crumble beneath him. Jabroal watched while his companion filled his flask, then both men drank from cupped hands.

A flicker of movement caught Pulsifer's eye. He snatched a scrap from the water — in his hand was a half-rotted oak-leaf, which had been tumbling swiftly past. Pulsifer held up the leaf and gestured with it upstream.

"That is our direction! This leaf is dead, but it grew old beneath the sun! We will follow watercourses whenever possible, and thereby find our way to the surface!" Dropping the leaf, he held the torch low to examine the stream.

"Broad but shallow. The footing on the other side looks more certain — and the grund we saw earlier will never cross running water. Follow closely, and try to step where I do." They hurried across, and the mage paused to bend and wring the cold water from his robes. Inside his lacquered over-clothes, Pulsifer was dry.

Jabroal shivered, glaring resentfully at Pulsifer. "Already the coolness of this region saps energy from my legs! Let us move, so that heat might be generated!"

Onward through the cavern they went, following the stream. Here and there they began to see patches of waxen fungi, but for its slight phosphorescence almost indistinguishable from the flowstone along the walls. At one point a group of the small pale beings they had seen before rose from a patch of fungi, to flee twittering before the light of their torch. The tiny things were swallowed by the darkness ahead.

Soon the darkness lessened and a warm radiance was reflected from crystalline structures jutting from the cavern walls. Pulsifer pushed back his hood. A warm, steady breeze ruffled their hair and clothing, hinting of a great cavity ahead. They came to a wide area filled with shards of jagged crystal, and walled with broken slabs of quartz; the light was reflected from an indeterminate source beyond this chamber. Pulsifer extinguished the flame at the end of the staff, and they entered the softly-glittering cavern of shards.

After a strenuous hour they had crossed the chamber; shattered walls gave way to those of another cavern, this one of a smoky, topaz-hued rock, a creamy-gold color. Still they stayed with the stream, which had cut a tunnel in the solid rock floor—Jabroal postulated that it was the remnant of a mighty subterranean river which had originally carved the caverns they were now in.

Jabroal also occasionally asked his companion questions relating to their respective identities, and their situation. More than once Pulsifer considered abandoning the mage and striking out on his own—after all, the man had not only once sought his life, but was becoming a hindrance as well. He watched the mage sidelong, lest the older man suddenly remember everything and attack his former employee.

For two more hours they trudged, pausing twice to relieve bodily urgings. Their bellies rumbled with hunger, their limbs ached with weariness. They neared a large, glowing opening, the impression of a vast expanse beyond.

Without warning there came a patter of tiny feet, and they were suddenly surrounded by twenty or more of the small pale creatures seen previously. In the greater illumination the things were revolting—stubby-legged, round-bodied, their skin texture had the appearance of colorless cheese. Their heads were almost entirely snapping, tooth-filled mouths, and their eyes were vestigial blue spots beneath unopened skin. Faintly, the impression of reptilian scales could be seen on their bodies.

Tossing the staff to Jabroal, Pulsifer drew his sword — the mage hardly grasped the staff before the things rushed them, long-clawed hands reaching to pull them down. Pulsifer hewed left and right, and Jabroal laid about with sweeping strokes — the leaping, hissing beings drew back in surprise, sap-like stuff spurting from amputated members and broken skulls. They scurried away, to vanish into holes in the nearby cavern-wall; the two men looked at each other in relief.

"Those beasties seem vaguely familiar," Jabroal muttered, "but I can remember nothing distinct about their classification. Perhaps they remind me of other beings, for I'm sure I've never seen their like before. Why is my memory lacking, do you suppose? I do not even remember my own name — or yours, for that matter!"

"You are Jabroal, I am Pulsifer! Come, we must move — I long for the increased light ahead. Hurry, before the imps return in greater numbers!"

They moved on, looking about nervously. The sound of falling water grew to a roar.

They entered an area consisting mostly of a deep, turbulent pool; into this a column of water poured, from a hole two hundred feet above.

Pulsifer cursed — his idea of following the stream to the surface was worthless! From the pool flowed the stream they had followed, as well as two others going in different directions, each apparently flowing into its own respective cavern. Across the pool from them was a huge opening, a hollowness which dwarfed even Zev Grotto. Glancing at one another with uncertainty, they began to inch along a ledge which curved around the pool.

Pulsifer looked down. The floor of the pool sloped down and away like a funnel, in the direction of the vast cavern — his eyes widened in surprise.

The pool's bottom was coated with water-polished stones — emeralds, topazes and rubies glittered in the depths. With a wince of regret, he abstained from entering the pool to obtain souvenirs for himself — the bottom was treacherous, and he thought to glimpse bones among the rocks where the funnel curved away. He returned his attention to the path, occasionally steadying Jabroal with the rope connecting the two of them.

They rounded the pool, to stand upon a wider shelf of stone, from which one of the pool's streams poured into a titanic, luminous cavern. They stopped near the brink, gazing with awe.

The cavern floor was eighty feet below, the ceiling three and four hundred feet above. The cavity vanished into distance, without even an intimation of a farther wall. The radiance came from a forest of tree-sized fungi which coated the cavern floor as far as they could see, and bat-like shapes dipped and fluttered among the glowing fronds. In a number of locations there were cones of igneous rock, some of them glowing with heat, or dribbling lava in orange streams. Flames flickered at the tops of some. Perhaps as far as four or five miles away, there was a mountainous brown-black mound, reaching two-thirds of the way to the ceiling of the grotto; a pleasant warmth radiated from the entire vista.

Pulsifer surveyed the alien environment with queasy intestines — unknown dangers in the cavern below, Morskured Montath assuredly behind!

He chewed his lip thoughtfully. Perhaps the *Stifling Spontaneous Generation* had not taken effect on the embattled Montath; on the other hand, the upper caverns could be teeming with mouth-generated toads! There was no way to know the condition of the hijret Firkui, but it was doubtful that it would be long before it tracked him down. Nevertheless, Pulsifer squatted on the ledge in contemplation, a hand on his thick-stubbled jaw. He turned suddenly to Jabroal.

"I believe a brief period of rest and forethought is called for, before entering the cavern below — dangers will likely be many! I also need a bath, and a shave. This stream will do. Stand guard while I wash the grime from my form and clothing, and I will do the same for you. Watch for the pale abortions which attacked us a few minutes ago — be alert!"

He untied the rope from the both of them, and began to divest himself of accoutrements and clothing; he kept his sword near at hand. In twenty minutes he had fastidiously washed the dirt from his body and his mane of hair, shaved, and trimmed his curling moustaches, which had begun to droop sadly. The fine blue-and-red outfit he had purchased in Yawamris was ragged and soiled to a blue-black color — squatting nude beside the stream, he beat pants, shirt, and jacket one the stone, raising a cloud of dust, then rinsed the clothing in the running water. Wringing them, he put them on still damp, and donned his traveler's clothes again, with the exception of gloves and kabeyui.

The protection his outerwear could provide against teeth and claws was not to be overlooked. Along his sides he unfastened vent-flaps, to allow greater circulation of air in this warmer environment, then fastening his other gear into place, he gestured for Jabroal to make use of the stream. Pulsifer stood surveying their surroundings, while the mage cleansed himself.

At length Jabroal finished his ablutions and redressed. Pulsifer gestured impatiently, and the mage hastened over, wearing his perpetual expression of confusion. Pulsifer retied the rope to their waists and looked over the edge of the cliff. A narrow, rock-hugging trail ran down to the cavern floor below. He handed the staff to the wizard.

"Here is your staff, old man — you may need it to steady yourself on the way down. Stay close to the wall, and cry out if you slip. I will start down first."

Jabroal raised a bushy brow. "Down?" He motioned back the way they had come. "Why not go in this direction? It appears less precarious! What is this place? You look familiar — you are a friend, are you not — ?"

"Indeed I am! We go downward; there are enemies in the caverns above us! Now come along…" He turned toward the cliff-face trail. An ominous rumble echoed through the cavern; the two men froze, looking for the source of the sound. The rock beneath their feet began to first vibrate, then shake. The pulpy forest below tossed as if in a windstorm, strange shapes bolting beneath its branches, and gouts of molten rock spurted from many of the volcanic cones. The mountainous shape they had noticed earlier lurched, shook violently, and lurched again — a blocky head, hundreds of feet in circumference, rose slightly for an instant from the cavern floor. It slammed back with an earth-shaking jolt which sent waves of force across the cavern.

Pulsifer and Jabroal were knocked from their feet, to lie quivering with fear until the tremors subsided. Jabroal's eyes were filled with terror, his memory more than sufficiently nudged.

"Rewelquian the Bound! Last of the Indefinite Hybrids, and a myth for millennia! Whatever dangers are behind us are preferable to entering the cavern of its sleeping imprisonment! Wisdom dictates that we return whence we came!"

Pulsifer rose, pulling the wizard up with a one-handed grip on the rope.

"The colossus has been bound for eons — Why worry? We'll pass beyond it, and perhaps our pursuers will be daunted. There is a great deal of fresh air, here — else the fumes of those cones would have made this a poisoned place. I seem to detect a moving mist, beyond the giant's mass; somewhere, there must be a large passage to the surface. I would stake my life on it — which is exactly what I intend to do!"

"Sheerest folly!" Jabroal sputtered. "I sense that you have been a good companion, but I cannot bring myself to trust you or your judgment. I must tell you that despite the dimness of memory I am experiencing, I will strike out alone rather than traverse the cell of this creature! The giant Rewelquian is lust, hunger, and hatred personified!" He untied the rope from his waist and handed it to Pulsifer, who shrugged. The mage waited expectantly for five seconds, then turned back the way they had come, saying:

"Farewell, my friend; I hope you reach the surface."

"Wait!" Pulsifer exclaimed. "Leave the staff — it is my only source of light in the event I find a passageway!" He stepped toward the older man. "Reconsider — my swordarm is quick, and a pair together doubles awareness of immediate peril!"

Jabroal paused. "Do not think of taking the staff from me — I seem to recall a flesh-shredding tremulation, or enough of it to rip you asunder. We will part in peace for the sake of our mutual survival."

Pulsifer made a wry face. "I will not light the staff for you, though I have both fire-kit and tinderbox. Your selfishness does not inspire courtesy!"

"Nor does yours. I will strike together stones of the appropriate type — eventually I will create a flame. Goodbye." The mage turned away, and began edging about the pool again; Pulsifer refrained from rushing him, wrenching the staff away, and shoving him into the water, for fear of the viability of the threatened tremulation. With a growl of disgust, the Velvet Knife wrapped the rope about his midsection and turned again to the downward trail.

The going was not as difficult as it had looked. He reached the bottom more swiftly than he'd anticipated, to find himself in a forest unlike any he had seen before — green, gold, and yellow-white were the tree-sized growths around him, apparently flourishing on the available combination of volcanic soils and plentiful water. Their shapes were similar to ancient corals he'd seen in the sealed cases of collectors, bulbous, arching, and almost disconcertingly unreal at times. He wandered between them haphazardly, attempting to travel as straight a route as possible by following the continuing stream. The waterway only occasionally deviated from a basically straight course, and along its banks the bizarre growths were almost like a wall — here there were also slender mushrooms taller than a man. Once he hid, while a troop of the pale little creatures he'd encountered in the caverns above passed by, moving in a mysterious and unmistakably orderly manner — they bore coils of crude rope. A while later he glimpsed something which appeared identical to a surface-dwelling jinmonander, and he found the remains of an enormous clawed annelid, its armor-like plates crushed by massive jaws; in the warm air, albino bats swooped and glided, feeding on large insects resembling dragonflies, and wasps as long as his fingers. Beneath his traveler's clothes he sweated copiously, but he did not remove his outer garments.

After a tiring hour of walking, he clambered high into the fork of a giant fungus, where he found a cup-like area in which to rest. Above and around were spongy boughs and twisting boles — soon he fell asleep, his bared sword in his lap.

Hunger tumbled inside him, but he still woke refreshed. His first instinct was to lie still, searching the air for the small, terrifying shape of Montath's familiar; after ascertaining that he had not been discovered while he'd slept, he stretched, sheathed his sword, and climbed down to the fungous floor of the forest. He had no idea how long he might have been asleep, for this lambent environment was as without the passing of day and night as the most lightless of caverns through which he'd already stumbled. Ignoring his hunger for the present, he decided it would be best to hasten. He set off in the direction which he thought led toward Rewelquian.

Somewhere, something screamed, either killing or dying. Pulsifer drew his sword as he slunk between the boles, his right hand on his knife-hilt. Bad enough were the known terrors — and sometimes unknown ones — which haunted Old Earth's frozen exterior; the unearthly appearance of this cavern heightened his anxiety tenfold. He rounded a twisting growth — With a wordless cry he leapt back, poised to fend or thrust. Before him swirled a spiraling cloud of glittering motes. A faint voice issued from the center of the swirl, in part comprehended without the use of his sense of hearing.

"We bring you the Lost One, in response to your command."

Pulsifer stepped away from the deity-mites with a mixture of suspicion and caution.

"I sent you nowhere — I recall no such command! I refuse this 'lost one! Return to the cask without delay!"

"The command was lodged five days ago, in a cavern near the world's surface — the Lost One, chosen randomly as you specified, is now brought to you, by reason of a brief image retained in a pocket of her memory. This persistent image is recognizable as yours, retained despite extreme metamorphosis on a cellular level in the foundling's brain. This persistence is perhaps due to a trauma in which you were directly involved. We were drawn to the creature by her powerful sense of loss, and have been with her for days — only a moment past did we perceive this record of your connection with her. Things are now made right — we have placed in her mind the impression that she belongs with you, to avoid her future displacement. Our task is done, and we return to the cask."

They swirled rapidly and vanished — his ring flashed bluely, there was a soft gasping sound, and turning, he caught the gleam of unclothed flesh behind a nearby outcrop of giant bryophyte. The sheen of luxurious red hair filled him with realization before she stepped into view, her blue-green pool-eyes wide, poised like a wary doe.

Sinfe the syleber stepped forward hesitantly, her every curve and line, each movement and quiver of flesh, exuding sensuality. Her jasmine aroma reached his nostrils even from ten feet away. She parted her lips, showing a white, unbroken tooth-ridge in a hesitant smile; her face seemed simultaneously glad and fearful. She came toward him slowly, reaching out as if she would take his arm —

Shaking his head he stepped away from her, and she stopped, confusion and pain playing as brief shadows of emotion across her unhuman yet human face. With her arms spread wide she implored him, her breasts heaving, her red-lipped face sultry and expectant. Her allure was more than natural.

"No, Sinfe," he said firmly. "Feel free to roam this warm land, but do not seek to accompany me! You would not understand, but you are a deadly distraction in a double sense! The constant temptation of your charms, as well as the poison caress of your love-talons, are luxuries I can ill-afford. Be on your way, and good luck to you!"

Leaving her, he resumed his trek — after an instant she followed silently, her demeanor puzzled. He turned and cursed her; she did nothing but blink long-lashed eyes and pout seductively. He thought of killing her with his sword, but although she was no longer human in any sense other than her basic appearance, he knew that he could not bring himself to harm her — unless it were in self-defense after love-making, an eventuality he intended to avoid. First looking about for threats, he unslung the valise from his back-harness and took out the Cask of Sranophaez. Sinfe sat crosslegged on the loam in a very unlady-like manner, and he looked quickly away.

Scowling, he consulted Dacdull in the usual roundabout fashion. He was unable to discover either a glyph-combination for returning him to the surface, or one which would rid him of Sinfe. He sent a dozen clusters of revived consciousnesses on ambiguous errands, so that they would not choose tasks of their own liking that involved him; at one point he raised the cask high to hurl it into the forest, but decided against that action. He chose to consult Dacdull once more, so he pressed the glyphs of opened clam and broken reed; the voice of the Interlocutor rolled forth, its tone petulant.

"*What now? Do you never stop? Can you not think for yourself? Incessant interruptions of my quiescence may drive me to silence! Ask, and be swift as you do so!*"

"I am the Master here!" Pulsifer retorted, reddening with anger. "Do not give orders in such a manner! I require procurers of clothing — my new companion needs covering!"

"*Why tell me? You know very well that the directives of the cask forbid my release of that information! I can no more tell you of shell and leaves than I can rise from this cask in physical form, to crush your annoying skull! Now leave me at rest!"*

"Go, O Unhelpful One!" Pulsifer snarled. Dacdull was silent; with a vocal command, he next touched the sigils for shell and leaves. A cloud of mites appeared, and after a few seconds of consideration, he directed them to garb the syleber in durable robes and a face-concealing mask. They swarmed about her like a cloud while she stood wondering, trying to catch them on her fingers as she would insects. The deity-mites disappeared, and the syleber stood clothed in dark green robes embroidered with cloth-of-gold, sapphires and emeralds sewn into the cloth in jagged patterns. On her face was a leathern mask, inlaid with gold and worked into the likeness of a green-eyed bird — she immediately ripped it from her head with a frightened cry, and strained to pull the clothing from her body.

Pulsifer stepped closer, his tones reassuring. "Here — leave those on, that's right." He gently took her soft hands and she gripped his tightly, thrusting her face close to his. The effect was almost overwhelming, and he pulled away; picking up the mask, he motioned to show her how to set it over her features and fasten it in the back. With a studious, confused expression, she stood still while he put it on her again; when he had finished she did not seek to remove her new apparel. He looked at her skeptically, wishing that he had specified that the robes be unimpressive and drab in appearance, rather than this glittering garb which might prove difficult to conceal. He sighed; if they were forced to hide, she could always take them off…

He thought of tying her to a fungus-tree and leaving her behind, but he knew that he might very well need the rope if he found a passageway leading upward. Again he got underway, pleased to note that she moved furtively in the manner of her kind. Occasionally she drew too near, and even made to run her fingers along his arm or back — at these times he admonished her with a stern face and voice, and for a while she would move away somewhat. He wondered about their sleeping arrangements with a mixture of anxiety and anticipation — surely, if rumor were to be believed, she would be more succulent than before, although even more deadly. Sylebers were creatures of instinct, and their instincts dictated that they sooner or later kill their human lovers — not necessarily at once, but without exception.

He reminded himself that many Collectors kept the creatures as caged paramours, binding the nymphs' hands and claws during dalliance — but he had neither a cage nor the appropriate equipment for such activity, nor the time to waste. In any event he was determined to never take such a risk; he had heard in the street-tales of Phontyque that by virtue of unique secretions, sylebers and merileuts were as addictive as the narcotic pollens enhaled by the hedonists of the great cities. With a glance at the graceful creature beside him, he decided that the only thing he would take advantage of would be the first opportunity to leave her behind.

Long they moved across the cavern-floor, passing through regions of dimness where the mushroom-trees were thick and high. Upon three occasions they saw groups of the pale imps, going in the same direction as they; Sinfe would sense them before they appeared and drop into a wary crouch, preceding the blue flash of the proximity-ring on Pulsifer's ungloved finger. The third group of the things had passed within twenty feet of where the pair lay, concealed by spongy growths — behind them they dragged a man, bound tightly with rough cords. Jabroal could not even scream, for his mouth was filled with the same fibrous stuff; Pulsifer watched the struggling wizard disappear behind an igneous boulder, and snorted softly in scorn. He had warned the man against striking out alone, and his problems were his own.

As they neared the mass which Jabroal had identified as Rewelquian, the air grew both more agitated and sulphurous. White-winged bats with pale pink bodies chased transparent, tube-like creatures as frail as mist, the latter riding the warm winds like yard-long wisps of fog. The phosphorescence of the tree-sized growths and the light from glowing, lava-tipped cones increased many times in brightness, creating a soft but substantial light which allowed few shadows; the entire landscape looked as insubstantial as a dream. The ground was covered now in a carpet of grass-like, narrow-stemmed mushrooms which were not crushed beneath their tread — at one point, one of the large insects Pulsifer had seen before hovered in front of the mask of Sinfe, and she touched it with one finger. After a minute of unguessable communication, the wasp darted away to vanish in the maze of the forest.

Eventually they could make out a distant mound. As if on cue, the cavern floor shook as the giant moved. Sinfe leapt to Pulsifer's side and took his arm in a fierce grasp — they staggered together, his arm slipping instinctively about her waist. The small tremor subsided as rapidly as it had begun, and they steadied themselves, still clinging to each other — with shocked realization, Pulsifer pulled away from the syleber.

She followed aggressively. He remembered, too late, Jabroal's warning of several weeks before — *do not stroke her back or torso — this would arouse her passion. She is totally syleber now.* Her odor increased, a subtle perfume of enchanting qualities. Even beneath concealing clothing, she radiated an insistent sexuality. Despite his unwillingness he felt a powerful attraction — taking her by her upper arms, he held her away from himself. Her arms were stiff at her sides, and three-inch, bluish claws were unsheathed from her fingertips. She trembled strongly. He made soothing sounds, and she began to relax.

"Sinfe, Sinfe — you were half human, once. Find restraint from your passion — do you understand my words? Think! If you know what I say, nod your head!"

She listened silently, then her head moved up and down in an uncertain motion. Still holding her by one arm, Pulsifer took the rope from his torso and slowly bound her wrists together; looping the rope about her, he drew her hands in against her body. His arm brushed hers and again she trembled, making a low, cat-like sound of longing. He took the other end of the rope in his grasp and leaned close to her masked face.

"I've never heard of one of your kind speaking — but you once were able to talk. Concentrate! Remember! You are Sinfe, or you were! Can you speak?"

He removed the mask from her face, her animal beauty raw and blinding. He tried not to look directly into her whiteless eyes. Her face was faintly haunted by pain, a hint of anguish usually unknown to her carefree species, and her simpler mind was apparently groping to follow the import of what he'd said. She opened her mouth, her voice first a soft and hesitant croak, as if her throat protested against an exercise for which it was ill-designed; then the sound of it changed modulation to become a gentle tone which was part whisper, part dove's soft cooing.

"I…I. Sinfe I was. Am not now. Now, I am not. I…" Her face filled with wonder. "I speak! Sinfe is gone, she has left me—but you can call me Sinfe, if you wish." She studied his face. "I remember you—man I ache for, now. Sinfe is gone, but I am here. Call me Sinfe, and have oneness with me…"

Pulsifer shook his head. "You are the syleber Sinfe. You have wild senses peculiar to your kind. Can you detect which of these growths around us are edible, and which are not? I am hungry—"

She moved uncomfortably near. "I hunger for *you*! You are warm, so warm—I feel the tide of your pulse, like fire! Share your heartbeat with me, I will love you unceasingly—"

"The love of a moth for a flame!" he remarked. "But in this case, I might be snuffed out like a candle if you had your wish. Still, you are bound…but never mind! I must eat! Which of these fungi are edible?"

Sinfe's eyes scanned their surroundings; she sniffed the air daintily. "The round ones, there—the small ones like turnips. Warm Ones much like yourself—you would call them deer, chamois—they could eat such. I am not sure about you, but I could eat them as well." Her gaze grew thoughtful, utterly uncharacteristic of a syleber. "More and more, my thinking grows clear. You have awakened me from a strange, mournful sleep! Life was a frightened dream of longing! I vaguely recall your face—and other parts of you as well. Oooh…We loved before, did we not?"

"Love is perhaps the wrong word. We've met." He put the mask on her once more, gathering an armload of the mushrooms she had indicated. It had just occurred to him that her syleber's senses might be capable of detecting a passage to the outer air. Leading her with the rope, he started moving again, ready in an instant to drop the food he cradled in one arm if he needed to draw his sword. They ate as they went. A short time later they had to lie low while a huge bear-like thing with saucer-eyes shambled past—Pulsifer huddled at her back for fear of an accidental scratch from her venomous claws, but to avoid the bear-thing's gaze he was forced to press tightly against her from behind. She sensed his growing passion and began to wriggle suggestively; with a frown he pulled away, though the backside of the creature they'd avoided was still in sight. Sinfe made a gasping sound of disappointment, and he quickly placed his hand over her mouth lest she alert the beast to their presence; she licked his palm hungrily, writhing again. He moved completely away from her with a mixture of disgust and fascination.

Soon after this they found shelter in the hollow trunk of one of the mushroom-trees, a roomy hole some twenty feet above the cavern floor. He tied the rope to a knotty protuberance so that she could not lie near him, and after a moment of indecision he removed her mask; rolling over, he was soon asleep. Occasionally he woke, to see her staring out the opening, for sylebers and merileuts did not sleep. Sometimes she would sense him looking and move her legs and torso expectantly, at which he would hasten to try and sleep again. It became increasingly difficult.

After this respite they began moving again. In very simple language he explained to her that they needed to find a passage to the surface, and she let him know that she could, indeed, sense the flow of air to and from the world above, fluctuating from some point ahead. She stayed as close to him as she could, and although he was glad he had thought to cover her face and form, he felt himself sorely tempted by her elemental allure to take the comfort she offered. In better days he had enjoyed the company of beautiful women whenever he had chosen to do so — as the Velvet Knife of Phontyque, he had been both admired and emulated for his roguery and audacity, his style and éclat. He kicked at a slender mushroom until it broke — the fickleness of existence was almost too much at times! His days as the darling of Phontyquen society were long past, and now he was trapped in a hellish, sunless cavern miles beneath the Earth's crust, tortured by the provocative nearness of a female he dared not touch!

He sank into a morose state, not speaking to his companion at all. More often now they saw pale little creatures of the type which had taken Jabroal, and hid accordingly. Only once did they encounter a large band of the imps face to face, and he wasted no time awaiting their assault — drawing his sword he ploughed into their midst, glad of the opportunity to strike out at something. This was a mistake which very nearly cost him his life — the twittering creatures clung to his legs like giant, loathsome leeches, seeking to drive teeth and talons into his lacquered outerwear. He chopped with equal viciousness, creating arcs of yellow ichor with each stroke.

Behind him a strange trilling began, and soon grew into a feminine wail, the sound of it half-buzzing above the noise of the battle. Pulsifer staggered now, for even after death the creatures retained their clinging holds on his legs, belt, and harness. The snapping jaws of leaping monstrosities neared his uncovered face, their breath fishy and hot —

Suddenly the air was filled with dazzling movement. Colorless wasps the size of his fingers, huge dark dragonflies with hundreds of wings a-hum, descended on the creatures in an angry cloud. Hissings of pain filled the mushroom-forest, as Pulsifer staggered away from the melee with wasps buzzing about his head; but not once was he stung.

Sinfe stood away from the carnage, the mask on the ground. Her head was thrown back, her eyes closed. Her lips were parted slightly, and from her issued the trilling sound that he had heard — part voice, part insect-song. He did not come too close to her — it was apparent that, despite Jabroal's efforts, she was not an ordinary syleber. She had retained a level of control over certain creatures which had been held by Sinfe the Witch, and ability so great that she had singled him out from the destruction she'd set in motion.

Scraping the dead imps from his clothing with his sword, he looked back at her handiwork — already the insects were vanishing. Tiny white bodies, covered with blisters and contorted by poisons, were strewn upon the sward. He sheathed his sword and looked uneasily at his companion — she was obviously a new elemental being of great potency.

Sinfe opened her eyes, and smiled — he smiled in return. Picking up the mask, he did not ask how she had removed it without using her still-bound hands; the marks of hundreds of tiny mandibles were still visible on the broken straps. Flinging it away, he took the trailing rope and she followed willingly, in an eager fashion he was becoming accustomed to; she wet red lips with her cloven tongue, its pinkness speckled with red, and tried to push up against him.

He allowed her to do so, wondering how long it would be before she realized that the insects at her command could free her hands as well. With his right arm about her shoulders, they moved off through the forest, skirting the scene of the fight.

His blood seemed to boil within his veins at her nearness; she leaned and licked the side of his neck. He clenched his teeth to maintain his self-control — he walked a tight-rope indeed, for he didn't wish to anger her!

Around them, several large dragonflies sped past on private aerial missions. Ahead, a dark mass loomed. The wind-like gusts of its breathing could already be heard.

Chapter III

Rewelquian

P ulsifer and the syleber Sinfe moved through the twilight forest with mixed attitudes, sometimes alert, at other times distracted by each other. As they neared Rewelquian the contours of the cavern floor changed, the fungi thinning out to at last disappear, and sharp-edged igneous rocks jutted like giant black bones from the ground. Miniature volcanoes festered like red-hot, running sores. Sinfe cut her foot on a ridge of hardened lava, and Pulsifer bound the wound with a strip torn from her gown; her blood was pink and watery on his hand. He wiped it on one leg of his traveler's clothes and they moved on.

Half a mile before them rose a frightening mass, a supine titan even larger than a mamonlex. Rewelquian was a slate-grey color, his head alone the size of a very large hill. His features were thick, striated, and rock-like, and he faced the pair with his eyes closed — thirty or more eyes were clustered like boils upon his face. He had no nose, just a jagged crack, and his cavernous mouth gaped wide, a sour wind issuing from its depths. The giant's body was covered by a sloping mountain of igneous rock — about it were many of the lava-cones, oozing molten stone. Rewelquian appeared very effectively restrained.

The pair crouched upon a hillside while Pulsifer studied the landscape, including the giant who was part of it; Sinfe pressed continuously against his side, making whispered overtures in tones alternately enticing and pleading.

He ignored her as best he could, but he knew his resolve was weakening, her magical allure undermining his best mental defenses. In the world above he would never be forced into such a prolonged period of close proximity with her... He studied Rewelquian with a serious lack of attentiveness, examining the colossus almost cursorily — suddenly he started, his attention focused on something other than his enrapturing companion.

In runnels along the sides of Rewelquian's enclosing mount, lava flowed in glowing streams. This in itself was astonishing, but the fact that the lava flowed *upward* rather than down was even more startling. The streams began at a moat of molten stone which surrounded the monster like a red-gold ribbon; reaching the summit, the lava apparently crested and cooled, while the mount's lower flanks slowly sank, melted again, and returned to the lava-moat.

Pulsifer shook his head — the genius of the extinct Nole civilization was indeed impressive! Rewelquian was bound by a perpetually-regenerating blanket of solid stone, which left no occasion for the establishment of weaknesses or soft points in the rock! Pulsifer fingered one moustache thoughtfully — perhaps the extreme heat of the topmost layer kept the giant from bursting upward, through what was probably the thinnest area of his imprisoning blanket.

A thread of movement caught his eye, a tiny column of whitish things — and there was another one, and there! Some of the imps were entering the giant's mouth, while others poured out like ants, or maggots. All seemed to give the molten areas wide avoidance, and many carried squirming living creatures into the titanic maw. He squinted — there, a procession of larger beings, clad in dark clothing! He could not make out their exact nature, but they also vanished into the mouth of the giant. His survey finished, Pulsifer pulled back from the vista, Sinfe following like a shadow. Her hands were still bound, so he helped her down the slope. When they reached the bottom, he asked her if she could sense a flow of air from the surface; gesturing at the area beyond the giant, she nodded.

"There, past the living mountain. I smell the chill of ice-draped boughs, firs and glens locked in frost! Somewhere in that direction is a large passageway leading upward."

He looked at her carefully; she seemed to grow more capable of expressing herself, more cognitive, as the hours passed. Either the actions of the deity-mites in her brain, the botched magic of Jabroal, or his coaxing of her vocal abilities, had set in motion a visible evolution toward higher sentience, completely unlike a syleber. Perhaps all three of these things had contributed to her rapid and strange evolution. She was becoming a type of being outside of his knowledge, as capable of thought as a human, ochdeviant, or darkling.

He nodded. "I think we should rest before attempting to squeeze past the giant. We passed an inactive cone a few minutes back, probably dormant for years. We can take shelter in its bowl and this will provide a higher vantage, and a defensible position." They headed back the way they had come, until they found the mound of which he'd spoken.

Soon they were nestled in the cone, a concavity some five feet deep. A blanket of pale moss overlay the ash and rubble of the interior. Pulsifer sat staring at Sinfe and she returned his gaze, her face definitely exhibiting a greater than animal intelligence. There was a long, awkward silence; finally she nodded down at her robes, or perhaps her bonds.

"I understand why you bound my hands — nor do I blame you. Leave me tied, if you wish! I admit to you that I do not know the limits of my self-control; I sense what might happen if we were to merge in pleasure. But since you awakened my awareness of — myself — I feel that I might control any later urge to sink talons into you! I do not really believe that such an urge would arise, anymore — I am not what I was, thanks to you! I only know that I desire you, as you desire me…"

Pulsifer rose without a word. Her shimmering glamour, her exaggerated impression of fleshly delights was too much. Had he not known enough hardship? A brief period of pleasure was surely his due! Was he not Pulsifer, clever enough to deal with any eventuality? He went to her and began fondling her neck on one side, kissing her on the other.

She smelled faintly of honey, and he began disrobing them both while she moaned lasciviously; her robes hung at her bound wrists. They fell together; the cavern floor shook slightly as Rewelquian moved.

They did not even notice.

Two hours later, Pulsifer, half-asleep, felt that his strength had returned sufficiently to allow him to stand. Rising, he peered over the rim of the cone — the view was bleak in one direction, weirdly verdant in the other. He turned to look at Sinfe, though he did not really want to — her beauty was now even more overwhelming than previously. Never had he experienced such raw physical pleasure, and he was far from uninitiated in the ways of a man with a woman! But Sinfe was more than an ordinary woman...

She sat cross-legged, studying him with a bold look, the hint of a smile on her face. Already he found himself longing for another inter-lude — his eyes ran over her unclothed form, and she lifted her arms to run her fingers through her thick tresses, her breasts rising —

He moved back, startled. Her hands were unbound. A number of the colorless wasps rose from the cone and shot away. She flexed her fingers, and her claws slid out, then back in. She laughed as he reached for his flung-aside clothing and the sword half-buried in his garments.

"Tie me again if it will put you at ease — but would you not have the caresses of my arms as well? Come to me again, Trespasser — we have only just begun to love..."

"We've wasted enough time," he warily replied. He dressed while watching her, keeping his sword close, but he still fought the tempta-tion to go to her again. He saw now the basis for the tales of her kind's addictive nature; and she was intelligent enough now to realize the power of her charms. He pulled his gaze away from her and his lust-ful urges subsided a fraction; then he began buckling on his traveler's clothes again. "You've cost me precious time, Sinfe — I did not intend so lengthy a delay. I have enemies who, even now, might be watching me as I dress! We must move." Her words of self-control did not reas-sure him — he watched her sidelong as she rose, lest she lunge. She brushed ash from her white flanks, and turned to display her posterior.

"Is the dirt gone from my backside? I would hope to always be pleasing to your sight —"

"You are presentable!" he snapped. "Put your robes on, and we will be moving."

Still smiling, she did as he directed, and he said: "Here, hold your hands up together! Make no sudden movements!" He tied her wrists against her body as before, then, buckling the valise into his back-harness, he lifted her over the lip of the cone. The feel of her flesh in his hands set his pulse to pounding.

As they moved again toward Rewelquian, he cursed himself for giving in to her sorcerous attraction. She was no less persistent in her flirtations than before, but now he felt an unnatural and almost overpowering ache to succumb again to her advances. Without her mask, his eyes were constantly drawn to her face, and each time she met his gaze and smiled knowingly.

Finally he tore his eyes from her and stared at the floor of the cavern.

Something glinted metallically against the black sands, throwing back the red glow of a lava-dribbling cone. He bent and retrieved it — it was a curved knife in a silver scabbard, of the type often worn by the durdelain-riders who guarded the caravans of Kalsurridin and Distidak. He scowled. What was such a knife doing in this place, miles beneath the surface of the world? Were there other human beings down here, lost as he was? He thrust the knife beneath his belt, pulling away as Sinfe strained to nibble at his ear —

"At last, Knave!" A powerful voice rang out, and a coarse bird-like squawk echoed the cry. Before them Montath dropped to the ground, his black hair floating in a circular nimbus about his head. Firkui squawked again and floated lazily down — it hiccoughed, flushing from mauve to purple, and back to mauve. Montath raised one redly-coruscating hand.

"There will be no more delays — I will destroy you on the spot and be done with it! I see you have a new companion — where do you find them? Never mind — Woman, stand away! This man is doomed!"

Sinfe moved closer, thrusting herself against Pulsifer. Beneath her breath, she droned almost inaudibly. Montath lurched and gagged as a dark, furry toad forced its way from his mouth. It fell to the ground with a nasty sound, and hopped away; Montath wiped his mouth with the back of his uncharged hand, and Pulsifer began to inch away as well.

"Almost have I rid myself of your latest blight!" The mage exclaimed. "With Firkui's help, the dimensional rift which allows the toads to enter my space is being closed, and —" again the wizard paused as another wide-bodied amphibian sought freedom from the inside of his head. After it had made its exit, Montath spat, his face filled with disgust. "Such indignities should never be known by one such as myself! Pulsifer, prepare to die!"

"Wait, Montath! This is totally inequitable! Would you rob this woman of her one true love? She will find life's only happiness with me — consider that you interfere with her interpersonal Equilibrium by your selfish pursuit of vengeance! As a mage, you are sworn to curtail Entropy in all its manifestations! Reconsider your violent threat —"

"Love?" Sinfe murmured in a confused tone, though Pulsifer hardly noticed. "Yes, that is the word — that is what I lost! You have returned it to me! I do love you…" She cried out shrilly in a wordless wail, and Montath looked at her in surprise, as if he were seeing her for the first time.

"An endearing consort, Pulsifer — perhaps the most beautiful woman I have ever seen! Her mind must be unbalanced, to cling to a worthless gangrel like yourself! But her mental disturbances can be cleared away, and she will grace my gynacaeum like a gem among trinkets! Think of that, as your soul goes howling into the dark!" He raised his hand, red sparks in his eyes.

"Woman, I said move away — I unleash a tremulation!"

Another toad wriggled from his stretched mouth, contorting his handsome features into a bizarre grimace. Pulsifer drew his sword, ready to rush the mage in a meaningless attempt to deal him death; Firkui settled on its master's shoulder in a gloating crouch, green flame licking about its evil little head.

Still Sinfe did not move away, but managed to grip his arm with her bound hands while a wordless song poured from her mouth. Montath gestured wearily.

"Firkui — remove the lady from the source of her distress."

The hijret floated forward and Pulsifer prepared to strike it as best he could, though he was quiet with the certainty that death was near. It flew toward them eagerly.

Suddenly Firkui hissed, as something swift-moving splattered against its scaled hide. Like night, a cloud of insects descended on the mage and his familiar, enveloping them by the millions. Montath cried out but was barely heard — the insects upon him burst into flame, but were instantly replaced by twice the previous number. Firkui was a wobbling, levitated ball, coated by angry wasps and the dragonfly-like insects from the cavern's expansive forest. Pulsifer and Sinfe ran, toward the bound behemoth Rewelquian.

He glimpsed one of the toads from Montath's mouth, sitting on a rock—its tongue lashed out to enswathe a passing wasp. Sinfe pulled away from him and he dropped the rope; her wrists were quickly covered by hundreds of her gnawing, winged servants.

"Run!" she cried. "Run far and fast—I'll slow them as long as I can!"

Tears streamed down her cheeks as she turned back toward the beleaguered wizard and his hijret assistant.

Pulsifer asked no questions—he sheathed his sword and ran, hurdling lava-ridges and rubble, dodging volcanic cones of various sizes, the furious humming of the insect-cloud behind him still loud. He felt a pang of pity at the thought of Sinfe's sacrifice—she would surely die, due to the feelings instilled in her by the deity-mites which she had mistaken for love. Still, he drew deep breaths, elated by the turn of events, although Montath would be only temporarily delayed; his long legs propelled him with fear-born speed over the barren terrain, as his eyes searched for a place to hide.

There was an intense sting as something struck his face—unable to stop, he ran full-tilt into a widespread net. Squealing like piglets, dozens of the imps fell on him from overhanging stones, instantly immobilizing him in their coarse-woven trap. He screamed and thrashed, but to no avail—ignoring his threats and pleadings, the little monsters hefted him on their bent backs and set off toward the mouth of Rewelquian. Pulsifer continued to curse them at the top of his lungs.

The creatures moved with surprising swiftness and coordination over the tortuous terrain. Pulsifer watched the cavern floor speed past, as the air grew increasingly hot and malodorous. Tears of rage welled into his eyes—he, the Velvet Knife, was to end as ingloriously as this! Little did Pammoth's gift avail him, now! He cursed the vindictive Montath and the others who had driven him into this situation.

Soon the air whooshed about them, first blowing one way, then another—the inhalations and exhalations of the giant. Pulsifer ceased crying and ranting, and strained to reach his knife. A deep, windy, rattling noise filled the air, and his captors began laboring up a slope—the light of the outer cavern diminished substantially, and he knew that he had been carried into the titan's mouth. It was a place of fetid gusts.

The light was dim, but he could see if he turned his head upward the slight amount he was able; the giant's mouth was a high-walled cave in itself, and they traveled along a granitic ridge which seemed to be a close-set row of teeth. The curve of the floor and wall — Rewelquian's palate and inner cheek — was dark, but spores of the luminous fungi had taken root in cracks and crannies, shedding faint phosphorescence. As they neared the throat the thickness of these pallid growths increased, as did the stench and humidity. For an instant he was held over a dizzying, glowing gulf, a sloping hall which was the giant's gullet —

— Then he was placed on the mushroom-covered surface, which was sticky with mucosal secretions. The creatures gave him a collective shove, and he slid, screaming, down the esophagus of Rewelquian the Bound, some of the imps sitting on him as if he were a sled.

It seemed that he slid for hours, though it was only a minute or two; he came to a rough stop, dropping eight feet into a room-sized cavity. The walls were slightly pinkish — still the fungi grew abundantly, shedding illumination. Three of the imps rushed forward and began to unwind the net from his body; this done, they scampered away, up the wall, and out.

He sat up, wiping slime from his face and shoulders with both hands.

"Up, up!" a squeaky voice commanded. Carefully he rose — across the 'room' from him were three of the fur-clad dwarfs called Sheft, from the forest miles above! In their hands were short stabbing spears, and they watched him with suspicion on their ferret-like faces. Their gender was unguessable. Behind them was a huge, twitching sphincter in the flesh of the wall, closed tightly like a puckered mouth. Pulsifer raised his hands in a gesture of peace.

"My friends, I am not an enemy! I, too, am a victim of this loathsome giant and his offspring! Let us work together, and formulate a plan for escape —"

"Silence, fool!" one of the dwarfs snarled. "Do not even speak of the Great Rewelquian, whom you are honored to serve as fodder!" It eyed him with a measuring gaze. "You look familiar — you are the rascal sought by the wizard Montath! No matter; you are Rewelquian's now. Even the wizard could not release you! What is in the bag you carry on your back? Valuables? You have weapons — weapons are not permitted here! Give the bag and your weapons to us — you no longer need either!"

Pulsifer drew his sword with a quick steely rasp. "Come and take them!"

The dwarfs brandished their weapons menacingly; their leader shook its head. "We will collect them later, when you are bones. Move to the opening — step carefully into the place beyond, for the portal area is sensitive! Angering Rewelquian will only hasten your demise!"

Pulsifer glanced up — the esophagus was reachable, but he would die with spears in his back if he tried to get to it, and the climb would be next to impossible. Also, the fleshy opening had puckered to a mere point.

Reluctantly he edged around the room and toward the sphincter, as the Sheft likewise sidled away to allow him to pass. One of them tapped the sphincter with the butt of its spear.

The pink-and-grey muscles quivered, then the wall opened wide. Pulsifer looked into another, larger area, curved and odious. He gagged, glanced uncertainly at the Sheft, and stepped through. As he passed into the next place, he stamped with deliberate forcefulness on the bottom of the sphincter.

The room convulsed, and he flew through the air as the wall closed behind him with a sucking noise. A distant rumbling sound was heard. He landed in an ignominious heap on the quivering floor — here the light was very faint indeed. He sat up with an oath, his sword still in his hand, half-wishing that Montath would follow him into the giant's belly and give him a quick death.

"Welcome to you, newcomer," a voice said. Pulsifer strained to see who spoke, and finally made out a group of dark figures, seated at the wall directly across from him. Warily he rose.

"Who speaks? Where am I? Why am I not immediately digested?"

"To be precise, you are in the first of the three stomachs of Rewelquian — or so the Sheft have said, and the imps support their statements. As you weaken from hunger, you will be moved downward until you reach the final, acidic compartment. The giant's interior has apparently evolved through the ages of his imprisonment, to a configuration suitable to his exact needs in this state. I suspect that Rewelquian also draws psychic sustenance from the gradual deterioration of our emotive forces, or the first two stomachs would not be necessary. We are your fellow captives, the last persons taken from a caravan by the foul forest-dwarfs. I am Gilgode Semmech; come sit with us! We trade tales, to pass the time."

Thrusting his sword in its scabbard, he joined them near the wall — three men, each haggard in the dimness. Nearby lay another, sleeping. Pulsifer peered carefully — the sleeper was Jabroal Glispert.

The man who had spoken nodded in a friendly fashion. He was blonde and narrow-featured, of slender build. "As I said, I am Gilgode, a mage of Ibret. This man is Ga-Ryellin the wubber-keeper; this other is Erzsange Phyroilic, of the warrior class. The sleeping man suffers from a malady, and does not know his own identity. You are — ?"

"I've been known by many names, none of them important now," Pulsifer cautiously replied. "If you are a mage, why are you still imprisoned? Surely magic can rescue us all!"

"Not so, not so," Gilgode answered sadly. "All magic is ineffectual in this entity's interior — apparently we are isolated from all causal and spiritual forces, either by the substance of Rewelquian's body, or the power which restrains him. Many a cantrip have I mumbled and roared — to no noticeable effect! We are all doomed." He looked at Pulsifer's scabbarded sword.

"Our weapons were taken by the Sheft when we were captured — how did you retain yours? Of course, the sword is worthless — the walls of the compartment are almost like rock."

"The imps captured me, not the Sheft — perhaps they have never seen an armed man, miles beneath the earth, before. You are certain that there is no possibility of escape?"

"Aye, we are beyond hope," Ga-Ryellin muttered. He was large and dull-featured. "Seventy-three others have gone before us, weakened by hunger and dragged down to the next levels by the pale things! Ah — do not step in that direction! Stay close by us!"

"Why?" Pulsifer looked back into the dark shadows of the stomach's farther end. "I wish to examine the limits of this cell — I refuse to embrace fatalism!"

"There are two other prisoners there, in the darkness." Erzsange Phyroilic nodded toward the other end. "One is a crippled talycent, unable to walk but still dangerous. The other is worse —"

"That is a certainty," Gilgode interrupted, apparently eager to tell the story. "Most of us signed on in Nishar, for passage to Kalsurridin, then Phontyque. In Yawamris we disembarked while new travelers booked passage. The city was yet in an uproar over the escape of Pulsifer the Uncursable, and many wished to leave the city lest the thief still be about. We left the plains of Distidak without incident, but once in the forests, well…"

He lowered his voice and glanced toward the other end of their prison.

"Several of the passengers were horribly murdered, mutilated in the vilest fashion! While we halted the caravan to smoke out the killer, the guards searched the cars for evidence, and that was when the Sheft attacked us! The identity of the murderer we did not discover until we were imprisoned with him in this titan's belly!"

Pulsifer nodded in understanding. "A madman, eh? The ferocity of an insane killer is to be respected! I will remain close by you; there is strength in numbers, yes?"

Ga-Ryellin eyed the water-flask at his belt. "You have water? Share it with us! Our last has been gone for many hours!"

Pulsifer placed one hand on the flask. "I sympathize with your misery, but the water is mine and I cannot share it. My own life is precious! But I will move away when I drink, so you will not have to watch!"

Gilgode Semmech shrugged. "Erzsange is a warrior, and Ga-Ryellin is still strong. We are three, and you are one. Share with us willingly, or have it taken from you and drink none yourself! I regret the unbalancing nature such a threat has on the Equilibrium of all involved, but life is precious to us all."

After a moment of consideration, Pulsifer nodded and took the flask from his belt. Taking one long, final drink, he handed it to the others, and they gulped greedily. Ga-Ryellin wiped his mouth with the back of his hand and glanced at Jabroal.

"What of him? Should we wake him before it is dry?"

Gilgode shook his head. "It would be more considerate to spare him the guilt and soul-debt we engender by taking another man's water. Here is your flask, friend — thank you for the drink."

Pulsifer returned the empty container to his belt, a wry expression on his face. "I only regret that I have no food for you to extort — we shall starve together. Now, do not disturb me while I work — any further attempts to take my property will be met with the edge of my sword! You have no weapons — even three can bleed!"

He squatted a few feet away and, removing the valise from his backharness, he took out the Cask of Sranophaez. While the others watched he pressed two glyphs at random, bringing forth an explosion of glittering deity-mites.

These desired to build a tower of gold, gem and skulls — he instructed them to construct the edifice on the forehead of the giant Rewelquian, and began considering another combination. Gilgode Semmech studied him with interest.

"You should have told me you were a mage! An invaluable relic, there — it could prove to be our key to freedom! It is a supply of encapsulated forces, is it not? Such things were common, fifty-six hundred years ago. Now the anti-magical properties of our prison are bypassed! Ah — What did you say your name was?"

"I didn't — be silent while I call forth the entities of the box!" The others gazed with growing excitement as he summoned cluster after cluster, but not one proved capable of assisting the prisoners and he dispatched them on meaningless errands. Manifestations created in their prison quickly disintegrated, probably cancelled by the same forces which halted other magicks. At length he thrust the cask back into the valise with a wordless growl. The other men said nothing, but Gilgode's eyes narrowed with suspicion. Jabroal awakened, sat up, and watched with curiosity as Pulsifer dug desperately in the bag for a helpful item.

His fingers closed on a bulky leathern object — the Cache of Indissolubles, stolen from Jabroal's workshop! He grinned; perhaps a specific ingredient, applied under the direction of Gilgode Semmech, could burst the giant Rewelquian asunder! He lifted the pouch from the valise —

"Thief! Varlet! Scoundrel! No-account! Offspring of incestuous ulmonders! The pouch is mine—give it to me!" Jabroal stood with his face contorted, jowls and nose jiggling. Even in the gloom his eyes seemed to blaze with wrath. Pulsifer stepped back, pushing the valise behind him with his foot, and drew his sword. He held the pouch in a firm grip with his other hand.

"This man is bereft of his senses—the pouch is my property! Sit down, old man!"

Gilgode Semmech spoke in a serious tone. "I know you now—I've seen sketches of you, often enough! You are the criminal Pulsifer! The infallible weave of justice has drawn you into our company! Be so kind as to surrender peacefully—though we all face death, yours shall come at our hands, as is proper! Any decent man would alleviate his soul-debt by bringing equilibration to your disharmonious skein! But first, return the pouch to the old man!"

Taking Gilgode at his word, his fellows Erzsange Phyroilic and Ga-Ryellin began to move purposefully forward—Pulsifer dissuaded them with a flourish of his sword, bent quickly, and caught up the valise beneath his right arm. As they moved forward again he backed to the opposite wall of their cell, where he set down the bag and dropped the pouch into it. Jabroal shook with fury.

"My memory returns! I am Jabroal Glispert, Mage Independent! He is indeed Pulsifer, trickster and despoiler! In the pouch is my greatest treasure, an elaborate compilation of runes gathered painstakingly over half my life's span! Kill him and gain great reward—" He looked about, surprise on his face. "Where am I? What is this place and how did I come here?"

"You are in the belly of the titan Rewelquian, and there is no escape," Gilgode replied. "But perhaps our spirits will receive some reward for engineering this dog's destruction! You will learn, Pulsifer, what it means to trifle with your betters!"

Biting his lip, Pulsifer readied for their charge as the four men moved toward him. Suddenly, however, Jabroal halted the others with an outflung hand.

"Wait! We must take him alive—listen to me! His essence represents the last component of the spell in the pouch—he must die in such a way as to assure that his departing soul can be driven into the pouch as it leaves his opened mouth! Someone must restrain him, and hold his mouth open — another must hold his nose, while another plugs his ears! Thus will his essential self depart through the desired orifice! When this is done, we shall have an effectuation of greatest potency—"

"Worthless in here, where magic sleeps," Gilgode Semmech said. "Let us kill him swiftly and be rid of him!"

"No, not worthless!" Jabroal's voice cracked with excitement. "This is an effectuation which even the immune-system of Rewelquian cannot stifle! The giant will be as a bug beneath my heel, when I have the complete spell! All of us will soon be free! Carefully, now — first take his arms and legs, and pin him down! You, big fellow, hold his head as I direct, and I will hold the bag to his mouth! When I give the signal, can you crush his windpipe with your knee?"

"I can," Ga-Ryellin said. Pulsifer sneered. Ga-Ryellin and Erzsange rushed from left and right — Ga-Ryellin fell away with a howl, blood spurting from the stumps of his severed fingers. Erzsange dodged a slash and backed away — Ga-Ryellin rolled at their feet, grasping his bleeding hand to his chest. The three other men stepped back to their wall, and the injured man began to cry. The smell of blood was thick in the air.

The proximity-ring flashed blue, its beacon unmissable in the darkness.

To Pulsifer's left, something moved — it stepped hesitantly forward, apparently drawn by the noise and the scent of blood. Gilgode noticed it with a shout.

"Careful! The murderer! Prepare to defend yourselves!"

Pulsifer took advantage of the distraction to grab the valise by its handles — he raised his bloody weapon as the face of the killer became visible.

Feature for thick feature, it was the face of Bolderge Grallko, the teamster — but its eyes were those of a bloodthirsty maniac. The kouool eased forward, its hands wide-fingered — with a delighted cry it sprang upon Ga-Ryellin, took his throat in its mouth, and dragged him away as if he were a lamb. The sounds of a brief struggle were heard, to be replaced by the slurpings and rippings of a grisly feast. Gilgode Semmech vomited up the water he'd taken from Pulsifer.

After this the other men fell to whispering among themselves, looking occasionally at the man with the sword. For long hours they sat in the murk, and Pulsifer managed to secure the valise in his back-harness again. Eventually there was a loud scuffling sound beyond the place where the kouool hid, and forty or more of the newt-like imps roiled into the chamber.

To Pulsifer's surprise, they spoke in chirping voices.

"Hurry, hurry!"

"Next, step lively! Schedules must be maintained!"

"The old man looks weakest —"

"Bad thing, prisoners eating one another!"

"Wasteful, that's what it is!"

"Grab the oldster — he is also feeble of mind!"

The imps approached the five prisoners — one indicated Pulsifer. "This one stands alone — an outcast has no defenders! Let us take him instead!"

"No, the big brothers said he is armed, and he is a fresh arrival — take the others, while he starves." They turned toward Gilgode, Erzsange, and Jabroal, and one squealed:

"You, old man! Come with us — we have prepared a place filled with pleasure and diversion for your enjoyment! Come, come!"

"I refuse to go with you!" Jabroal stated defiantly. "Take the rogue, there, or the killer in the wall-cranny behind you! I have only recently regained my complete awareness, and am not yet prepared to relinquish it!"

Ignoring his words, the creatures massed in preparation for an attack—

Pulsifer edged away from them, toward the wall-sphincter through which he'd entered the first stomach. The kouool — replica of Bolderge — eased into view, met his gaze, and smiled. High in one hand it held the heart of its last victim, and said:

"You and I shall be the last! It is destined that I bathe in your blood, for the greater glory of the ochdeviants! The imps fear me, and I remain well-fed —"

"Leave the old man here!" Pulsifer blurted. The imps turned in surprise at his outburst. "I volunteer to go to the next level — open the passage, and keep the creature behind you away from me! As a gesture of goodwill, I abandon one of my weapons — but do not seek to remove my others, I warn you…" The other prisoners gaped in wonder as he pulled the curved knife he'd found from his belt, and made to toss it to them. It landed beyond the creatures, and Erzsange Phyroilic moved swiftly to snatch it up, practically ripping it from its scabbard.

"A knife from one of my brothers-in-arms!" he exclaimed. "Come now, little devils — I'll slice you to bits!"

To his surprise and apparent disappointment, the things ignored him, for they still looked at Pulsifer. One of them eased forward, and said:

"You go willingly, with no struggle? Come then, that's a good fellow! We will protect you — you will earn no violence at our hands! What a happier place this would be, if all prisoners were so cooperative!"

Pulsifer stepped forward uneasily and they closed about him in a protective swarm — as they shuffled toward the rear of the chamber, Jabroal spat at him.

"You have earned my undying hatred, Pulsifer! You repaid kindness with betrayal most foul! You cannot flaunt your turpitude forever — the retributive flow of Equilibrium will drown you in its torrent! Remember my words, as you die in the bowels of Rewelquian —"

"Speak not to me of justice!" Pulsifer snarled. "I saved your life — you sought mine! The pouch is scant reimbursement for the hardships you have caused — I would not even be here, if it were not for your treachery! Share reminiscences of me with the kouool — he, too, is an old adversary of mine, and good company for you!"

Jabroal's face went bland. "Kouool?" he half-whispered, glancing toward the dimly-seen figure. Pulsifer, too, now watched the monster with care as they passed, his hand ready on the hilt of his sword. Once molded into permanent human form, the creature's strength would be uncanny.

The face of Bolderge nodded as he passed, displaying a sophistica-tion of emotion unknown to the coarse man from which it had been taken. "In my gut, the brain of Bolderge screams for your death — his distress is savored! I am robbed of you for now, but sooner or later I, also, will pass downward. Perhaps we shall meet again!"

"Particularly enjoy the older mage," Pulsifer rejoined. "I have it from the observation of a parsennoc that his nose is a sweetmeat of great distinction!"

The kouool vanished as the wall curved, and they neared the next meaty dungeon. There was no sign of the talycent, which had apparently been removed. Behind in the gloom, Jabroal screamed in rage. Before Pulsifer and his teeming escort, the wall opened like a blossom of flesh.

For long dark hours Pulsifer sat in his new place of confinement; having paced its dimensions, he had determined that he was alone. Smaller and even dimmer than the previous cell, its convoluted walls glowed faintly with a pink radiance. Once he drifted into a light sleep, partially soothed by the warmth of his heavy clothing and the soft throbbing of the giant's pulse — almost immediately, several of the imps crept into the stomach with the obvious intention of disarming him, and dragging him to the next level. The flashing of his ring awakened him and he kicked wildly, bursting one of the creatures open with his heel — jumping to his feet with his sword in hand, he sent them running, carrying their companion with them.

They screamed back imprecations as they went, then disappeared.

After this he did not doze. He took the Bowl of Shigandure from his bag and examined it in the dimness. Surely Shigandure the Immolator could burn for him a path to freedom! But Rewelquian was vast and powerful; the heat required might destroy all the beings in the giant's body, himself included.

And if he escaped — Shigandure had his price. What if Pulsifer were the only available human being to serve as payment? He decided against releasing the bowl-entity for the present, and thought of Montath, who surely searched for him with bewilderment.

Even if the wizard deduced that he was inside the titan, Montath would be foolish to follow him within, and probably would not. But he would almost certainly be waiting if the Velvet Knife were to somehow win free of the giant's digestive tract — His stomach growled insistently at the thought of another's digestion. How long could he survive without food, water, and sleep? He returned the bowl to the valise, refastened the bag into his harness, and got to his feet.

He poked the pink wall with one finger; it was tough as saddle-leather, but definitely composed of living tissue, not nearly as hard as the cartilaginous walls of the first stomach. With a fierce two-handed thrust, he drove his sword-blade into the wall — the whole room palpitated queasily but he clung to the swordhilt with both hands. Bracing his feet, he began working the blade in a saw-like motion; soon he held hanging in one hand a large, fat-marbled steak, almost bloodless, carved from the wall of the stomach. Thick blood, black in the murk, began to well slowly into the wound, coagulating almost instantly.

Wrinkling his nose in revulsion he ate, cursing between rubbery mouthfuls; soon he heard a pattering commotion and jumped to his feet, sword in one hand and meat in the other. A score of the pale things rushed into the room, screaming savagely.

"Desist this vandalism! You cause Rewelquian considerable discomfort!"

Pulsifer laughed. "I also am uncomfortable! Hunger is a sensation I find particularly annoying. Ah, not too close! Come nearer, and —"

Bracing his feet again, he drove the sword-tip into the wall — the chamber quivered, and a distant sound like thunder rumbled some-where above. The imps fell to the floor in a jerking mass, clutching at their abdomens and hissing like lizards. After Rewelquian's spasms had passed, the things scrambled to their feet, embryonic faces bent with fury — they approached him with predictable intent.

Again he stabbed the wall — again, they fell in agony. He repeated this until they lay gasping like fish on a bank; walking over, he began stepping on their little heads. Their skulls popped like gourds, spilling yellowish fluids — they had no brains. A few managed to stagger up and away, and he watched them flee with amusement.

Forcing himself to eat a few more bites of the rancid-flavored meat, he eyed the darkness carefully. In a matter of minutes the entrance-sphincter gaped, and a band of spear-wielding Sheft crowded in the opening. With all his strength, he buried his blade to the hilts in the soft tissues he'd already uncovered — the room leapt and the sphincter snapped shut, crushing arms, legs, trunks and heads. Pulsifer observed with interest. The Sheft, too, had no brains.

Striding quickly to one broken body, he ripped away the conceal-ing furs — beneath was a pale white form much like those of the imps, only slightly more man-like. Toward the neck the skin grew pink, in mimicry of human complexion. He backed away from the area and moved cautiously toward the rear of the chamber, and the next portal.

To his surprise it was partially opened — he peered into the region beyond.

A faintly-glowing hall-sized tube dripping with secretions curved down, up, then away to the left; moving swiftly, before the stunned Rewelquian could recover, he forced himself through the opening and into the tube. His foot scraped as he passed, and by reflex the wall snapped shut behind him; with a grin, he started down the tube. There was no logic in waiting to die — he'd take this route as soon as the other, rather than sitting inactive, waiting for a fatal sleep! Besides, he did not wish to see any of the inhabitants of the first stomach again! He encouraged himself by thinking of the fact that all previous newcomers to this section of the giant's body had been much weaker than he, when brought here.

A foul wind hit him in the face and he fastened on his kabeyui, then his thick gloves as well. He moved with haste but carefully, scrambling at times to go up slick rises. A scuffling issued from somewhere — coming around a bend, he met a veritable horde of the imps, among them many others in intermediate stages between larval imps and fully-developed Sheft. They rushed forward with horrible cries.

Furiously he jabbed the wall of the tube, which was much softer and wetter than that of the compartment before it, and the crowd of things rolled in misery as he plunged the blade hilt-deep again and again — squeals and hissings echoed in the narrow space. Clear ichor gushed into the tube from the wounds he made, and the whole place lurched with every stroke. Finally the creatures grew still; walking on their senseless, mushy bodies, he rushed over and past them. As he stepped away, a few already began to stir. He decided to run.

Now he sped along with the fingertips of one gloved hand graz-ing the wet wall. The tube curved more often now, first one way, then another; he slid down a declivity with his weapon upraised, crouched like a skier. Still glissading, he rounded a turn, where he met more of the little monsters — he jumped, sailed over their heads and reaching hands, and landed well beyond them. They followed with screams — he dug his sword into the floor as he slid, ripping a gash some eight feet long. Again the imps collapsed in pain behind him.

That action ended his reckless slide, and it was a good thing — ahead the tube branched in three directions. He stumbled to a halt just short of flying into the center branch, which plunged precipitously downward. The splashings and hissings of stomach-acids issued from the depths. He looked into the left-hand tube — it was virtually packed with hundreds of writhing, recovering imps. Without hesitation he went to the right. The tube narrowed and grew even darker, the walls a deep, pulsating red.

He gouged the wall for good measure, and then crouched as the convulsing tube contracted dangerously. In his mind's eye he pictured the thrashings of all the Sheft and imps, wherever they were at the moment, and the earth-shaking screams of the titan in the cavern, which he could hear as a sonorous rumble. The quaking subsided and he moved along, searching for other branchings. Both the lack of imp-traffic in the stomachs from which he'd escaped, and the logic of anatomy, spoke of other exits from the giant's body. He winced in disgust at the thought of the possible nature of these exits, but hurried on.

After awhile the tube abruptly terminated — he stepped into a gigantic cavity, its walls, floor and ceiling covered with blue and red veins as big as his arms and legs. On the walls were hundreds of protruding cells, irregularly shaped and capped with half-solid mucous — through the opacity of these could be seen tiny fish-like things, fluttering and turning. He hurried from the place of incubation with his stomach fluttering as well.

Traversing a short stretch of tube, he waded through a round organ half-filled with dark, copper-colored liquid; then he clambered up into another place where writhing worm-things covered the walls. The air was acrid and eye-burning. Next he came to an area where the ceiling lowered and he had to bend deeply to pass along a bumpy route — as he stepped on dark protrusions, the walls quivered in agitation. He slammed his heel on several of these nodules as he entered the next open space—here, bare bone like tree trunks half-emerged from fleshy walls. Gleaming strangely as if with interior fire, gem-like incrustations grew from the meaty area above his head. Unable to resist, he ripped several from their settings of cartilage and thrust them into one of the compartments of his pouch-belt—Why not profit from this experience, if he survived? Many mages on the clandestine market would pay handsomely for a piece of the colossus…

The arching passage went a brief distance, then he met a membranous wall. Looking up, he saw ridges of rock-like bone, and a length of hanging, burbling intestine—the interior of the titan seemed more arranged as a dwelling-place, than the body of an anthropomorphic creature! As if in confirmation of his thought, the darkness was filled with a sinister scurrying—he wheeled, slicing three imps in half with one stroke. A huge number crowded behind them, filling the low area he'd just left—he jabbed at the floor below, and his sword grated on bone.

The imps, unaffected, rushed forward. Suddenly he was covered by them, and he lurched about with ferocious swings of his sword, his right hand ripping them loose to be flung away. The dim cavity was filled with a frenzy of noise and motion—his wide-swung blade cut deep into the membrane behind him, and the creatures dropped like broken toys. Shaking them off, he turned to the area he had struck.

The wall rippled and shuddered. He hacked at it like a woodsman, to uncover another layer a foot behind the first, and then another. Strange grey-white bursts of energy accompanied the destruction of each layer, and illumination increased with each one he destroyed. At last he stepped into a roseate chamber, aglow with red-gold light.

He eased forward cautiously. This area was filled with softly-glowing heaps and rounded shapes of a transparent material, from which the radiance issued; encased in each was an immobilized being. He looked about in amazement—these were entities almost certainly beyond the ability of the imps or Sheft to capture and restrain! It was like an illustrated scene from a section one might find in a grimoire, on the classifications of potent supernatural beings. A male silver djinni, golden-haired and purple-eyed, nude in the fashion of his kind, stared from one pile; another contained a dread ochdeviant, three-headed and horrible. Small hijrets, larger, apebodied, reptilian-headed jrets, a scarlet empusa, two cat-faced demons — even a grey viodom, his massive pinions folded on his back — all these and more were imprisoned, an impressive collection of the entities which haunted the deeper concentricities of the Earth. Pulsifer shook his head in wonder — how were they taken, much less held?

Above and behind he heard a creak of movement — turning, he saw above him a protuberance some six feet in circumference, growing from the wall. As a heavy curtain of skin slid up, he realized that this was an eye — leaping with all his strength, he drove his sword into the center of the freshly-uncovered pupil. The room shook as if in an earthquake, and he was thrown free, sword in hand, to land with a painful jarring impact on the floor. Clear liquid poured from the injured eye, and it snapped shut; Pulsifer rose uneasily to his feet.

He looked about for a path from the room — there was none. Soon, he knew, the imps behind him would revive — should he attempt to go back, and retrace his steps? He cursed in frustration, wheeled in rage, slashed the air with his sword. His eyes met those of the silver djinni —

There was a leap of light between their gazes, an instant of coursing contact which thrummed with mutual awareness. Pulsifer instinctively jerked his head away, but not before a single word rang in his skull —

"Wait!"

Warily he looked again at the ifrit. "What do you want? Speak quickly! I have no time for conversation!"

The thoughts of the unmoving entity poured into his mind, resonant and musical. *"Remove your mask — your eyes are shadowed. There! Now, listen — there is no escape from the things you flee — they are in fact Rewelquian, or impressions of his personality, generated from his body while his mind is in a half-dream state. The dream-mind of all beings is the most potent — each of us here learned that to our misfortune! We each came here out of curiosity, and were snared by our own crystallized avarice for knowledge, or for plundered pieces of the giant! Had you not blinded Rewelquian's greed-finding eye, you too would have been imprisoned in this fashion! The only escape for you will come from helping me win my freedom — Do not look at the ochdeviant! He would draw your soul from your eyes with an effectuation of blackest malice!"*

Pulsifer gazed at the djinni with distrust, but he did not look directly at the ochdeviant. "Why should I trust you? Know that I am Pulsifer, betrayed in the past by others of your kind! No wise man believes the word of a djinni…"

The djinni simultaneously emanated surprise, curiosity, and eagerness.

"You are Pulsifer! Of course you would be — only such a chaotic agent could bypass the Hemen-Klurstic Ponderations of Probability! The Net of Equilibrium is doubtless snarled hopelessly! Set me free — I swear by the All-Inundating Eyes of Pammoth and Hymakki, by my Sphere of Grome-Urul, and by my Truest Name, that I will aid you in achieving your grandest aspirations! But first you must travel back the way you came, and farther, to enter the skull-cavity of Rewelquian — his sinuses should provide the most direct access! There you will find a fist-sized crystal, black as coal, the essence of the colossus — destroy it with your sword-blade, but prior to this you must smear the edge of your weapon with human blood! A bit of your own will do —"

"Desist your directions! Surely you do not expect me to make such a journey! I may have other methods of doing what you describe — but first, your Name! I will hold you to your oath!"

"My name is Piristil — now, do what you will!"

Pulsifer shook his head. "Not so fast — an agent of veracity lurks in my brain, a gift of the infallible Pammoth! Your True Name, if you please!"

The djinni apparently believed his lie. *"You are indeed the astute Pulsifer! I am Aflauncu — hold me by that calling! Destroy the giant and I will remove you safely, showering you with riches —"*

"Wealth is not necessarily my greatest desire, and I may have several —"

"Choose only three fulfillments, but nothing as elaborate as those Pammoth gave you. I am by no means omnipotent, and I am also weakened by my months here. The emanations of my sphere are vital to my potency."

"I will be more specific later — I am not yet certain that my plan will prove successful. In the event you are freed, be prepared to carry me to safety!" First he sheathed his sword, then he half-unharnessed the valise, opening it slightly. Twisting awkwardly, he managed to take out the bowl. Setting it down, he squatted above it, dug his fire-kit from a pouch, and put a bit of tinder in the vessel. He struck several sparks, and a tiny flame grew. He quickly backed away.

The bowl filled with a familiar glow — the blazing face of Shigandure rose to fill it. The cavity was now suffused with heat and radiance, and Shigandure spoke, his voice booming as always.

"WHAT NOW, O UNTACTFUL ONE? REMEMBER, PAYMENT WILL BE REQUIRED FOR THIS DISTURBANCE!"

"You will receive what you require! Do you sense the size and nature of the giant around you? Can you destroy a being of such magnitude?"

Shigandure's features brightened blindingly.

"AN ENTITY OF ASTOUNDING TENACITY! ITS ESSENCE WOULD ENORMOUSLY STABILIZE THE FLOW OF ENERGIES AMONG THE VERTICES, MORE THAN THOSE OF TEN-MILLION HUMAN BEINGS! TLEOCAUZUALC WILL SING WITH BINDING FORCES! BUT I AM NOT SURE I SHOULD RISK SUCH AN EXTENSION INTO THIS PLANE..."

"What?" Pulsifer exclaimed. "You are surely not intimidated —"

"YOUR INSOLENCE IS BOUNDLESS!" Shigandure roared. "BUT I UNDERSTAND THAT IT IS A RESULT OF YOUR PUNY AWARENESS. TO TAKE THIS BEING, I MUST EXPAND TO AN EQUIVALENT SIZE, DRAW-ING ON THE ENERGY-FLOW OF THE TESSERACT-STRUCTURE — AT LEAST FOR A MOMENT, REALITY ITSELF MAY VERY WELL BE AT RISK OF DISSOLUTION! BUT THE BENEFIT TO THE VERTEX WOULD BE SO GREAT — ALL IS CONSCIOUSNESS, O IGNORANT TEMPTER OF THIS DEED..."

"Surely a worthwhile risk!" Pulsifer eagerly cried. "But hasten, else your help is useless! Do not expand here — I, too, would be destroyed! Blaze through the flesh of this giant, and unleash your full force within its skull — there you will find its center of being! Wait, before you act — will the giant's death cancel the spells which hold these beings around us?"

"THEY, TOO, WILL PERISH — THEIR CELLS ARE APPARENTLY OF THEIR OWN MAKING, YET ARE PART OF THE GIANT'S MATRIX. WOULD YOU HAVE ME PERFORM ANOTHER TASK AND FREE THEM? YOUR COST WOULD BE TABULATED ALONG WITH THE FEE FOR THE DESTRUCTION OF THE COLOSSUS."

"Only this one, the djinni — your full power would be too much, but just a crack or a pin-hole in the crystal might do. The others are malefi-cent and can burn, for all I care."

"THEIR ESSENCES, TOO, SHALL BE WELCOMED TO THE CON-DUITS!"

Shigandure grew out from the bowl only enough to allow his shoul-ders and arms to swell free. He pointed a flaming digit in the direction of Aflauncu — a burning white beam shot forth, instantly burning a hole the diameter of a grass-stem in the red-gold substance surround-ing the ifrit.

Aflauncu melted into a silver mist and billowed like smoke from the opening; reforming beside Pulsifer, he took him by the arm.

"Come, Pulsifer — ah, how good it is to speak aloud! Unleash your hot friend, so that we may be gone from Rewelquian's suppressing fields!" Pulsifer nodded and gestured — Shigandure shot from the bowl with an ear-aching roar. In a second a sizzling tunnel was burned in one wall, inclined upward, straight and long to the point of vanishing. Pulsifer knew that, already, the demiurge was in the skull-cavity of Rewelquian —

Rewelquian's body was racked by a mighty spasm. Pulsifer left the bowl where it lay, for the floor of living tissues tilted crazily — he scram-bled for footing, as one of the rock-like prisons which contained a russet jret slid toward him with crushing potential. His heart seemed to leap as he realized that he was about to die — then Aflauncu, effort-lessly standing straight on the sharply-tilted surface, thrust out one hand and halted the transparent mass.

Again the giant around them shook massively, and a low, thundering scream reverberated distantly; Aflauncu wrapped one arm about Pulsifer's shoulders, and he grew weightless. They sped up toward the meaty ceiling.

There was a red coolness, a fog-like haze. There was no sensation of motion, though they rapidly ascended, and Pulsifer suddenly looked down on the mount of Rewelquian. The cavern shook, vibrating with rock-shattering shock-waves as the titan slammed his head repeatedly against the ground. His many eyes, ocher orbs with oblong black centers, were opened wide. There was no sign of the tower which the deity-mites had been instructed to build upon his head—they, too, had been unable to escape from the giant's body.

The magma-prison covering his body trembled and bucked, and the titan's voice, visible as a heat-like air disturbance, rose from its mouth in waves.

Great slabs of rock began to break loose from the ceiling, to sag and fall to the cavern floor. The volcanic mounds about the giant erupted with red-hot spray. Rewelquian's eyes suddenly melted and ran like butter.

Pulsifer floated beside the glowing djinni, who now grasped his shoulder with one hand. About them to a distance of two feet was a hazy blue field of protective force. Even the sounds in the cavern were muted, and it seemed that they gazed upon the tumultuous scene through the waters of a placid pool. Aflauncu drifted, and the surrounding field moved with them.

"Here comes your servitor," Aflauncu observed in a sardonic tone. The head of Rewelquian grew red as the lava of the cones, and began to melt like a mountain of wax—out of this rose Shigandure, growing higher and broader, a blazing being of sun-bright intensity. Despite the protective field, Pulsifer looked away. The fungi-forest was instantly shriveled and gone, and he wondered if Montath had been there, and had been evaporated. The thought of soft Sinfe, burned away in an instant, brought an unfamiliar feeling of remorse—but, he reminded himself, she was a soulless syleber, perhaps even less than an animal!

Still Shigandure continued to swell, until he threatened to fill the cavern—it grew warmer within their shield, and Aflauncu shot with lightning-speed to the farthest reaches of the grotto.

They looked back at Shigandure—he was nothing more than an amorphous blaze of white plasma. Suddenly he began to shrink, his lower portions vanishing into one point, the bowl, as the demiurge sent to Tleoucauzualc the forces he had assimilated.

The mass of the bowl-entity dwindled, the cavern grew dark with an inky blackness. Streams of lava shed some light, flowing over the cavern floor in a web-like pattern. In a daze, Pulsifer peered toward the place of Rewelquian's imprisonment—the spot was leveled, melted flat. Shigandure still stood there, a blazing dwarf-giant some fifty feet tall, but shrinking in size as they watched. With a windstorm of whorling particles about him, the entity followed the last of his energies into the bowl. The watchers waited — the voice of Shigandure the Immolator rang out, and Pulsifer trembled at the sound of it.

"*TWO HUMAN LIVES — THESE I REQUIRE OF YOU! NOW I RETURN TO TLEOCAUZUALC, WHERE I WILL INTEGRATE THE NEW FORCES INTO THE JUNCTIVE SUB-VERTEX. SUMMON ME AGAIN WITH YOUR PAYMENT AT HAND — OR WHEN NEXT I VENTURE INTO THIS PLACE, I WILL MOST ASSUREDLY SEEK YOU OUT — REGARDLESS OF WHETHER OR NOT YOU ARE THE ONE TO CALL ME FORTH!*"

The darkness became total; Shigandure was gone. Pulsifer and his supernatural protector were bathed in a blue radiance. He looked at the violet-eyed ifrit.

"What think you to be the odds of the discovery of yonder bowl by an intelligent being?"

Aflauncu pursed his lips and creased his brow. "I daresay the likelihood would be high; a disturbance of such magnitude as we have seen will draw the attention of a million minds — human mages, djinn, and others. The question many will ask is: Has Rewelquian burst his bonds? Others, ignorant of the giant's place of imprisonment, will simply seek to establish the origin of a vast upheaval in the planetary flow of forces. If you wonder as to the likelihood of the demiurge's re-emergence into this plane, I would say that it is almost a certainty."

"I request the first of the fulfillments you have sworn to deliver! Remove the bowl — bury it a thousand feet below the frozen sludge on the floor of the Raskurye Sea, away from all lifeforms or sources of heat — nor ever speak of it, or seek it yourself! Does this qualify under the terms of our agreement?"

Aflauncu smiled. "Pulsifer, Pulsifer — your devious mind is a delight! Wait here — I shall do as you have specified." The djinni disappeared; to his shock, Pulsifer found himself hanging alone in the black cavern, surrounded by the blue energies. In ten seconds the elemental reappeared, still smiling.

"It is done. The unspeakable item is beneath the Roskil Sea, locked in the heart of a block of granite. The Raskurye Sea is above a pocket of hot gases, the same which heats the enclosed Maji Sea to boiling. There it would not have been utterly isolated from heat. The Blazing One will never again burst forth from the tiny particle it calls home, and you are beyond its reach."

Pulsifer reached over his shoulder with one hand and tightened his backharness.

"Then let us be gone from this dead place! I would eat and rest before I make my other choices, if it would not be asking too much of you — Aflauncu."

The djinni laughed, a musical sound that echoed endlessly in the blackness. He inclined his head graciously. "I would be honored by your company, O Master."

The next instant, they were not there.

Part Four

Taut and Tangled

Chapter 1

Bargains Binding

Calim Pulsifer, the Velvet Knife, fugitive from the justice of all mankind, lounged upon a soft divan in a golden room. Both he and the room were in the Concentricity of Grome-Urul, some three hundred miles beneath the surface of the aged Earth. Nearby was a fountain of aventurine, surrounded by statuary formed in the likeness of water-dipping maidens; their round-limbed forms were of clear rose quartz, their eyes were of opals and jade. The water splashed and gurgled, and Pulsifer occasionally found himself listening closely, for it seemed that the liquid actually spoke in a number of tongues, their words unknown to his ears. He took a goblet of wine from a passing djinniyah of fiery beauty, raking her with an appreciative eye as she backed away, bowing, an amused and flirtatious smile upon her lips.

He wore new clothing of his own design, fashioned in a second by Aflauncu; the topaz-colored material was thin but warm, embroidered richly with blue samite and emeralds. His boots were fashioned of the horny red hide of a teltinc, polished and supple, and nearly untearable. Nearby, his bundled traveler's clothes were restored to newness, as was the shagreen valise; rising, he went to the bag, took out his pouch-belt, swordbelt and weapons, and buckled them on. An amused voice rang out behind him.

"Ever ready to flee or fight! Are you so soon restless?" Aflauncu drifted beneath an archway and into the room, disdaining the use of his legs for walking. "I trust that Lurulzehede has seen to your comfort and nourishment."

Pulsifer smiled. "She provided both food and drink of wondrous goodness, as well as the enchantment of her beauty. I thank you both for your marvelous hospitality."

"No thanks is necessary — gratitude is neither given nor received, among my kind. Existence is a business, and all interpersonal activities are viewed as transactions. I feel much better, now — I bathed in the fires of Penderoth, and my essence hums with renewed vitality! You have two fulfillments left to you — have you thought about the possibilities?"

Pulsifer nodded and strode over to the scintillant fountain, where he gazed at the talking waters. Amorphous, child-like shapes swept into and out of substantiality beneath the surface. "I must gain access to certain information before making any decisions. First I would know the whereabouts and activities of certain persons..."

Aflauncu raised his hand and a colorless cube, clear as glass, appeared in his palm. "Look into the Cube and ask your questions — you will come to know all that you require."

Pulsifer regarded the cube with a pensive expression. "Great care must be taken to generate complete protection as we eavesdrop — I can leave no chinks in my defenses! To begin, I must know the activities of my enemies. Show me anyone who currently speaks ill of me!"

The cube clouded, and thirty faces were shown in rapid succession, while Pulsifer leaned near to look. The face of Moilerve Sulshaine flitted past, and he saw the features of Azahad Zuzirco as well. A wizard he thought to recognize as the archimage Porvul Shuk, an old acquaintance, was shown also. His eyes shot wide and he pointed, his voice cracking with surprise.

"There! The droop-nosed man! That is the mage Jabroal Glispert! He can not be among the living — I left him in the belly of Rewelquian!"

"Obviously he lives. I will expand the view." The cube grew until it was a foot wide in every dimension — within could be seen the parlor of Jabroal's forest home, and the wizard himself dressed in clean blue robes. Two other men moved into the scene — the warrior Erzsange Phyroilic, and Gilgode Semmech the Mage. Pulsifer gaped in astonishment as the voices of the three men emanated from the cube. Pulsifer listened for a minute to their discussion, then waved his hand in dismissal.

"They somehow escaped — they must have availed themselves of the moment when Rewelquian was weakened! But they speak of my certain death with a despicable satisfaction; there is no threat from their direction. Now show me the wizard Morskured Montath and his hijret familiar—these are my deadliest adversaries!"

Aflauncu cocked his head like a bird. "The name of Montath is as familiar as your own—he is an awesome architect of sorceries! It will be difficult to spy on him without his sensing it...but I will try. Among Seeings, the Cube is one of the most undetectable vehicles. Behold—the pinnacle Vomanction, and the stronghold Krikenvaxi!"

A misty crag grew in the cube, a dark finger of stone which brooded like a monstrous raven over a low, slightly-rolling countryside. A dome-covered city gleamed below and behind the crag, fracturing the rays of the setting sun into colorful beams. The domes were fogged with interior heat, and snow lay without the convex coverings. Pulsifer knew that city—it was Neshgrel, in his homeland of Phontyque. Closer and closer the image loomed, as the Seeing swooped about the castle on the crag with the speed of a starling, showing balconies and turrets, observatories and bartizans, giant merlons and smaller, jutting, iron-edged crenellations. As the image of the citadel seemed to rotate in the cube, he glimpsed the intimation of bodies, limbs, and faces, horribly twisted and compressed into blocks of grey-black stone. The voice of Aflauncu spoke softly.

"Now we enter the citadel—there is an unprotected spot in the roof-tiles on the west tower, a hole made by the gnawing of attic mice. This created a leakage of containing forces, and now there is an instability in the overall protective field—Ah, here it is." The conical rooftop drew closer, perspective shifted; the rooftop became a vast plain of rugged slabs, with a diagonal horizon. A ruptured, rough-edged hole appeared and suddenly the cube went black. After a few minutes of this inchoate view, a crack of light appeared; beyond this spread a grey vastness. Again the perspective changed, and the huge space became a small, round chamber. Aflauncu laughed lowly.

"Ha, now we are within! Think no turbulent thoughts—the hijret might sense that something is amiss. Let us find the wizard—Krikenvaxi is large, so this could take some time."

Pulsifer assented with a wordless grunt, his eyes fixed upon the cube—he was seeing inside Montath's private sanctum, built by djinn in the span of a single night! Such a revelation as this had not even been accorded to the other wizards of the Brotherhood of Mages, for not only was Montath secretive and reclusive; none dared risk his ire by even asking admittance. There was little doubt in sorcerous circles as to who was the most powerful man in Teumdoth!

The scenes in the cube changed rapidly—first out the door, then down spiraling stairs and through chambers both austere and opulent—at one point Pulsifer saw a sparkling room, hung with cages which were filled with living birds of gold, their eyes jewels of flashing colors. Here there were tapestries, fountains, cushioned alcoves—and dozens of women, beautiful and strangely docile. Their apparel was rich and varied, and unmoving. He peered closer; they did not move, but stood, sat, knelt, and reclined in a variety of poses, each apparently awaiting the occasion of Montath's desire to free them from enchantment. An atmosphere of profound sadness hung over the assembly—the Seeing Cube moved on.

Finally the vision showed a high-vaulted chamber, located in the topmost portion of the stronghold's central tower. On the walls, brass glacier-lions grappled with bronze snowdevils, their clashing forms in relief against inlaid mountains of jade and lapis-lazuli. Four feet above the floor, in the center of the room, Morskured Montath floated between two giant polyhedrons of amethyst. Slowly he rotated like a roast on a spit, his eyes closed, hands folded against his chest, his solemn, handsome features weirdly tranquil.

Aflauncu made a surprised sound. "Aha! He will never sense us! Not only are we beyond the ambit of his power, but he is also engaged in a rejuvenation process—his mind is in stasis, while his body absorbs concentrated terrestrial energies! We can destroy him now, if you wish—none of his defenses have been triggered by our etheric intrusion! The hijret is not to be seen—Quick, what say you? I can blast him through a momentary opening and wither him as he sleeps! Make your decision—if he awakens before I act, his power could be excessively difficult to overcome!"

Pulsifer only considered for an instant. "He would do worse to me! Destroy him in the most effective manner at your disposal!"

"As you wish — this is your second fulfillment! Watch joyfully — the dreaded Montath dies!" The djinni fixed the cube with a fearsome stare, his lips moving soundlessly. Pellets of yellow light flew from his mouth, penetrating the cube — the runes continued into the space of the tower chamber as though the room were one with that in which they stood. The tremulation sped toward the oblivious wizard.

Suddenly the image of Montath was surrounded by a blanket of blue fire — the runes of the djinni vanished in tiny explosions. Montath began to stir as if he fought for wakefulness — a brilliant purple spark rose from his hair, and darted toward the watchers. As it came, it began to grow, to change —

"Hijret!" Pulsifer yelled, diving away. Aflauncu made a gesture with his free hand, and crackling pink lightnings fluxed about the cube. The face of the hijret Firkui seemed to slam against one of the interior planes — it looked for a moment as if its form were compressed into a block and held in the djinni's hand. Aflauncu again spoke soundlessly — the cube faded and disappeared, the aggressive hijret vanishing as well. Pulsifer rose uneasily from the floor.

"The little beast nearly had us —"

"He is a nasty one," Aflauncu agreed, "but scarcely a threat to me. You, however, he could completely destroy. We will find another way to deal with Montath, but we will have to tread gingerly. I could never openly attack the mage — he is bound in a pact of alliance with the djinn of Yurdash. Not only did they build his citadel; they are sworn to aid him against hostile djinn of Grome or Calambriel. In return, he is to assist them against the viodoms, or so he says, and the occasional ochdeviant looking to enslave weaker djinn of the Yurdash Sphere. The Yurdashi are clods, but an interconcentric war is best avoided. Such a conflict hasn't arisen since the First War of Wizards, some six thousand years ago."

"How then to deal with him?" Pulsifer grumbled, sitting on the divan again. "He clutters my life with pain and frustration!"

"Every man has his secrets, his weaknesses," the djinni replied, somewhat smugly. "Montath, for all his strength, is a human being. I will find his secret — this is an entertaining game! Involvement with mortals is usually so tedious! Wait here; if you need anything, call for Lurulzehede and she will provide for you. I go to seek Montath's unraveling."

Before Pulsifer could speak, Aflauncu vanished. The Velvet Knife reclined on the divan, closed his eyes, and drifted off to sleep — the image of Firkui haunted the edges of his awareness, before he slipped away into a blackest night.

⁓

Water whispered and laughed. Pulsifer paced the chamber, circling the fountain repeatedly. His rolled traveler's clothes were upon his back, and the valise hung at his side, from a shoulder-strap provided by the djinniyah Lurulzehede. According to the periodically-appearing ifrita, seven hours had passed since Aflauncu's departure; when Pulsifer tried once to leave the chamber, he was met with an invisible resistance which had a consistency like thick mud. Lurulzehede explained that this was for his own well-being, for it would be unsafe for a human being to wander the endless courtyards, halls and chambers of Grome-Urul — djinn other than Aflauncu and his subordinates were not bound by laws of hospitality.

It was with an exhalation of relief that he greeted the returning ifrit. The djinni appeared in a flash of silver light, instantly seated on the edge of the fountain, a half-mocking smile on his beautiful features.

"Aflauncu!" Pulsifer exclaimed. "I thought you would never return! Did you find his weakness?"

"Fear not for your safety, Pulsifer — I am yet obligated to you. I discovered possibilities, instabilities, disequilibriums of minor yet significant potentiality. But if you refer to Montath's secret — yes, that I uncovered."

Pulsifer gestured flippantly. "I am a straightforward person, despite my reputation for devious deeds. Do not cajole me with riddles; elaborate on your statement."

Aflauncu grinned. "The haste of flesh and blood! Very well. Montath holds a hijret in subservience, a being of particular potency. Much of the wizard's power is focused and channeled through this devilkin, having as its source an ancient Force in the Concentricity of Riolda. The Force I speak of is the archviodom Salanque, equally an enemy of djinn, ochdeviants, and men. Salanque was known in the world's youth by the men, and djinn, of that time — he is a demon of fearsome power, most potent of viodoms, perhaps only weaker than the Singularity Pammoth. His appearance and activities have changed throughout the eons, but his hatred of all beings not under his sway has not changed; he would only have struck a bargain with Montath if he saw in the mage a potential servant — something I'm sure Montath would never agree to! I have been informed by a renegade jret that, in order to guarantee the return of the hijret in the event of a contractual dispute, Salanque holds the core of Montath's soul, the Center without which the other components of his spirit would shred into aimless longings and urges."

Pulsifer started as if he had been slapped, comprehension spreading across his face. "His soul! That I must have — he would be at my mercy! How do we bargain with the viodom?"

"That is not easily done, but a meeting has been arranged, under the guidelines of a truce which you would not understand. You must attend the meeting — your chaotic vibrations may assist in some way, perhaps clouding the deviousness of Salanque. But do not dicker with the archviodom, I warn you — he will accord you the same respect he gives the earthworms he feeds to his vesps."

"Reason enough to leave the dickering to you," Pulsifer said. "That is your second assignment — procure for me the soul of Morskured Montath, while providing me complete protection from all perils — including the whims of the archviodom. I do not wish to obtain Montath's soul, only to be destroyed the next instant by the demon!"

Aflauncu nodded. "You are ever specific."

"Experience has taught me to be exact when dealing with your kind." Pulsifer smiled in a self-satisfied manner. "Shall we go?"

"So we shall." Aflauncu rose, reached out, and lightly tapped Pulsifer on the arm — suddenly the beautiful chamber was gone and, protected by the blue field, the pair passed through layers of rock as if they were strata of vapor. Upon their journey to Grome-Urul, Aflauncu had explained that the density of their bodies grew more vaporous to accommodate lower spheres; now, Pulsifer supposed, their density increased as they moved upward. They passed through caverns filled with fire, unaffected by the fearsome heat of the undying flames. They entered a dim cavern-region where dreamlike meadows rolled away all around, and contented people lounged and disported; in the distance was a shining palace of gorgeous metals. Pulsifer asked the identity of the owner of the keep, and Aflauncu waved a hand — the glamour was removed, and the meadows became ulcerous, cratered rock covered with scrawny figures in agonized poses; the palace was a heap of broken rubble, and giant, monolithic bones. The voluptuous form of the ifrita Lijjelda was seated like a white flame in the center of the pile, apparently watching the man and djinni pass through the High Hells. Aflauncu waved, and she returned the gesture. The djinni explained that she was an aunt of sorts, and they passed to the level above.

At last they reached a realm of complete blackness. Pulsifer felt the fingertips of the djinni graze his eyes — the darkness fell away. They were in a palely-lit world, either covered with forests of orange and golden trees, or by plains of basaltic slabs. Above was a deep-green sky, flecked with clouds — seven moons, honey-colored, rolled languorously in the firmament. For an instant Pulsifer felt a twinge of suspicion — had Aflauncu carried him to a distant world circling another star, such as that from which it was said the ochdeviants had originally come? He assured himself that this was not the case — if anyone would have the power to create an illusion of space such as this, then Salanque the Archviodom would have that ability.

They alit on a shimmering plain. Around them the emptiness stretched for miles. Still they were surrounded by the blue force; Aflauncu touched his temple with one finger, and the intensity of the field's brightness increased.

A hundred feet overhead a red fire-ball shot past, paced by five or six smaller spheres of blue-green fire. Pulsifer, more than a trifle nervous, lifted a brow uneasily. Aflauncu followed his gaze and smiled.

"A jret in its truest form, besieged by yapping hijrets. Does this surprise you? In purest essence, all beings are aspects of Mind-Energy — even yourself. Forms taken in the field of Time are not necessarily meaningful. Be hopeful that you will not see Salanque as he essentially is — your brain would be jarred in a most uncomfortable fashion."

Pulsifer looked sternly at the ifrit. "Concern yourself with the preservation of my body as well. Before we embark on the final stage of this enterprise, assure me again as to your ability to provide me with protection."

Aflauncu shrugged. "Salanque the Archviodom is a formidable enemy; equally-potent entities of demonic classification presently exist only on nonearthly planes. Your defense is dependent neither on my strength, nor upon that of my brethren in Grome, but rather on a mutually-conciliatory clause of a subjunctive nature; this is buried in the Koriamshir Accordance of Interconcentric Truces. I have invoked this clause to our advantage — do not strain its protection! Salanque and his kind have shattered agreements before! The sense of honor which melds a djinni to his word is unknown to the demons of Riolda. For this reason, do not address me by name while we are here — this could weaken me and tempt the viodom to treachery."

"Have no worry as to my conduct. Let us get to it! I must initiate an immediate change in my life!" Pulsifer scowled at the thought of the indignities and humiliations he had endured, primarily because of the hatred of Morskured Montath and other wizards and collectors. Aflauncu nodded.

"I sought only to alleviate your worries, Pulsifer," the ifrit said in an unpleasant tone. "Rudeness, and the lack of humility you so often display, are the very things which might bring Salanque's ill-favor upon us. Look above — see the moon-disks of Riolda! There we will find Salanque, Lord of Viodoms."

Pulsifer looked at the disks. A shadow seemed to shudder across them, settling on the center circle — this flushed to a ruby hue, emitting a red radiance. Aflauncu acted on this apparent signal and they began to rise, soaring weightlessly toward the reddish disk; Pulsifer felt his throat constrict with fear. He wondered if it were too late to cancel their meeting with the demonlord of Riolda —

They rushed toward the disk, yet he still felt neither the sensation of motion nor the passage of the air outside their protective aura. The ruddy circle grew until it filled their view; it seemed almost of metal, its surface revolving like a reddish-bronze wheel. They shot toward it with their upturned faces foremost, and Pulsifer suddenly cringed at the prospect of imminent impact —

They entered an orange, liquid environment. Here, rat-like creatures with human faces swam through a turbid atmosphere. Pulsifer recognized them as the imps called vesps, often summoned and dispatched by wizards; he had left some of their relatives buried in a bottle, some-where on the plains of Distidak…

As Aflauncu and Pulsifer moved, walls became visible around them.

From niches in the stone, hijrets of many colors watched them pass with ophidian gazes. They came to a great round entranceway, flanked by squatting jrets the size of men — just within the portal stood two scimitar-wielding viodoms, their yellow cat-eyes smoldering against the dark grey luster of their skin, their bat-like wings slightly unfolded. They stared with contempt at both the djinni and the man; Aflauncu addressed them with an air of icy disdain.

"Tell Salanque that Piristil has returned with the human pilgrim; we await his indulgence, under the fifth Seriaptic Adjunct of Koriamshir."

The pair of demons bowed and moved to either side to let them pass. Pulsifer and Aflauncu entered a spherical chamber of enormous size — sitting cross-legged in its aqueous center was an unexpectedly incongruous figure. They moved toward him.

Of human appearance, he was old and frail, naked but for a humble cloth twisted about his loins. He looked to Pulsifer like the shriveled philosopher-hermits he had seen in the Zabathi Mountains, in Distidak. On his head was a tight hermit's coif; over his features was a crude bark mask of abstract, angular design. Pulsifer did not know why the demon affected such an unimposing form, but he was not misled — it was evident from the caution of Aflauncu that Salanque was formidable, regardless of any innocuous appearance he might assume.

"I am Salanque," the viodom said in a feeble voice; "I am the unac-knowledged lord of this expiring Earth. Come closer, Pulsifer — I would see the man who, I have heard, is responsible for a reprieve from death for this weary planet."

Pulsifer bowed with a mellifluous grace, respectfully averting his eyes.

"Forgive me if I remain by my escort, O Archviodom — I will allow Piristil to speak for me, as I find myself unworthy to converse with a Power such as yourself."

Salanque said nothing, but nodded once. Aflauncu smiled and bowed as well. "I have returned, Mighty One, on an errand which might prove mutually profitable. We desire from you a singular essence, and I will pay you handsomely for it."

"What can I have, that the djinn of Grome might desire? Viodoms and Djinn cut our ties long ago!" The voice of Salanque had a wheedling tone to it. "Do you seek to take advantage of an elderly relative? Very well: I will listen to your offer. Speak."

Aflauncu steepled his fingers, tip to tip. "I will not waste your time. We require the soul of the mortal Morskured Montath, which we have heard you hold in a matrix of fragile gypsum. Transfer it to us free of liens, and I will hand you the indefinite use of a pocket of Void which predates Creation. It is contained in a grain of matter created by the Great Outbursting, but through its non-temporality you would be able to visit any previous age."

Salanque shook his head. "The first being I would call upon would be myself—however, no such visit occurred in eons past, so obviously I do not accept your offer in the present. I have an obligation to the man Montath; I must guard his soul until such time as he releases one of my children from his service. If he invalidates his contract with me, I may find uses of my own for his essential self—but that has not yet come to pass. No transaction is viable between us; our meeting is ended. I am not interested in further bargaining."

"But I must have his soul!" Pulsifer exclaimed, and Aflauncu shot him a warning look. "He disequilibrates my life with his petulant persecutions! Reconsider—perhaps my friend has other services to offer you!"

The frail figure regarded him silently from behind the mask. A chuckle like thunder rolled around the titanic room, and both Pulsifer and the djinni moved back. The figure shimmered like a flame—giant, black, claw-tipped pinions sprouted from the viodom's shoulders, spreading to an awesome span. A bright red light began to emanate from the eyeholes of the mask, and tiny white wraiths fled from beneath it as if in terror.

"You state your own case after all!" Salanque observed. His small figure was ridiculously overshadowed by his viodom wings. "Would you perhaps be willing to haggle for yourself? I understand that you are quite proud of your puny individuality—trade it to me! Give me your soul, in exchange for that of Montath! Immortality is what you make of it — you lack both the breadth of experience and a purpose to your existence, to warrant such a gift! However, an unaging human could prove useful to me in the world above…"

"I could not!" Pulsifer protested. "My individuality is my most prized possession — it may be the source of both my triumphs and my difficulties, but it sets me apart from all other men, for that very reason! I am not bound by any laws other than my own — that is what makes me the Velvet Knife!"

Salanque shook with rumbling laughter. "I followed another being, long, long ago, beside whom you would be less than a nit. He, too, spoke in such a manner, and he led viodoms, djinn, and others to their devolution from a Perfect Ascension. Your soul would be quite comfortable here, Pulsifer; conquests beyond measure would be yours in the world above! No wizard of mortal lineage can stand against me — they are but dying candles against the wind of my will! You belong to Entropy as much as I —"

For an instant Pulsifer's mind reeled, as he was tempted by the offer of the Archviodom — but then he shook his head. "I stress my right to self-determination, even if this means my destruction! What is the use of my feelings of justification, if I relinquish my soul to you? Perhaps blind Equilibrium will rule me in the end, I do not know — but I must struggle even against such impersonal Law as that! It looks as though I have nothing to offer which you would find useful…"

Salanque nodded thoughtfully. "If I wished, I could rip your protesting soul from your body; but I will honor the terms of this meeting. One moment more, though — I sense the fluctuation of strange energies about you…You carry components of cause and being. Perhaps we can discuss a different manner of transaction. What is in the cumbersome bag?"

Pulsifer stared stupidly at the demon for a moment, then fumbled at the bag at his side while Aflauncu pursed his lips uneasily. "Yes, Salanque! Herein I carry a wondrous conglomeration of runes!" He pulled out the pouch containing the Penultimate Postulation, and held it high for the demon to see.

"Herein is an unrepeatable effectuation, which grants godlike power to a human mage — what then might it do for one such as you?" He dug in a pouch, pulling out a folded, tattered page. "On this paper are listed the creator's formulations, and his determinations as to the spell's potency — the only ingredient not negotiable in this would be my own essence."

Salanque made an interested sound; Aflauncu waved one hand, and the page appeared, floating, before the mask of the viodom. Salanque glanced at it for one second, then it burst into flame and disappeared.

"I will accept these runes — but they are not enough. You carry a metallic box as well; explain the essences I sense locked within."

Pulsifer nodded eagerly; Aflauncu waved again, and the pouch of runes was transferred to the lap of the archviodom. Pulsifer pulled out the Cask of Sranophaez.

"A most-effective collection of dead deities, O Salanque; they are dispatchable servants, ever-willing to please! Would you care to examine the box?"

It vanished, to reappear likewise in the viodom's shallow lap. Aflauncu looked simultaneously surprised and intimidated — apparently this had been done by Salanque, and showed the djinni's defensive powers to be ineffectual before the archviodom. The Lord of the Viodoms examined the cask, turning it rapidly in his withered hands. His head snapped up.

"We have an agreement! These items are mine — Montath's soul is yours!" Salanque's statement was peremptory; Pulsifer exclaimed in relief, surprised at the ease of the acquisition. Aflauncu laughed aloud. A blue-green hijret appeared, bearing in its grasp a hollow pyramid of crystal — suspended in the pyramid's center was a jagged white mass of delicate mineral flowers.

"The soul of the wizard!" Salanque said. "Bear it with care! Shatter the casing, and the minerals crumble — Montath dies in body and spirit!" The hijret floated through the field and to Aflauncu, and placed the pyramid in his hands. The hijret vanished, and the djinni and Pulsifer exchanged grins of accomplishment.

"Some final words," the archviodom said; the pair looked again at the demonlord. "In the interest of fair-dealing, Pulsifer, I tell you this — you have given me a spell of tremendous power. With its integration into my being, I shall unleash death and destruction upon the world of men such as they have never known! Know also that, with yourself being the final ingredient of the spell — a component which I, not being mortal, do not require — you have had within your grasp a source of salvation all along! You were, indeed, the final ingredient — had you simply swallowed the runes, you would even now have Power rivaling mine! As for the cask, it does carry helpful essences — they are the final concentrations of energies, left by the self-devouring of two-thirds of my viodom kin, gone dormant and forgotten! Originally among the most powerful of our kind, they tied themselves to the worship of men through the ages — when worship dwindled and ceased, they found their out-flowing power unreturned and consumed themselves in desperation. But they could never totally die — now with my newfound power, I will resurrect them to rule with pain and hate over mankind, and all others!"

Aflauncu looked resentfully at Pulsifer. "Thank you so much. I should have remained in the giant's belly —"

Pulsifer shrugged. "What Salanque does with his possessions is not my concern! We have what we came for — let us be gone!"

Salanque leaned forward suspiciously. "Wait! Do not yet leave! Pulsifer — what do you carry in your belt? I sense a significant import of an ontological nature — a singleness of being, yet expandable. Do you seek to short me in this transaction? Empty that pouch, there — the second one from the left!"

With a confused expression, Pulsifer fumbled at his pouch-belt as the archviodom had instructed. Digging into the pouch, he pulled out a handful of dusky stones, glittering with smoke-like hues; they were the encrustations he had cut from within the body of Rewelquian. He grinned uneasily.

"Pardon, O Salanque, but these are my property — I would never seek to deceive you! These are growths from the interior of —"

"From the interior of talycent skulls!" the demon roared. "These are the brain-nodules of talycents, as specified in the spell! It is understandable that the mage Jabroal might have acquired extras — I sense that they can only add to the potency of the effectuation! You removed them purposely from the bag, before you arrived! Do not lie — return them to the pouch! I estimate they will multiply the effectiveness of the compilation sevenfold —"

With an expression of indifference, Pulsifer tossed the stones toward the demon. The bag opened as if of its own power, the stones floating unerringly into it, and it closed. Salanque began, again, to laugh.

Aflauncu leaned close to Pulsifer. "I am afraid this looks unpleasant..."

Around them the forms of jrets, hijrets, worm-headed bipeds, and other entities, as well as grinning viodoms, began to congeal and take shape from the thick atmosphere. The pair were surrounded in every direction by the vassals of Salanque. The demonlord chuckled, and his minions laughed with him.

"Observe as I embark on Conquest!" the archviodom roared. "You shall be the first to feed my greater hunger! Behold the hate I have nurtured for this world!" He threw off his mask — his face was a pulpy, oozing mess. His body began to swell and darken, to become that of a viodom twelve feet tall, thickly-muscled and handsome of face and form. From his skull grew a majestic set of jet-black antlers. He hefted the bag of Indissolubles before his face, and pressed them against his forehead — Pulsifer grasped the cool arm of Aflauncu with all his strength, his mouth dry and tasting of bile.

In less than a second the demonlord absorbed the runes. There was deep and expectant silence as both his servitors and prisoners watched. The viodom smiled with relish, and a strange, windy sound began to issue from his midsection.

"*Power,*" he whispered, his yellow, red-centered eyes half-closed. "*Such power! The cosmos opens before my gaze...*"

He swelled even more — suddenly his eyes stretched wide. The cask of Sranophaez, which had floated before him, was catapulted like a projectile of war across the room and out of sight. He started to shake, and the rack on his head began to coil and writhe. His head lurched forward as his mouth opened.

Grey-green flames jumped from his astonished face. His body bulged outward in several directions, but did not burst — he began to spin violently, head tossing, spitting mouthfuls of the unnatural fire into his crowded attendants. Dozens were shriveled on the spot, and the rest fled the throes of their convulsing liege. Aflauncu threw back his own head with a laugh of delight, as he and Pulsifer began to rise and speed away.

In an instant the disk was far below. Around it swarmed a cloud of agitated entities. As they shot upward, Aflauncu looked at Pulsifer. "What were those last stones you gave to Salanque? Surely they were not fundamental to the notation of the effectuation! They seemed to have had a more than disruptive effect on the runes' intended function —"

Pulsifer burst into laughter. "No wonder, that! They were stones formed of secretions from the intestinal tissues of Rewelquian!"

Suddenly they halted; Aflauncu wore a worried frown. "This situation bears watching — such an integration of elemental energy, with the concentrated forces of dark human emotions — Rewelquian — has never before occurred. Rewelquian was a living being comprised of festering unconscious desires — the viodom epitomized overt and blatant evil of a purely spiritual nature. Let us see which shall emerge triumphant!"

Below them, the disk started crumbling, sending out spiraling bolts of force. Its pieces dissolved into mist as they fell. The creatures of Riolda swirled like bees about a dying hive — a monstrous, familiar form was revealed, floating in place of the vanished disk. The viodoms, jrets and hijrets darted away.

It was identical to one of the imps of Rewelquian — but it was forty feet long from crown to heel. It opened its embryonic face and screamed like a cyclone, then fell to the ground below with a distant thud. It lay spread-eagle and face-down, as if dead; it began to move, then rose uneasily. Looking around hungrily, the Indefinite Hybrid set off for the nearest forest, visibly growing as it went.

Aflauncu sighed. "Salanque is fundamentally negated. A new Rewelquian is born — probably more powerful than the first one, due to the pouchful of runes, not to mention the essence of the viodom! This is bad news for Riolda, and several concentricities farther down. Fortunately for the upper world, the Sphere of Outer Fire, with its tides of magma, will keep the colossus from bursting upward. Ah, well — this has been interesting! Now we go, to complete the last phase of your fulfillment!"

Pulsifer nodded in readiness and they sped upward, two dwindling specks. Below them, the viodoms began their battle for rulership, clashing for possession of a small metallic box; on the ground, the young giant paused in its trek, to gaze up as if enthralled at the bat-winged forms, and blazing explosions of light.

Chapter II

A Balancing of Love and Hate

The last days of the Chill gripped old Teumdoth in a frozen hold, but mankind was far from dormant. From Nishar in the southwest, to Jesbidan in the far northeast, the underclasses scoured cities and hamlets in search of Pulsifer — Pulsifer, the Uncursable, Pulsifer, the Velvet Knife.

The Eight Upper Classes directed the search with rigorous enthusiasm — Warrior-Philosophers sought to determine the whereabouts of the outlaw through exercises of strategic thought; Lord Merchants offered great monetary rewards for information; Mages and Collectors combined their resources of magic and knowledge, in an attempt to pinpoint Pulsifer's location. His continued freedom made an unprecedented mockery of the equipoised social system which had stood since the Ochdeviant Invasions, eighty-five hundred years before.

His escapades in Yawamris had generated unforeseen repercussions, inspiring social revolt of an unthinkable degree. In Kalsurridin, a retreat of the Aesthetes was burned by disgruntled servitors; the semantic sculptors and their works were thrown into the icy river Iteg. In cities such as Kebbege in Jesbidan, Lygoem and other cities in Phontyque, and Jeb in bleak Nishar, various artisans and craftsmen had taken to wearing masks and had also adopted other conventions of their betters — some cities had even had their governing councils stormed by mobs of the lower castes, who went so far as to demand equal representation in the business of government. These upstarts were put down by the power of the mages and warriors, but the lower classes still grumbled — now, all members of the ruling aristocracies agreed upon one thing. Calim Pulsifer had to be captured, punished — and destroyed. Their determination was evident — not since the Wars of Wizards had such a massive undertaking as this search been shared by the entirety of mankind.

Despite their vengeful bluster, even the mages of the Brotherhood were uncertain of the possibility of Pulsifer's capture. Other things of unsettling aspect clamored for their attention. Just over two months previously, the lower chambers of Mt. Yawamris had filled with an unexplainable, residual radiation which scorched the flesh of hundreds of miners and metalworkers — it was hypothesized by Tatimoi Murlda, the Sorceress-Overseer of the mine-complex, that the radiation had its origin in a release of tremendous forces far beneath the Earth, and had seeped through the Lower and Upper Cavern Realms until it reached the volcano. Many hundreds of dangerous life-forms, hungering for human lives, or simply maliciously mischievous, had somehow burst free of the vast menageries of Moilerve the Lord Collector, as his home and belongings simultaneously disintegrated around his ears. The culprit behind this dastardly curse had not yet been discovered, but the shock of the tragedy sent Moilerve into infirmity, and he now rested in a home for Unwell Aristocrats. His daughter, the somomorph Erhis, had escaped as well, and with the other denizens of the menageries she terrorized the countryside around Lake Syragen, and about the cities of Skurpe and Skiggen. Some of these creatures wandered into the Forests of Iskiruen, and were seen no more.

Searchers sent into the southern Forests in quest of the hiding Pulsifer returned with a strange tale — weird folk, more or less human, but with transparent skin which gave them a ghoulish appearance, had emerged from caverns beneath the forest. Now they dwelt on an aboriginal level of cultural development beneath the darkest trees, shunning the sunlight — when approached by a party from Jesbidan, the glassy-skinned people pelted them with stones and vanished into the shadows of the wood. The mages Jabroal Glispert, of the Forests of Iskiruen, and Gilgode Semmech of Nishar, came forward with a strange story which attested to Pulsifer's demise beneath the Earth — but the particulars of this tale were so outrageous, and Jabroal's reputation so disrespected, that it was discounted as a complete falsehood.

Porvul Shuk, the great archimage, stated that he had detected a massive upheaval of terrestrial energies which supported the story of Rewelquian's demise; but he also said that a war raged in the Concentricity of Riolda between a similar, unbound titan, and the viodoms, who were now led by a previously unknown demon called Dacdull. In fact, he said that the numbers of the viodom host had swelled by the many thousands. Shuk could not determine what had happened to the fearsome archviodom Salanque, however. The dreaded, self-isolated Morskured Montath was asked for his opinion on the Riolda matter, but had no comment; however, it was said that when Pulsifer's name was mentioned in connection with these mysteries, the young mage threatened to transform the messengers of the query into silver-furred snow-monkeys, and keep them in his garden of growing ices. Some thought that Montath was still irked by the unexpected rebellion of his hijret familiar — inexplicably released from whatever bound it to his will, it had tried determinedly to destroy him. After a prolonged combat in the air between the towers of Krikenvaxi, he had transformed the hijret into a chunk of black onyx, and then placed it in one of the courtyards of his citadel. He hadn't yet taken another familiar of any type, and those who knew him said he seemed inordinately pensive about something.

Even the city of Neshgrel, close as it was to the stronghold of Pulsifer's self-proclaimed nemesis, was not free from the coordinated search for the fugitive. The streets beneath the domes, the wide-stretching causeways and glittering minarets, were ablaze with the lights of the hunters, as were the outlying, uncovered streets of the slums and tract-houses. In the latter places the lights, if anything, were brightest.

On the summit of the unnatural peak Vomanction, in the black citadel Krikenvaxi, one dim light burned in the central tower. From their vantage far above in a bubble of levitational force, Pulsifer and the djinni Aflauncu gazed at the distant window — from Pulsifer's brow there dripped a sweat of anxiety, and in his hands was the pyramid containing the soul of the wizard. Aflauncu wore an expression both aloof and amused.

"Our partnership nears its end, Pulsifer," the ifrit observed; his tone was curious and almost unreadable to his companion, but more than sorrowful, it was sardonic. "Before you confront the mage, however, be warned — the instant you leave the influence of my field, you will be almost instantly detected by a dozen wizards — among them will be Morskured Montath. Observe that cloud, and the mist which obscures the moon; within each lurk many minor wraiths and djinn, attentive for your possible appearance. Also, you have one final fulfillment yet outstanding — what will it be? Remember that my power is limited, even as yours is, within your environment — consider carefully, for this request is definitely your last."

Into Pulsifer's mind a score of possibilities competed for realization — then the image of the somomorph, Erhis Sulshaine, leapt to the fore. For an instant he considered requesting a reversal of the terrible condition imposed upon her by the djinni Kethil — of asking Aflauncu to return her to her former state of beauty and humanity. But the face of Montath intruded on his thoughts — he was too near his goal to jeopardize success for the sake of a sentimental gesture!

"Is it not obvious? I desire a field to render me undetectable to supernatural servitors and sorcery in general. Thus may I take Montath unawares! I must see the defeat on his face before he dies!"

"You have spoken — it shall be so." Aflauncu tapped him with one long finger. "You are now surrounded by an obfuscating vibration; its duration is seven weeks. That is the best I can do, for I will not be here —"

"Remain, and maintain the field indefinitely!" Pulsifer exclaimed.

Aflauncu laughed at his outburst.

"Such a condition was not specified — we are now free of each other. Remember, seven weeks."

Pulsifer half-scowled, then grinned. "Good enough, O Djinni — if you will deposit me inside yon bartizan, I will bid you farewell."

"That I cannot do — Montath's home is completely sealed, even to me. Getting within is your own task; I will place you on the eastern battlement, close by a latched window. Farewell, O shrewdest of human creatures."

The next moment Pulsifer stood shivering on the shadowy battlement.

Aflauncu was gone. A perilously cold wind bit through him, making him wish he'd put on the traveler's clothes which were still rolled upon his back; he crouched behind a merlon and surveyed his surroundings. In a nearby wall was a shuttered window. First he unstrapped the encumbering, empty valise, and threw it far out over the wall; then, half-bent, he ran swiftly to the window, grasping the soul-pyramid to his chest with one hand.

Before even touching the sill, he paused — Krikenvaxi was charmed against supernatural intrusion, but what about burglars of the mortal variety?

He surmised that, since the citadel was inaccessible by air without one's unnatural flight being detected, there might not be any conventional safeguards. It was said that Montath himself came and went upon a great black fottermee, and worried about thieves not at all... Pulsifer looked about nervously at the thought, then took the chance. He placed the pyramid in his squatting lap, then took small tools from his belt, setting to work with windnumbed fingers at the latch.

After a minute the shutters sprang loose. Deftly he slipped inside, closing and re-latching the window. In one hand he now carried his sword; in the other, Morskured Montath's crystal-ensnared soul. He was in a musty chamber, filled with stacks and heaps of books and unsavory items — wrinkling his nose at the mildewed odor, he went to the door and out into the gallery beyond. He was wary beyond any caution he'd ever known, suspicious of the ease of his entry, and the absence of the wizard. He looked about nervously — where was the arrogant young mage? Determinedly he set out to find his enemy.

For two hours or more he wandered the vast keep, eyes darting cagily for traps and snares. He passed through a broad menagerie filled with a superlative variety of beings — night-walking darklings stared from behind panes and bars as he passed, and a broad-headed prainquel made a somber sound, ruffling its feathers. He saw his face reflected in its great owl-eyes; then he was out of that chamber, and in yet another long hall. Through rooms heaped with treasures, through chambers of torture, pleasure and labor he went, until at last he reached the stair which, he was certain, led up into the central tower. With a step at first apprehensive, he started up.

Up and up, legs untiring, he went, fueled by a mounting hate which imparted fierce energy. He anticipated with grim delight the smashing of Montath's soul upon the floor at the mage's own feet, the strangled look, the spasms of a most total death. Soon, the wizard would trouble him no more!

Abruptly he came to a narrow landing. Before him was an oaken door, slightly ajar — purple light danced beyond. He eased to the portal, gazing at the giant amethysts he had seen once before; suddenly the door swung wide and he jumped back, teetering on the brink of the stairwell. Thirty feet away, Morskured Montath stood in the center of the room.

Holding the ensnared soul behind him, Pulsifer stepped into the purple light. Montath regarded him with a calm expression, his black brows raised as if distantly amused, the hint of a smile at the corners of his mouth. He spoke in a relaxed voice, yet mockery laced his every word.

"Pulsifer, Pulsifer! Welcome, old friend! What took you so long — did you tour the grounds before coming to pay me a visit? I detected your entry the instant you unlocked the window — although, I admit, I did not detect *you*. Perhaps you can explain that to me, before I kill you."

"You are the one about to die," Pulsifer said uneasily, raising his sword. His voice was thick with suppressed emotion, strange to his own ears.

Montath laughed.

"Really! I told you, did I not, that the forces of Equilibrium were undeniable? I tired of the pursuit — we are bound together inextricably, you and I, opposing planets whose orbits cross again and again. I knew that you would be drawn to me by the weave of predestination, and I will now sever the cords which connect us. You surprise me with both your entrance, and your final unflinching audacity — but ready yourself! I reduce you to atoms!"

The mage's eyes began to burn with a hellish glow; his hair rose about his head, strands twisting like snakes as a violet light emanated from his skull. He raised one arm, and his cheeks began to pulse with the power of the runes he held in his mouth. His lips parted —

"Wait!" Pulsifer cried triumphantly. He held up the crystal pyramid for the wizard to see. "Destroy me and I smash your soul, obtained from the viodom Salanque!" He raised the pyramid as if he would hurl it to the floor —

Montath lowered his arm, the lights dying in his eyes. Instead, Pulsifer saw fear flickering there in his gaze.

"Oh, Pulsifer, how I long to destroy thee!" Montath whispered; but his face was unsure. "Place the pyramid gently on the floor — only three years of jagged pain will you endure. This is better than the death-sentence of a moment past!"

"Not better than your death!" Pulsifer retorted. "I am completely in command at this point, Montath — this you should at least admit! You set yourself against me with unwarranted vindictiveness; again, you have been proven my inferior! I can destroy you as I please, and you are powerless to stop me — at this moment, you know but a fraction of the apprehension you have given me!"

"An oath, then," Montath gritted, his teeth clenched. "I give you an oath unbreakable, to forswear any violence, any personal retribution against you. Return me my Self, and we will be at counterpoise!"

Pulsifer laughed. "That would not be nearly enough, for a mineral formation as rare as this! If I were to even think of bargaining with you, I would have your personal guarantee of safety, against all the efforts of the Eight Upper Classes; I would have your wealth, your keep, your public apologies! But more than these, I will have your life! Goodbye, Montath!" He raised the pyramid.

"Wait, I beg you!" the mage cried. "By Pammoth's Eye, by the first and last breath of the living Earth! By the star Illunwher, which influences all magical activity! By Equilibrium's Net itself, I forswear my claims against you — I give you all that you have named as well! You have done me a service, bringing me my soul from the Archviodom — we will now be friends! Only do not destroy me, I implore you!"

Morskured Montath's fists were tight at his sides, his face was twisted with terror — Pulsifer laughed loud and long. Here was a revenge sweeter than execution! Montath could live long — yet he would always carry this humiliation like a brand upon his memory!

"You will stand by your oath? All I desire is peace between us, between myself and the world."

"I will, I will!" Montath smiled eagerly. "And anything else you desire, so long as it is within my power, I will give you! Return my soul to me, and I will always be in your debt!"

"I do not trust you," Pulsifer remarked. "But still — would you square matters between the Brotherhood, the Collectors, and myself? Also giving me Krikenvaxi, and all else I request?"

"I would! My soul, if you please!" The mage reached for the pyramid — after a second's hesitation, Pulsifer placed it in his hand. A mage, even one as mighty and vain as Montath, would never break an oath such as he had sworn! Montath clutched the pyramid to his chest with both hands — within it, the gypsum containing his essence throbbed with a faint golden light. His face instantly changed to a hateful one again, but he spoke without threat or malice in his voice.

"As you have directed, so shall it be," the wizard said. "You have me by my word — to a mage, one's spoken word is one's power, and there is nothing more binding than this. Allow me to place my soul in a safe place and gather a few articles of clothing — unless you begrudge me that — and then my citadel, and all it contains, becomes your property. You can make further requests of me before I depart, if you wish."

"I shall, do not doubt it." Pulsifer watched cautiously as the mage left the chamber — but apparently the game was won! Montath would do as he promised, no matter how greatly it enraged him to do so; soon Pulsifer knew that he would be free of all threats and charges! If anyone had overriding influence among sorcerers, and the upper echelons in general, it would be Morskured Montath!

Pulsifer sheathed his sword, a deep sense of satisfaction settling over him. He moved about the room, peered into the giant amethysts — he pulled back with shock, for it felt as though he had been about to plummet into a bottomless violet pool. He tinkered with a curious mask of bronze and gold, apparently worn by Montath during particular rituals — there was a sound behind him, and he wheeled.

Montath grinned without humor or goodwill. "I gave you my oath — I will not dare break it —"

"The proverb says: The Serpent sheds his skin, but he remains a snake."

"So it runs. What else do you need, before I go?"

Fingering his curled moustaches, Pulsifer evaluated the situation. "Hm. All things must be considered. I cannot leave myself open for retribution. Are you certain that you will obtain a pardon for my crimes?"

"I will, for none will gainsay me. But you will still be in danger from men such as Jabroal, who are free agents of sorcery. He is not of the Brotherhood, and he desires your death as much as I — as much as I once did. Also, assassins may be hired, or recruited from lower castes; some ambitious guildsman may even take it upon himself to earn the gratitude of society, and kill you. Your situation will be somewhat better, though, than it was before tonight."

Pulsifer stared at the mage with a candid look. "Where can I take refuge from all my foes?"

Montath shrugged. "Krikenvaxi is safest, impenetrable by mage or spirit. I can activate defenses for you against fottermees and other flying things — Vomanction is unscalable up or downward, and blood-loving grigets nest along its sides. Here, and probably only here, will you be isolated from justice…"

Pulsifer nodded thoughtfully — he wanted badly to rest. He did not have to remain here for good, only long enough to have a respite from the world. Here he could recuperate, think, plan his coming life — which would be long indeed, with the final boon of Pammoth! He smiled at Montath.

"Provide me with a supply of both food and drink — I shall stay here for a year. Return in twelve months' time to see if I am ready to temporarily depart — in the interim, I will explore my new home and its treasures, study my new books, dally with my — No." The memory of the mage's frozen seraglio halted his spiel. "Take your women with you, or better yet, set them free. I only request that you find for me a few willing paramours to share my self-exile; be certain that they are renowned for their beauty and grace, but make them interesting of personality as well! And see that they stay of their own free will — unlike you, I am capable of persuading women into love, rather than force them into bondage! Also, remove all creatures from the menagerie, and from this place. Do all as I have directed, and perhaps, bit by bit, this keep and its treasures will be returned to you; but I intend to make Krikenvaxi my home for quite some time. You see, I am eternally youthful through Pammoth's intervention — but you heard the talycent-queen say as much! Someday, when you are grey and doddering, you might return to this place, for by then I will have found fresher fields in which to roam. Now go, and return in one year — do not forget my companions, for someone must cook for me — I am in need of good refreshment, and relaxation! Do not fail to do everything precisely as I have specified!"

"Word for word. The pantries and the storerooms are continuously stocked by the djinn of Yurdash. The furnaces will be well-stoked as well. You will have both sustenance and comfort. I will return one year from tonight, to see what further service I may provide. Until then, Pulsifer."

Montath bowed tersely, turned, and walked into the blackness of the stairwell. Pulsifer felt a vague disquiet; something in the tone of the wizard's farewell, his face, his stride, had seemed unconquered and dangerous. He shrugged — Montath was tamed by the oath he had laid upon himself!

Clapping his hands with a laugh, Pulsifer set out to locate a place to rest. On the morrow, he would inspect his new home!

The sun's first rays roused him. Leaving his things in the bedchamber, he spent the day's first hour lazing in the heated marble baths; growing hungry, he went to the kitchen and prepared a fine breakfast for himself. Without the fear of pursuit, the worry of death, he felt truly free, despite what amounted to a year's upcoming confinement! Krikenvaxi was large, and offered diversions and explorations to interest him continuously.

He flipped through his priceless books for a while, then he ranged the halls, admiring the works of a thousand painters, sculptors, friezemasters and tapestry-weavers. At noon he bathed again, and, practicing a bit of legerdemain with the proximity-ring, he dropped it into the grating which covered the drain. Resolving to retrieve it later, he left the bath and had chervillion tea of greenest clarity, and hothouse plums coated with sugar and the jelly of quinces. In the afternoon he toyed with singing boxes, and moving mannequins which danced when he clapped or whistled; then he examined the menagerie. The cages were empty, and spotlessly clean. Toward evening he sat with a hot cup of harsh rac-rac, watching from the window as the sun lowered to a blue-white, curving Earth, a sense of contentment welling up within him. He thought of the travails he had undergone, since he came to Yawamris months before—he grinned with satisfaction, tapping his foot upon a gilded skull. This was the life that he, the most persecuted man of the Age, surely deserved! Yes, it would be a most pleasant year! As he sat in this state of quiet contemplation, he became aware of movements on a portico across from the room in which he lounged—he spied a slender form, retreating within and into shadow. He suddenly remembered his request of Montath for feminine companionship—in that location would surely be the chamber of pleasure he had glimpsed through Aflauncu's cube! There his ladies would be waiting!

Smoothing his unruly hair with a golden comb, he cleansed his teeth with a small brush and a silver toothpick, sprinkled fragrances on his curls and shoulders, and went to the nearest pantry, where he selected a bottle of the golden vintage of the Imonber greenhouse-wineries; then he sauntered, by a curving route, through his house and toward the area he had espied from above. Soon he heard the tinkle of fountains, the sweet chirping of the metal birds, and he smiled with confidence. At the end of the dark hallway, the ostentatious room gleamed, a vision of erotic indulgence and delight…

There was a quick and sinister sound, a scamper in the dark. Pulsifer leaned to one side as the knife plunged past his ear, and a falling wrist made contact with his shoulder. Grabbing the arm, he assisted his attacker's momentum, and a form smaller than his flew over his shoulder, to land with a jarring thud on the tiles. He rushed forward to finish his assailant with the upraised bottle, and pulled back in surprise.

"Azahad! What are you doing here—?"

Azahad Zuzirco staggered to her feet, still grasping a ten-inch dagger; her body was covered by rags, her fair flesh was soiled and chafed, and there was an iron collar about her neck. Her blonde hair was matted with filth. She smiled with hate, her voice dry and rasping.

"The wizard delivered me from beneath Yawamris—where I was sentenced to the miners' brothels, for conspiring with you! Sir Montath said that I met the standards you had set, being most popular of the girls pawed by the wretches in the mines—this blade, which I found in a chest upstairs, meets my standard! It is more than fit to cut out your heart! You cost me my life's dreams and desires, and you will die!"

She lunged, and he knocked the knife from her grasp. She turned, and dashed into an adjoining passageway. Picking up the knife, he looked in after her — he heard the echo of her footfalls, then silence. He called to her in the blackness.

"Your anger is unfounded! It is clear that your life's ambition was realized!"

Cursing Montath for his trickery, he moved to the chamber of concubinage with a cautious tread. Now there was a madwoman loose in the place, intent on killing him — probably while he slept! He swore a loud, violent oath, and entered the draped and cushioned chamber.

Here all was tranquil. The metal birds sang in their cages, the water laughed ceaselessly. He looked about for other surprises, but he seemed to be quite alone. He placed the wine-bottle on a table. Warily he went to one wall, where a huge mass of soft cushions was piled, and set himself down to think —

His back-flung hand met quaking flesh. He threw himself across the floor and the knife flew from his other hand, as the massive body of the somomorph Erhis Sulshaine, once called the most beautiful of living women, thrust herself erect from a ponderous repose. Beneath flowing black tresses, her eyes lit with a frightening joy, and she took one ton-heavy step forward. Her voice was deep, crude, yet understandable.

"P-Pulsifer! My Pulsifer! O my Light! My duck, my love! We are together at last!"

At this he sprang up and turned to run — the somomorph would not be able to follow him into the higher levels of Krikenvaxi! He took one long stride toward the doorway —

His jaw dropping, he halted. Wrapped only in scarlet hair, the syleber Sinfe stood in the portal, more beautiful than the mind could imagine. A strange hum filled the air. She smiled, licking her lips with relish; from her outspread fingers, her long, poisoned talons slid into place. Behind her, a cloud of buzzing wasps framed their queen with a backdrop of many colors.

She pursed her lips seductively, and her voice was husky with desire. "Hello, Trespasser, my Love. Come to me, Love. Come."

Her gaze was anything but loving. Talons outstretched, she stepped into the room.

From the back of a hovering fottermee, Morskured Montath watched through a ball of amber, a smile of satisfaction on his smooth-shaven face; snapping a word, he turned his mount to the west, toward Pegres and his other residence. Wondering what he would find in a year's time, he left a chain of dark laughter in the sky; behind him he left Pulsifer, the Velvet Knife, with his companions renowned for their beauty and grace…but interesting of personality as well.

Colophon

This book was printed using 11,5 pt Adobe Arno Pro as the primary text font, with NeutraFace used for titles.

Special thanks to Steve Sherman.

Book composition & Typesetting: Joel Anderson
Typographic design: Howard Kistler
Management: John Vance, Koen Vyverman

www.ingramcontent.com/pod-product-compliance
Lightning Source LLC
Chambersburg PA
CBHW050421260626
47156CB00003B/1107